# FORGED FROM ICE

*New York Times* & *USA Today* Bestselling Author

CYNTHIA EDEN

This book is a work of fiction. Any similarities to real people, places, or events are not intentional and are purely the result of coincidence. The characters, places, and events in this story are fictional.

Published by Hocus Pocus Publishing, Inc.



Copy-editing by: J. R. T. Editing

# CHAPTER ONE

She'd escaped from him three times before. She wouldn't be getting away again.

Titan Everett kicked the door shut behind him, blocking the fierce wind that had been at his back and shutting out the howl that had followed him inside. The promised storm had been chasing him for miles, and he'd made it to his destination just in time.

*Got you.*

Titan slowly approached the worn bar. He was in the middle of nowhere—literally, a dot on the map called Nowhere, South Dakota. He'd been tracking his prey all across the US. He had to give the woman credit—Cassidy Jacobs was damn good at running.

Too bad for her, he was damn good at hunting.

Country music blared from an old speaker that had been perched up on a nearby wall. The place looked like it had once been a barn with a tall ceiling and broad, wooden rafters. Titan was pretty sure he even saw some leftover straw on the floor.

Not exactly the Ritz, but then, when you were running from a murderer, keeping a low profile was probably far more important than living a life of luxury.

Her back was to him as he closed in, so he couldn't be one hundred percent certain she *was* his target. Not yet. She was humming along to the music and moving her hips in a little sway exactly in time with the beat. Every now and then, her head—adorned with thick, dark hair that spilled over her shoulders—would bob to the left or the right.

The woman's situational awareness was shit. With her past, he expected more. She seemed completely oblivious to his presence in the bar.

He was almost on top of her, and he still hadn't gained her attention. Those hips of hers kept swaying and his gaze was on them—probably focusing too *much* on them, dammit—and Titan whipped up his eyes to see—

Her, staring at him in the mirror. The big, wide, and very long mirror that hung on the wall behind the bar. A shelf full of bottles waited beneath that mirror.

Fuck. He'd been the one not situationally aware. A tight ass in a pair of equally tight jeans had just distracted him. Talk about humiliating.

His hands rose and flattened onto the bar.

She smiled, a wide flash that sent dimples winking in both of her cheeks. "See something you like, handsome?"

*Handsome?* The word had him stiffening. Okay, fine, it was dark in the old bar. The lights overhead were dim as fuck. Probably a deliberate tactic to hide the aging surroundings. But given the dim lighting, maybe his prey hadn't been able to see him clearly. Especially since she'd just been peering at his reflection in the mirror. But even as he had that thought, she was spinning around to face him and stepping up to the bar.

No way could she not get a good look now.

At him, and the scars on his face. A face that no one in their right mind would call handsome. More like the stuff of nightmares. That had been the actual description given by his ex once upon a time.

*How can I possibly stay with you? I look at you and—God, Titan, it's a nightmare. You're a nightmare. I need to wake up.*

But the bartender—slender but curved in all the right places—just kept swaying slightly to the music. Her gaze didn't stray from his. Usually, curious—or horrified—gazes cut helplessly toward his scars. Toward the long, white scar that bisected his right eyebrow and climbed toward his forehead. That knife slice had nearly taken his eye.

And if people didn't look at that scar first, then their gazes tended to fall to the slice that hit his cheekbone and disappeared under his jaw. His attacker had been determined to carve him up.

*He'd succeeded.* The scars on Titan's face were just the tip of the iceberg.

"Uh, hello?" she prompted as she waved one hand toward him. Her eyebrows rose. "Something I can get for you?"

She still hadn't looked directly at the scars. Meanwhile, he was drinking her in. To make certain she was the correct target—that was why he was studying her so carefully. Why his gaze had started at the tip of her head—dark, thick hair with a faint curl—and was slowly lowering. Deep, dark eyes. Not really brown, more a gold so complete and deep that her gaze appeared dark. Heart-shaped face. Perfect cheekbones. Disarming dimples.

She wore a plain, white T-shirt that stretched over small but nicely rounded breasts. No nametag on the shirt. And she—

A long sigh slipped from her. "Didn't your mother ever tell you it was rude to stare?"

His eyes jumped right back up to find hers.

She leaned toward him. "It's even ruder..." Her tone went lower. Huskier. "To lust after someone you've just met. You're not supposed to gawk at strangers."

Holy fuck. He most certainly had not been—

Her smile widened. Her dimples deepened. "Are you blushing? I think you are. That's sort of cute."

No. He was *not* blushing. Titan didn't blush. Not ever. And never in a million years could someone seriously claim he was *cute*. He growled.

She bit her lip, as if fighting her smile. Or stifling a laugh. "Okay, Mr. Tall, Muscled, and Blushy...are you going to be rude and keep staring or are you going to order something?" She motioned toward the otherwise empty bar. "As you can see, I am having one majorly slow night. Probably because a real nasty bit of weather is scheduled to hit at any time, and people in their right minds aren't out."

Was she telling him that she didn't think he was in his right mind? Insulting him in that sweet, husky voice? A voice that seemed to be stroking right over him and—

Sonofabitch. He *was* lusting after his target. He was even more hard up than he'd thought.

Thunder rumbled. A long, loud rumble that seemed to shake the bar itself. Titan was sure he noticed a few glasses trembling on the shelf behind the bar.

She shook her head and sent her thick hair sliding over her shoulder. "That is not a good sign. Probably gonna be just like the local weatherman predicted on the five o'clock news...'Severe thunderstorms with the threat of tornadoes. Torrential rainfall. Dangerous lightning strikes.'" A pause. "In light of all that and the fact that I can now *hear* the rain pounding against the roof, I just have to ask...what brings you out on a night like this?"

*You.* She'd brought him out. He'd been chasing her for a very long time. And, yes, he was staring straight at his target. Her hair was longer than it had been in the picture he'd been given, but then, that picture was over a year old. Longer hair and darker, too. Her body seemed more slender, as if she'd lost weight while running and hiding. But the smile was the same. The killer smile that had been like a punch to his gut the first time he'd seen a photo of it—of her.

But in real-life, that smile of hers was even more powerful. Even more disarming.

Only her smile dimmed as he stared at her and said nothing. What could have been fear began to stir in her dark, dark gold eyes.

Now *that* was the typical reaction people had when they encountered him. They stared at him, and they feared. But then, she had a reason to fear, didn't she? A beautiful woman, alone in an otherwise empty bar with a stranger. He towered over her because he knew his prey stood at five-foot-five. He probably outweighed her by more than a hundred pounds, and with the storm amping up to violently rage outside, no one would be rushing in to join them.

They were all alone.

The fear deepened in her eyes even as her hands began to casually lower behind the bar.

*Hell. She's going for a weapon.* He had to speak, even though that act was probably going to scare her even more. "Whiskey." As always, his voice emerged as a growl. A rough, twisted, gruff request. Titan knew that he looked scary as hell, and when you added the wreck that was his voice—the package became even more terrifying.

She blinked. Her hands stopped reaching for the weapon.

More thunder rumbled.

She held his stare a moment. "Anyone ever tell you that your voice is even sexier than Vin Diesel's?"

He could feel his eyes widening. No one had *ever* told him that. He'd made children cry before, but no one had ever said anything about his voice being—

"No? It is. Know it. Own it." With that, she swung away, went back to swaying with the music, and grabbed some whiskey from the shelf beneath the mirror. "You didn't specify what kind, but I believe I told you it was a slow night, so I'll be giving you the most expensive drink I have. Considering that you might be the only sale I make tonight, I'm sure you understand." She splashed some whiskey into a glass for him. Never missed a beat with her swaying. The woman had a rhythmic gift. *I need to stop staring at her ass.*

Titan swallowed. His eyes lifted. Very reluctantly.

"I know most of the folks in town." She whirled back toward him and put the whiskey in front of him with a graceful movement of her hand. *No rings. Slender fingers.* "You're not from around here, are you?"

He shook his head and didn't reach for the whiskey. He did settle onto the bar stool near him, and Titan found that he couldn't take his gaze off her.

Rude to stare? Yep. But everyone who knew him would agree that Titan tended to be one rude sonofabitch.

At least he wasn't staring hard at her ass anymore. He was locked on her face. A dark secret he had? Her face had been haunting him for ages. Ever since he'd first been given her picture and he'd found himself taking a cold case that *shouldn't* have been his.

But one look at her, and he'd been hooked.

"Passing through town?" she asked as her dark eyes seemed to sparkle.

How did she do that? Get her eyes to sparkle when they were so dark? He could have sworn that sparkle lit up not just her eyes, but the whole damn bar. Crazy. Impossible. Yet he studied that sparkle as he tried to puzzle things out.

Her brows stayed up, all expectant-like.

Hell. He should answer her question. Um, was he passing through town? Nope. He'd gotten what he came for. She was right in front of him. So Titan shook his head.

A bubble of laughter spilled from her. Freaking adorable and infectious. "You are not one for talking, are you?" She grabbed a white cloth and wiped down the bar top on her side, then bent and swiped it lower *behind* the bar, too.

No, he wasn't much for talking. He liked silence. Liked to watch and observe.

She gripped the cloth in one hand as she tilted her head to study him. "If you're not passing through and you're clearly not *from* here, then what brings you to Nowhere?"

He eyed the cloth in her hand, and, for the first time, he smiled. He'd been a bit worried about her. A woman alone in a rundown bar. She *should've* had a coworker with her. No way was it safe for her to be working alone. And with her past, the lady should know better than to be unguarded. But it was nice to see she had a few hidden talents. "Gonna shoot me?" Titan asked.

She took a step back. Then she also looked down at the cloth in her hand. A cloth that he knew was wrapped around a small gun. He could see the outline of the weapon. She'd grabbed it while acting like she was cleaning.

"Sorry," she told him, not even hesitating as she boldly lied to his face and said, "I have no idea what you mean. I don't know—"

In a flash, he was off the bar stool, partially over that bar, and he'd snatched the cloth—and the gun—from her fingers. He unwrapped the cloth to reveal his prize even as a startled cry burst from her lips.

"Gun," Titan stated simply. He lifted it up and checked the chamber. A *loaded* gun. Shaking his head, he unloaded it for her.

And she ran for the door.

Hell. He was definitely not handling this situation with any finesse. *Typical.* "Cassidy, wait!"

With her hand reaching for the front door, she jerked to a stop. Her head whipped back toward him. Her gaze met his, and he saw the terror burning in her eyes. If possible, the gold had gone even darker. "How do you know my name?"

Simple. "I'm here for you." He started to reach inside his coat.

Her terror-filled eyes widened even more. "The hell you are." Then she yanked open the door and ran into the stormy night.

***

She'd known he was trouble from the minute he walked into the bar.

Of course—*of course*—the bar's manager had gotten stuck out at his cabin because the road had washed away with last night's rainfall. *Of course,* Cassidy would be there alone. And, *of course,* the worst kind of trouble would walk his way into her bar *when* she was all alone.

The rain pelted down on her as Cassidy hauled ass through the parking lot. One big problem with this fleeing run of hers? She didn't have a car. She'd taken the bus to Nowhere. All right, fine, she'd taken the bus to the bigger town *near* Nowhere, then she'd hitched a ride over with a trucker. Shortly after arriving in the tiny dot of a town, Cassidy had gotten a job at the bar, and one of the perks had been that she got to use the small apartment behind the main building.

She'd been saving up some cash, hoping to buy herself a ride and—

"*Wait!*"

His cry—deeper than thunder—jolted Cassidy as she scurried across the deserted lot. His vehicle—a big, black beast of an SUV—was the only ride there. Not like she could hotwire that thing and make an escape. She had zero hotwiring skills.

At his booming cry, Cassidy didn't look back because looking back would be an utter waste of time. If she could get to the trees across the road, she could have some cover. She'd twist and turn her way through the woods and maybe lose the guy after her. Then if she got extra lucky—a situation that rarely happened in her life—Cassidy would be able to make it to the small sheriff's station that waited about three miles away. She knew a deputy there who could help her out.

She scampered forward and—

Arms that felt like tree trunks wrapped around her, caging *her* arms against her sides, and looping around her body as the big, dangerous stranger yanked her up. He held her easily against his chest even as she squirmed and kicked. With her arms pinned, she couldn't quite reach the knife that she had strapped to her ankle. She was trying, though, and Cassidy heaved up her right foot, twisted, and managed to get her fingers around the small handle of the knife on her third attempt. *Yes.*

"US marshal."

She yanked out her weapon, and Cassidy jabbed the knife into his leg because, unfortunately, it took her a wee bit too long to process his growl.

But he dodged the blow. Mostly, anyway. And the knife sliced to the side instead of sinking deep into muscle and bone.

"*Fuck!*" He spun her around in a flash and yanked the knife from her. He tossed it somewhere—she heard the clatter as it hit the pavement.

He'd managed to toss the knife and still hold her. Kinda impressive. Majorly scary. Her feet dangled off the ground. *This. Was. Not. Good.*

Since they were dangling...Cassidy kicked him. Hard and fast. Over and over. She aimed right for his di—

"*US marshal!*" More of a roar than a growl. "US marshal! US marshal! I'm a marshal! Lady, *stop!*"

Too late. That last kick had landed hard right on target—with, uh, his dick being the target. His teeth snapped together. Did his eyes roll back into his head a bit? Oh, yes, they did.

She winced.

*Did I just attack a US marshal?*

He slowly lowered her to the ground. His teeth remained clenched, and his body completely rigid. One of his hands remained clamped around her arm while the other reached into his jacket—he'd been reaching back that way when they'd been in the bar, too. But then, she'd thought he was reaching for a weapon, so she'd hauled ass.

Her particular motto was...*When in a threatening situation, haul ass first, and never stick around to ask questions.*

But he didn't pull out a weapon. He pulled out what looked like a black wallet. He flipped it open, and she saw a shiny, gold star surrounded by a circle. One side of the wallet contained the star, and the other side held some official-looking ID card.

So...going back to *her* mental question...

*Did I just attack a US marshal?*

It would appear that the answer to that was...Yes. In fact, she had. She'd sliced him with her knife and potentially broken his dick. If a dick could be broken. This could not end well for her. Cassidy cleared her throat. "You really should have ID'd yourself first."

He shoved the wallet back into his coat. *Didn't* release her.

Dammit. She'd freaked when he yanked the gun away from her so easily. She'd only gone for the weapon behind the bar because he'd been setting off every alarm bell possible in her head. Again, as far as she was concerned, *his* fault. "Talking more would help, too. You can't just enter a bar, eat a woman alive with your eyes, and then expect her to be completely relaxed and chill when you disarm her in five seconds flat. That shit is scary, just so you know."

He blinked and finally let her go.

She realized that they were both soaking wet. The rain had drenched them. Her hair and clothes stuck to her body, and seeing as how she was wearing white...

*Fantastic.*

She was her own walking, talking version of a wet T-shirt competition.

His gaze dropped to her chest.

A muscle flexed along his ever-so-hard jaw, and then his eyes immediately flew back up to her face. She could feel water dripping down her face. Cassidy felt like she should apologize for the knife attack. And the dick attack. "I, uh, hope I didn't hurt you."

His hand rose, and he shoved back the wet hair that had fallen forward. The man had some seriously thick, dark hair. "Fine," he gritted.

Fine...as in he wasn't hurt? Nah. She didn't buy that. "I know guys like to brag, but I'm sure your dick isn't indestructible."

Lightning flashed overhead, and she jumped.

"My dick is *fine,*" he rumbled.

Her gaze darted upward. "I don't like lightning," she whispered. And here she was, running around while it flashed overhead. "Almost got struck when I was a kid. I could smell the scent of ozone, and I swear, I could feel an electric charge in the air all around me. It terrified me." Oh, if only lightning was all she had to fear these days.

Thunder roared.

Automatically, she grabbed his hand and pulled him toward the bar. "Let's get back inside."

He didn't move.

"Lightning storm," she said as she tugged harder on his hand. "We need to seek shelter and—"

Headlights. They cut through the rain and the darkness and locked right on her as the vehicle came rushing across the lot. For just a moment, those lights pinned her and her US marshal. She squinted against the light but didn't let go of her stranger's hand.

*Why not? Why am I holding him so tightly?*

But then lights flashed from the *top* of the approaching vehicle, and Cassidy realized she was staring at a patrol car. Or, to be more precise, a deputy's patrol car. Her gaze narrowed against the rain and light as she tried to make out the vehicle more clearly.

The brakes screeched a little as the driver stopped. The swirling light bar on top of the patrol car remained on even as the driver leapt from the vehicle, leaving his door open. "Cass!"

She knew the voice. Deputy Maverick Thomas. A year or so younger than she was, a nice enough guy, even if he did ask too many questions that she didn't intend to answer, and he flirted with *everyone* who—

"Who the hell is he?" Maverick demanded. "Cass? What's happening here?"

More lightning. She flinched. "We're going inside. You should come, too—"

Maverick bounded forward. He put his hand on her shoulder and tugged her away from her marshal.

Wait. Was it her imagination or had the marshal just growled?

Maverick put her behind him. "Who the hell are you?"

She was getting drenched. "He's a marshal. You're Deputy Maverick Thomas." Introductions had been made. "I'm soaking wet. We're all going inside." Done. Wasn't that the way to take charge? She thought it was. Not waiting on them—because she wasn't just going to stand there now that she was no longer running for her life—Cassidy headed back for the bar.

Behind her, she heard... "Marshal?" Maverick questioned as his normally jovial voice turned gruff. "You better have some proof of that on you, buddy."

No response. She suspected the marshal had just nodded.

The bar's front door was open, so she hurried inside. There was a slam behind her. Had Maverick finally closed *his* car door? Hopefully, he'd turned off the flashing lights, too.

She shook her head, sending drops of water flying across the bar. Goosebumps rose onto her skin. A marshal had just tracked her down. Not like she was some wanted felon or anything. Cassidy had broken zero laws. So there was no reason for him to be hunting her.

*Don't lie to yourself. You know why he's come.*

Footsteps. Heavy. Right behind her. She whirled. The marshal filled the doorway. As in, seriously filled it. The man's shoulders bumped the frame. She swallowed. "You are a big one." So big that he'd easily lifted her into the air and held her against him like it was nothing during their struggle outside.

He took a step forward.

His eyes pinned her.

The man's eyes were *insane*. Not in a bad way. In a crazy, hot, intense way. As in, she'd never seen such an electric shade of blue. Another shiver swept over her as she stood there, dripping, but this shiver had a whole lot less to do with the cold and a whole lot more to do with his unforgettable eyes.

The whole man was an unforgettable package, to be honest. That jaw? Killer. So hard and strong. Chiseled. That was the word. A chiseled jaw. The kind you wanted to lick.

*Nope. Stop. You are not licking anything. You just were running from him, for goodness' sake. Get some control woman.*

Obviously, she had been without a romantic partner for too long. But, given her track record, that was probably a good thing.

In addition to his killer eyes and his chiseled jaw, her marshal had a little cleft in his chin. A strong nose, a noble brow, and a lion's mane of dark hair.

He cleared his throat. "You need a new shirt."

He'd just said five words. Five whole words. Cassidy tugged the clinging, wet shirt from her body. "You are just getting super chatty on me now." She had another shirt—in her little studio apartment. But going to retrieve said shirt at the moment didn't seem to be a possibility because now Maverick was pushing against the marshal and coming inside.

"I want to see that ID!" Maverick blasted.

She should probably look at it again, too. A thorough look to make sure it was legit. But who would fake being a marshal?

*Like you can trust him—or anyone—blindly? You know better, Cassidy.*

The marshal headed toward her. His blue stare swept over and hardened with what looked like anger. Why was he mad?

Oh, right. She'd stabbed him. And kicked him in the dick. Cassidy winced. "I can get you some ice."

"I want that ID!" Maverick's voice rose even more.

The marshal rolled his blue eyes and pulled his ID from his coat. A big, dripping raincoat. They were all making puddles on the floor. The marshal tossed the ID to Maverick.

Maverick stood at least five inches shorter than the marshal. He was a whole lot leaner, too. He had his weapon holstered at his hip, and his uniform had dark splotches covering it—wet spots from the rain. His bushy brows rose as he checked the ID. "Titan Samson Everett?"

"Titan," she repeated. "That fits."

Titan took off his coat. More water dripped. Then he put the dripping coat over her shoulders. It *swallowed* her. "Um..." Her head tilted back. "I think raincoats are more useful when you're outside. You know, in the rain."

He lowered his head toward her. "I could see your nipples."

"You should have looked elsewhere then." Dammit, not her fault. And she was blushing. Great.

"*He* could see, too." His big hands reached out and tugged the front of the coat together before he zipped her up.

Cassidy shook her head. She also popped her arms out of the sleeves because otherwise, she was just standing there feeling like a burrito. "Do you have issues I need to know about?"

His lips tightened. God, his lips were sexy.

*Why* was she noticing sexy things about him? Why, why, why? Talk about the wrong time. And had she *not* learned her lesson before? Getting swept away by a sexy stranger was a bad thing. A terrible thing. A wreck-your-life thing.

The coat smelled like him. Her nostrils widened as she caught the scent. Crisp and fresh. It reminded her of the ocean. She was far, far away from the ocean. But she'd once spent her days running on beaches and watching the waves crash into the shore.

*Home. He smells like home.*

Nope. He did not. She was too tired, and this was madness. Cassidy licked her lips. The marshal—Titan—had said he was at the bar because of her. Her whole life could implode in the next minute if she didn't handle things very carefully. "Don't tell him about my past," she whispered to Titan. Then, hating it, she added, "Please."

His blue eyes narrowed on her.

"Ahem." From Maverick. He headed forward, moving once more into Cassidy's line of sight. "What's a US marshal doing in Nowhere? My office wasn't notified that you were here." He held out the ID to Titan. "You after a criminal? Someone dangerous in my town that I need to know about?"

*Please.* Mentally, she made the plea again. *Please, don't tell him. Please, don't wreck this little life that I've created.*

"No," Titan said.

Just that. Just no.

Her heart slammed into her ribs. Was Titan telling her no? Denying her plea? Or was he—

"No, what?" Maverick asked as he scratched his chin. Maverick was an attractive guy. Never seemed to lack attention. She'd seen several ladies hit on him each time he came into the bar. The guy had a reputation of always providing a fun night for the women who were interested. He had a quick grin, easy charm, and he looked good in his uniform.

But as he stood next to Titan, he just seemed...weak.

"No to your last question," Titan rumbled.

Her breath released in a relieved rush. *Someone dangerous in my town I need to know about?*

Good. And Titan was telling the truth. *She* wasn't dangerous.

It was her ex. He was the dangerous one—a real nightmare. Not that anyone had believed her when she'd tried to tell them the truth.

Titan shoved his ID into the back pocket of his jeans. Then he crossed his powerful arms over his chest and stared at Maverick.

Maverick's gaze kept jumping between the scars on Titan's face. "What the hell happened to you?" A low whistle escaped him.

"A knife."

Just that. Brutal and cold. And she flinched.

Maverick shot a questioning glance her way. "I don't understand what's happening. Why is a US marshal in your bar?"

"Came for her," Titan said.

Oh, no. Now she was worrying again. She wanted to close her eyes and pretend all of this wasn't happening, but that trick had never worked for her before, so why would it work now?

Titan's arm brushed against her.

Maverick grunted. "Oh, I get it."

She very much doubted that he did. Very few people would ever *get* what was happening in her life.

But Maverick nodded, all sage-like. "This the boyfriend? The one you told me about?"

Titan stiffened.

Oh, crap. She'd forgotten that lie. When Maverick had first hit on her, she'd told him that she had a boyfriend who'd be visiting town soon. The lie had been an easy way to keep him at a distance. To keep all the guys who might be interested away.

"The one you text sometimes?" Maverick continued because the man seemed determined to share her info with Titan. "The one you told me would be coming to visit you soon?"

Titan's face went dark.

"This him?" Maverick's fingers rested along the top of his holster as he took Titan's measure. "Because when I pulled up, I saw you holding hands outside."

They hadn't been holding hands. She'd been trying to get him out of the storm.

Titan opened his mouth—

"Yes!" Cassidy blurted. Once more, she grabbed Titan's hand. Probably held it a little too tightly. "This is my boyfriend, Titan. Titan Everett." She sent him a beaming smile. "So glad that you made it into town. I have missed you."

His brow furrowed as he took in her smile.

"So much," she added. "Just...so much." He was going to blow this. And why wouldn't he? He'd call her a liar right in front of the deputy, and her whole new life would go up in smoke. She'd have to move again. How many moves had it been in the last year? She couldn't get settled anywhere. Couldn't make any friends. Couldn't have a life. Pain and fear were eating her up, and she wanted it to stop.

She surged toward Titan. Wrapped her arms around his massive form—as best she could—and shot up onto her toes. She tried to yank him down closer to her. "Please," she whispered again, aiming for his ear.

But his head turned. Her lips skimmed over his jaw. To Maverick, it probably looked as if she'd given her boyfriend a tender kiss.

But…

No.

She hadn't intended a kiss. And she didn't know what to do with the sudden need that blazed through her. The kiss had been nothing. A brief touch of her lips against his chiseled jaw. A jaw that had a little stubble on it. She was—

Titan's eyes met hers. The warmth of his body—of him—surrounded her. One of his hands rose and cupped her jaw. A careful touch, but she could feel the calluses on his hand. His head dipped close to her again, and she realized that he was about to kiss her.

*He's going along with my story.* Relief had her feeling lightheaded. This stranger was going to back her up. She would owe him so much as soon as they finished this scene and got Maverick out of the way. She was going to—

His lips brushed hers.

*He's actually kissing me.*

Heat surged through her body. A sudden, fierce, sensual awareness that had every part of her feeling electrified. Like he was the lightning, and he was igniting her senses. Her lips parted more for him. His tongue dipped into her mouth.

A siren blared.

*A siren?*

"Oh, shit," Maverick exclaimed, utterly ruining her unexpected moment. "That's the tornado siren. We need to get the hell down into the shelter, now."

# CHAPTER TWO

Why had he kissed her?

Titan hunched in the tornado shelter—one that was hidden beneath the bar-slash-barn. Cassidy had led the way down the narrow staircase, and he'd barely fit as he wedged and twisted his way inside.

The siren had blasted for a time, and they'd huddled in the dimly lit interior. Cassidy hadn't looked his way, even though his eyes had remained locked on her.

*She'd told Maverick that her boyfriend would be coming to visit her soon.* As soon as the deputy had said those words, suspicion and dread had settled heavily in Titan's gut. He'd thought that he was chasing a victim. A fleeing witness.

Surely...surely Cassidy wasn't still connected to the lover from her past?

*She can't be.*

Maverick's radio crackled. After taking the fast update, he told Cassidy and Titan, "Okay, we're all clear here." Relief was apparent in his voice, and he quickly added, "I need to go check the town." He moved toward the narrow stairs, then stopped. "You two going to be all right?"

The tornado had passed. There'd been some creaks from upstairs. The moan of wind. But otherwise, ten minutes had elapsed in tense silence. The crackle of the deputy's radio had been a welcome blast.

"We're fine," Cassidy said, her voice overly bright. "Just gonna...uh, shut down the bar for the night. Not like anyone else is coming." Then, lower, Titan caught her mutter, "Should've had the damn thing closed earlier."

A closed bar wouldn't have kept him away from her.

Maverick glanced back at her. The guy didn't exactly look reassured.

There was no need for him to worry about Cassidy. "I've got her," Titan said simply. Nothing was going to happen to her on his watch.

Maverick sighed. "Figured you'd show up sooner or later." He climbed the stairs. "Was hoping for a lot later."

Because the deputy had a thing for Cassidy. Noted. That was one of the reasons Titan had put his raincoat over her. He hadn't wanted the deputy gawking at her as the material clung so tightly to her breasts. *I could see her nipples.* That had been another reason he'd covered her up. His reaction to Cassidy was a whole lot more intense than he'd expected.

The floor creaked overhead with the deputy's departing steps.

Cassidy didn't move. She kept staring at the floor, like it held all the secrets in the world. She'd stopped dripping water, though. So had he. The bar's door slammed.

The deputy was gone.

"We should see about your leg," Cassidy finally told him. "You might need stitches."

"You didn't cut me."

Finally, her head whipped up. "I did." She pointed at his left leg. "The jeans are sliced open. I didn't drive the knife deep, but the blade hit you."

He shook his head.

She took a step toward him. "Don't play the hero."

His jaw locked.

"You're hurt," she said with a determined lift of her chin. "Let me help you."

"Not hurt." Was she worried about him? Or just feeling guilty? He suspected guilt motivated her. "I know what the slice of a knife feels like." He waited for her gaze to stray to his scars.

Only, her gaze didn't waver.

He had to swallow. Probably from the dust in that makeshift shelter. It was making his throat tight. "You didn't cut me."

Her gaze fell...far down. "What about other areas?" Cassidy bit her lower lip. "You need an ice pack."

The woman was overly concerned with his dick. Huh. Maybe that was a good thing. "It's working fine." No worries on that score. When he'd seen her nipples outlined by the thin, wet shirt, his dick had sprung to eager attention.

"Good to know." Her long lashes flickered. "We should go upstairs."

And he was pretty much blocking her path. But not like there was a ton of room down there for them. He shifted a bit to the side, and when she went past him, her body brushed against his.

*There it is again.* A surge of pleasure. Just touching her sent heat streaking through his body.

She sucked in a quick breath at their physical contact, and he wondered if she felt the same flare of awareness.

Cassidy double-timed it up the narrow stairs.

He also wondered just who the fuck her boyfriend was…*Is it the sonofabitch I want to toss into a cell?*

Slowly, he followed her back up to the main level. The country music still played. A man sang about a woman who'd broken his heart in the worst way. The man crooned he wasn't complete without her.

Cassidy stumbled a little. "I hate that song," she mumbled, but she didn't move to turn off the old radio. Instead, she headed for the door and opened it to peer outside. "Your ride is safe. No damage in the parking lot. The tornado doesn't seem to have hit anything around here." Her shoulders sagged as she flipped the sign near the front window to CLOSED. She shut the door. Locked it. Then turned toward him. "I hope everyone else was as fortunate as we were."

So did he.

Silence.

A silence that stretched.

Cassidy's hands twisted in front of her. "Thanks for lying. I mean, I'm sure you don't lie to deputies as a rule. That's probably against some marshal code or something, but I really appreciate you doing it for me."

She shouldn't be thanking him. "I didn't lie."

Her brow furrowed. "But..."

"You're not dangerous." The deputy had asked if he was in town because Titan was looking for someone dangerous. Cassidy wasn't dangerous.

At least, she wasn't supposed to be.

*She'd fought like a tigress in the parking lot.* No fear at all, even though he was pretty much double her size. And she'd had a gun at the ready, hidden within easy reach behind the bar.

The Cassidy Jacobs in his file had been a happy-go-lucky kindergarten teacher. Her sunny smile had greeted kids and parents when they came into her classroom. No one had an unkind word to say about her. Her friends called her the life of the party. Her neighbors had said she'd give you the shirt off her back.

No one had said she was dangerous. She was supposed to be the good girl...who'd had the unfortunate luck to attract the attention of a very, very bad man.

"I'm not some pushover." She sniffed. "I can defend myself. You have no idea what I've been through—" Cassidy's words broke off. Once more, her lashes flickered. "Or, I guess you do. That's the reason you're here, isn't it?"

Titan nodded.

"*He's* the reason?" she pushed with fear breathing into her words.

Again, he nodded.

She paled and swayed, and for a moment, Titan thought she might faint on him. Acting on instinct, he leapt forward and scooped her into his arms. “I’ve got you.”

“What?” Her eyes widened. “What are you doing? Put me down!”

But she felt right in his arms.

*And that is wrong*. He let her go immediately, putting Cassidy back on her feet. But he kept a hand on her shoulder. “Thought you were fainting.”

“No. Absolutely not.” She seemed horrified by the idea, but she lingered against him for a moment, and her hands fluttered nervously over his body. “I’m just still shivery from getting soaked in the rain. I’m cold and, a few moments ago, I thought a tornado was going to take us all out and—*God, is he killing again? Has Blake hurt someone else?*”

She seemed breakable beneath his hand. Her bones delicate. Her build too fragile. He’d come after her because she was the key to stopping a string of murders. But in order for her to be that key...

Her hair trailed over her shoulder as her head tilted to the right. “Are you okay?” Cassidy suddenly asked him. “You look...sad.”

In order to be the key, Cassidy Jacobs would be placed in mortal danger. “I didn’t lie.”

She inhaled and backed up a step, shaking free of his hold.

Titan’s hand dropped to his side. His fingers flexed, oddly missing the warmth of her body.

"No, no, I guess you didn't lie to the deputy." She turned away and walked toward the bar. Her hands drove into the pockets of the raincoat. "I did that part. You told him you weren't here for anyone dangerous, and I was the one who lied and said that you were my boyfriend."

She'd pleaded with him. The sound of her whispered *please* had made his chest ache. Cassidy—with her sunny smile and those deep, dark eyes—he'd had the thought that she shouldn't be begging anyone for anything.

"You went with my ruse, so I owe you." She eyed the whiskey still on the bar top. His whiskey. "You're not planning on drinking that, are you?"

Titan shook his head.

"Then don't mind if I do..." Her hands eased from the pockets. Her right hand curled around the glass. She lifted it up, took a gulp, then grimaced. "Burns like good fire." Her fingers trembled as she put down the still mostly full glass. "I owe you, so how do you plan to collect?"

She'd turned around, propping her elbows behind her on the bar as she lounged back and waited for his response. As he stared at her, an all too vivid image danced in his head. Of them, on that bar, finishing the teasing kiss they'd started.

*What. The. Actual. Fuck?*

"You keep looking at me like I have two heads. It's weird." She shrugged. "And a little insulting."

He knew exactly what it was like when someone looked at you in an insulting way, and that had never been his intent with her. Never. "Sorry." Gruff.

A roll of her shoulders. She still wore his raincoat. A good thing, because he doubted her shirt had dried. "It's odd because I could swear, one minute I think you want me, but the next, you're staring at me like I'm some new form of life you've never seen before." A faint smile teased her lips. The dimples didn't show because her smile didn't stretch far enough. "I can assure you, I am nothing special. Probably just like every other woman you've ever met."

Not exactly. "There's a notable exception."

She swallowed. "Right. The boyfriend."

*The boyfriend.* "You're still seeing him?" Titan found himself surging forward. Almost stalking her. "After everything that happened, you are still with—"

She shot away from the bar. "Of course, I'm not still seeing him! I'm *running* from him! I don't have a death wish. I also don't have a giant wish to spend my life with a psychotic bastard who gets off on *killing women who look way too much like me.*"

And there it was. The truth in all its dark and twisted glory.

Her eyes closed. "Do you ever think you're in a nightmare and if you could just wake up, everything would be okay again?"

He was the nightmare, so no, Titan didn't usually think that.

"I'm scared of silence."

Had he heard that right?

"The night I learned what Blake was doing...I couldn't make a sound. There was a dead body on the floor. *The floor of his kitchen.* I'd found her, and..." Her eyes opened. "I knew she was dead. It wasn't like I didn't try to get help for her. You can't lose that much blood and still be alive. Her neck was sliced open. There was a *pool* of blood beneath her." She cleared her throat. "On the plastic beneath her. It was the plastic that I didn't understand at first. I mean...why was the plastic there? Then it hit me. He'd *planned* to kill this woman. He'd put the plastic down so the blood wouldn't stain the fancy tiles in his kitchen. I wanted to scream but, before I could, he was there."

Her voice had lost all emotion. So had her eyes.

"I heard the back door squeak open. I heard the sweet music from the wind chime that I'd given him—the chime that was on his back porch. I knew all he had to do was walk through the mudroom and he'd be back in that kitchen. Back with me. I wasn't supposed to be there." A shake of her head. "I wasn't. But he'd given me a key the night before. We were...God, he wanted me to move in. I was going to move in *the next day*. But I was excited, so I'd come by unannounced and...there was a dead body on his floor."

"How did you know he'd killed her?"

Cassidy's lower lip trembled. "Wh-what do you mean?"

"How did you know someone else hadn't done it?" Each word grated and rumbled, and she flinched.

But he didn't think she was flinching because of his voice. It was her own memories that made her flinch.

"He was whistling. I heard him whistling when the back door opened. His whistle. My wind chime."

Yet how had she *known* he was the killer? "Someone could have broken in."

"The front door showed no sign of forced entry. I used my key to get inside. His car was in the driveway." Another swallow, and this time, he heard the faint click of sound. "Do you ever meet a person and think...you're too perfect?"

No. That hadn't happened. And no one had ever met him and thought that.

"Blake was perfect. Like everything I thought I wanted, all tied up in a perfectly handsome bow. He said the right things. He was always the perfect gentleman. It was like he was reading my mind and knowing what I wanted before I even knew myself." She wrapped her arms around her stomach, and the raincoat crinkled. "Too perfect. Inside, I knew that no one was perfect. When I saw that body...when I saw *her*...it was like I was staring down at myself. She was naked and dead, and it could have been me. She could have been me."

A tear slid down her cheek.

Titan didn't like that tear.

"My first reaction was to hide. Maybe that wasn't what I should have done. Maybe a better person—a braver one—would have fought him. Grabbed a knife from the block that was on the kitchen counter. Gone at him. Grabbed a chair and hit him with it—*something*. I didn't. Because I have never been brave." Her chin lowered. "I hid in the pantry. I didn't make a sound. I clamped one hand over my mouth, and I stood there crying while he…"

Again, she stopped.

He should do something. Comfort her? Fuck. He didn't know how to comfort anyone.

"There were slats in the pantry door. I could see through the slats. Little cracks. So small. But I could see everything he was doing. He stopped whistling. The chime didn't reach me because the door had closed. He…bent down toward her and he…" Her teeth chattered. "It's cold in here. No, no, I bet it's the wet clothes. I have to get out of them." She spun and rushed toward a black door marked STAFF. Her hand lifted and curled around the doorknob. "My apartment is just beyond this building. I-I'll change. You can wait here. I'll be back in a few minutes."

Not like he planned to leave Nowhere without her.

"I couldn't make a sound. He didn't make a sound either. He just…Silence," she said, with her back to him. "I had to stay there in total silence, and I kept praying that he wouldn't notice me. That he wouldn't come to the pantry. And I couldn't make a sound, and it took so long and…" Cassidy whirled toward him. "I hate silence now," she told him as her voice broke. "So I talk too much. I play my radio too loud. I keep the TV going when I shouldn't. I do all kinds of things that probably seem weird or odd and so…you should know that it's just going to get worse from here on out. You have to understand that about me. You look at me like I'm some strange specimen already, and that's just the surface. You should know—"

"I'm sorry." The words were pulled from him, but they had to be spoken. She feared silence. Hell, wasn't that all he was?

"For what?"

*Tell her.* "If I'm looking at you...too intently..." And he was. Titan knew it. "It's because you look at *me* differently."

A few fast blinks. "I do?" Then her cheeks pinkened. "I—"

"You don't stare at the scars." He rubbed the line that dipped below his jaw. The raised skin looked so much better now than it had when he'd first woken in that hospital. But the truth was that even the *better* version still made him look like a monster. The lines on his face were just the start of what waited on his body.

A little furrow appeared between her brows. "I saw them. Same way I saw your chiseled jaw and your thick hair and your gorgeous eyes." Her dimples flashed for a moment. "You have the bluest eyes I've ever seen. Bet you hear that a lot, don't you?"

No, he absolutely did not. No one ever talked about his eyes.

"Ugh. Is it possible to get drunk off so little whiskey?" A negative shake of her head. "I must be drunk. I am oversharing like crazy with you. This doesn't usually happen. Yes, I talk too much, but I don't make a rule of telling men that they have beautiful eyes."

*Don't stop.* Fuck. "Cassidy..." They needed to get back on track. Back to talking about the case and her ex and why Titan had tracked her across the U.S.

"I'm going to my apartment. I'm ditching my wet clothes. Getting dry. Once I've changed, I'll give you back your raincoat. Thanks, by the way, for the loan. Maverick, um, he hit on me a few times, so I gave him the excuse of a made-up boyfriend."

Made-up. Some of the tension slipped from Titan. "So there is no real boyfriend?"

"With my past?" A bitter laugh. "Not likely."

Why was he relieved to hear she wasn't seeing anyone else? It shouldn't matter. *Maybe you're relieved because it makes things easier. If she has no ties, then it will be easier for her to leave Nowhere and come with you.*

Only that didn't *feel* like the reason he was so relieved.

Her brow furrowed as she peered at him. "What am I supposed to do with you?"

*Anything you want?* Nope. That wasn't the right answer. "I need to talk with you about my case." It was more about what *he* was supposed to do with her. *Take her back. Bring out the killer.*

"Talk. Right. We will do that. Definitely. Just...give me a few moments first, will you?" A sad smile. "We'll talk. I just...I need to change first."

Not like he could force the woman to let him into her apartment. With her past, she was wise to play it safe and *not* let him get too close. "I can give you a number so you can verify my identity. Don't want you thinking the ID is bullshit."

"That was a lot of words from you." She licked her lower lip. "Are you doing that for me? You seem to be getting chattier."

*I'm afraid of silence.* Yeah, he was doing it for her. Awkward as hell. "I'm doing it because I want you to trust me."

"I don't trust anyone."

Titan knew that feeling.

Her cheeks puffed out, then Cassidy released a long breath. "Has he killed again?"

"Yes."

She flinched as if Titan had just hit her.

"He's not going to stop," Titan added. The words had to be said.

But her gaze cut down to the floor.

"Not unless you stop him," he said.

She staggered back. "How do you—" She shook her head, sending her hair flying, and there were *tears* in her eyes. Tears that made the gold gleam and swirl and that made his chest ache even more.

"Cassidy?"

"I have to go." Another fast shake of her head. "Go change. I have to go change. I'll be back. Just—you stay here. It's safe in here. Too dangerous outside." With that, she whirled away once more and rushed through the employee door.

He stood there and fought the urge to chase after her. He'd hurt her. That hadn't been Titan's intent, but he'd made her cry.

*She's terrified, and you just brought her nightmare crashing back on her.*

But Cassidy was a necessary component of this case.

*Because she's the one the killer wants. The only victim to get away from him.* Cassidy Jacobs was the woman who the killer wanted. She was the one woman Blake Normandy actually seemed to care about. If it was even possible for him to care.

Some people weren't born to love. They were born to destroy. To tear the world apart. Titan had encountered many of those people in his life. But even monsters could feel an attachment to something. To someone. Titan had an FBI buddy named Oliver Foxx who spent most of his time tracking serial killers. Oliver swore that it was possible for even twisted murderers to form attachments with certain people.

In the case of Blake Normandy—not like that was the guy's real name, just another in a long line of aliases—in his case, Oliver believed that Blake had fixated romantically on Cassidy. Even though she fit his victim profile, Blake hadn't hurt Cassidy. Instead, he'd seemingly fallen for her. Had asked her to move into his house. Had even planned to marry her.

That had all been before Cassidy had discovered the truth about him.

Too bad the local cops hadn't believed her when she'd run to them. But, by the time Cassidy had gotten the cops from Cresent Beach, Florida, back to the scene of the crime, the victim's body had been long gone. Blake had been the picture of innocence, and Cassidy...a hysterical Cassidy had been put in a seventy-two-hour psych hold.

He glanced toward the STAFF door. Cassidy hadn't made it through the seventy-two-hour hold. She'd escaped during the first night and vanished.

The man calling himself Blake Normandy had vanished, too. And the body of the supposed victim that had sent Cassidy running to the cops? She hadn't been found.

*Until recently. And then the cops had to suddenly believe the woman they'd pegged as delusional had actually been telling the horrifying truth.*

His gaze fell. Then slid around the bar. Thunder rumbled in the distance. The bottles on the shelf trembled faintly. The storm wasn't over. Not by a long shot.

Titan knew he wasn't going anywhere that night. *There is no way I am leaving her*. Not just because of the storm, but because he'd discovered that Cassidy had a real talent for vanishing.

That was why tracking her had been tricky. Each time, he'd thought he was closing in, only to have her vanish.

She'd cut out of her gig as a blackjack dealer in Biloxi two days before he found her.

One day before he'd arrived in Nashville, she'd left her waitressing job at a small diner. Side note, the place had served some damn good grits.

And her tour guide gig in Colorado? She'd given up her river rafting routine *hours* before he'd rushed into town.

He'd started to think someone might be tipping her off. But everything he knew seemed to suggest she had no ties, not to anyone. She was all alone. Running. Scared.

*And very, very good at vanishing.*

Only she couldn't vanish now. He'd found her. He would *not* be leaving town without her. While she was changing, he'd go to his SUV and grab his bag. Maybe after she'd verified his identity, Cassidy would let him bunk down on the couch in her apartment. He certainly wasn't going across town to the dilapidated motel on the edge of Nowhere. Not like he'd trust her out of his sight—

*Fuck.*

She was already out of his sight and sudden fear had him slapping his hands against his front, right jean pocket. The pocket that *should* have contained his car keys. Only those keys were gone.

He remembered lifting her into his arms. Remembered the way she'd leaned against him and her hands had fluttered over him when he'd put her down.

Sonofabitch.

Cassidy was making a run for it already. And planning to use *his* ride.

Oh, hell, no.

***

She hadn't really planned to change clothes. The little room she'd entered in the bar was a storage area. One with its own back door. Cassidy ran through that door and then got in and out of her apartment as fast as she could. She snagged her go bag in about thirty seconds and then huffed it toward the parking lot.

She'd started keeping the go bag after she'd had to leave Biloxi. It made sense to have a change of clothes, some hair dye, and her cash waiting for her. Biloxi had been *too* close. She'd almost been caught there.

The rain fell lightly, but she still wore the oversize raincoat, so Cassidy was protected. She felt a *wee* bit guilty for stealing the marshal's coat.

Her right hand lifted, gripping the keys she'd lifted from his pocket.

She felt even *guiltier* about stealing his ride. But her life was on the line, and desperate times called for some law-breaking measures.

She didn't bother using the remote to unlock the car. Cassidy knew if she hit that little button, the SUV would probably honk and its lights would flash. No way did she want the sexy marshal hearing the horn blare. That blare would alert him, and he'd come chasing after her.

She was almost to the vehicle. Raindrops slid down the driver's side window and—

A gravelly voice asked her, "Are we going somewhere?"

Cassidy screamed and spun around.

"Because it looks like *we* are." The giant wall of muscle that was Titan stood less than two feet—maybe just one—away from her.

Oh, shit.

He reached for her right hand. His fingers swallowed hers because he had a bear-sized hand. "Wondered where these had gone. It's the wildest thing. I could have sworn they were in my pocket."

"So weird," she whispered. "I found them and was bringing them to you."

"That's how they wound up in your hand? You found them?"

"Uh, hmmm."

It was too dark to be certain, but she thought his lips might have twitched. "Did you, by any chance, find them when you lifted them from my pocket?"

Oh, God. This was going badly. Very, very badly. Because that was precisely where she'd found them.

"You should have checked the other pocket," he told her as he released her hand. "You would have found something useful in there, too."

She'd just been caught—seriously *red-handed*—trying to steal the vehicle that belonged to a US marshal. There was no way this ended well for her.

"See?"

Her gaze flew to *see* just what he'd taken from his other pocket.

Only for him to snap a handcuff around her wrist.

"Super useful," he assured her. "Sweetheart, you're not getting away from me."

# CHAPTER THREE

The tree had almost smashed straight into the front of the truck.

Deputy Maverick Thomas flashed his bright lights as he pulled to the side of the road. From what he'd been able to tell, this two-mile stretch had been hit by the tornado. Trees were uprooted. Part of a nearby wooden fence had been smashed to bits. But, luckily, no homes were in this area. His people were safe.

Except for this driver?

Climbing from the car and pulling on his rain poncho, Maverick noted the barcodes on the back window that marked the truck as a rental. He didn't see any damage to the rear of the vehicle, but he hadn't gotten a good look at the front yet. The big, fallen tree appeared mighty close to the front bumper.

He clutched his flashlight in one hand and headed for the driver's side. The windows were darkly tinted, and his knuckles rapped on the glass as he kept holding tightly to his light. "Hey! You okay—"

The window rolled down.

Maverick automatically tensed. Even as his left hand gripped the flashlight, his right stretched to hover over his holster. He'd learned long ago that you never knew what danger you could find waiting for you on a dark night.

"Officer! Thank you for stopping." The man's voice held relief as he rushed to say, "A tornado flew right in front of me. Scared the hell out of me. Never seen anything like it in my life! There was this roaring and the whole world was shaking, and I thought for sure I was dead..."

"You need to get off the road, sir," Maverick told him even as he felt tension slither down his spine. Tornadoes scared the ever-loving-hell out of him. "The bad weather isn't done for the night. You need shelter. There's a motel not too far from here. If you don't already have a place to stay, you can find a room there." Though that rickety place wasn't exactly the most secure location. Still, it would be better than being in the open.

"I-I think my front tire might be flat."

Maverick swung his flashlight toward the front tire near him.

"The one on the right," the driver told him quickly. "I looked at it a moment ago—after the roaring stopped—and it seemed to be sagging straight into the road."

"You got a spare?" Maverick asked.

"Yeah, yeah, I think so."

"I can help you change it." They needed to move, fast. The sooner they got off that road, the better. "Come on." Maverick's hand moved away from his holster. He headed around the front of the truck, then shone his light at the front, right tire.

Not sagging at all.

The truck door slammed. The driver had gotten out.

"The tire looks fine to me," Maverick called to him. Perhaps the man had just gotten confused in the dark.

"Really?" The guy's footsteps shuffled closer. "Oh, that's great. I was pretty shaken up, maybe I was mistaken."

Maverick shone his light toward the fallen tree. About three feet away. "You got lucky. The tree seems to have missed you entirely."

"I have always been lucky."

The man was almost right beside him. A little too close for Maverick's comfort.

Maverick jerked his light toward the guy's face.

Behind the thin frames of his glasses, the man's eyes squinted. "Uh, do you mind?"

Maverick didn't lower his light. Not yet. The guy was bigger than he'd realized. Tall. Short hair. A tight beard covered his jaw. "Sir," Maverick said, making his voice flat, "you need to get back in your vehicle and get to that motel I mentioned. It is not safe for you to stay out in the open during this kind of weather."

"Oh, I'm not going to a motel. I'm here to find a friend."

"It's the middle of a damn storm. Your friend can wait." He lowered his light and stiffened a little. Had he just started to hear—

"Maybe you know my friend," the stranger added, speaking quickly. "Her first name is Cassidy. She usually goes by Cass. Really pretty. About five-foot-five. Has these incredible dimples when she smiles and these deep, golden eyes—"

The tornado siren roared again. *Shit.* "We got to get out of here!" Maverick snapped. "We need shelter. We need—"

"Cassidy—"

"Yeah, yeah, I know her. She's with her damn boyfriend." He ran around the vehicle. Heard footsteps behind him.

The man grabbed Maverick's shoulder.

Maverick spun back around. "Listen, buddy, you need to—"

Something hit him in the stomach.

No, not hit him. *Something drove into me.* Maverick glanced down. He saw the handle of a knife. A handle that the stranger was gripping. As he stared in horror, the bastard pulled out the knife, only to stab Maverick again.

"She's not with her boyfriend," the man snarled. "Because I'm fucking right here."

Too late, Maverick tried to grab his gun. Everything felt slow and his fingers weren't working right, and he couldn't get the thing out of the holster. He—

The knife pressed to his throat. "You're really not my type. So I'd prefer not to kill you."

Maverick could feel the blood pumping from his wounds.

"Let's get back to *my* girl, Cass, shall we? Tell me where she is. Tell me right now, and I won't cut your throat from ear to ear."

The wailing of the tornado siren grew louder and louder. And then...a rumble. Like a train coming toward them fast and hard as it picked up speed. Getting stronger and stronger and...

Wind whipped around Maverick and sent his hair flying and his poncho fluttering against his body.

The knife sliced across his throat, and the whole world spun.

***

"I shouldn't have called you 'sweetheart' just then."

Cassidy gaped at him.

"That was my bad," he added grimly.

"Your bad?" Her voice rose to a near shriek. "*Cuffing me* was your bad. Do you hear me, *sweetheart?* You can't just—" She broke off, and her mouth dropped open even more.

He knew why she'd stopped chewing him out.

Sonofabitch. The tornado siren was going off again. Titan locked the other cuff around his wrist and lifted Cassidy up against him. He held her with one arm wrapped around her body as he rushed back to the bar.

"What the hell?" An angry cry from Cassidy as she broke from her momentary stupor. "You can't do this. You can't—"

He heard a rumble. A whoosh. Could have sworn a pounding waterfall or an oncoming train was barreling toward them. When he looked into the distance, he thought he saw the darkness of the sky swirling. Lightning flashed and sure the fuck enough—

"Run!" Cassidy screamed. "Run a whole lot faster!"

He hauled ass. Got them inside and back down into her shelter. He yanked the small door closed behind him and twisted and shoved his way down the stairs. The dim lights above them flickered, over and over again, and the whole building seemed to shudder.

Cassidy turned her cuffed hand and grabbed his. She linked her fingers with his and held on tight.

Screw that. Titan did better than a hand hold. He drew her in close against his body, huddled over Cassidy, and covered every single inch of her.

***

Silence.

Cassidy's drumming heart slammed into her ribs. She could feel Titan everywhere, against her back, beneath her legs...because she was sitting on him.

Her eyes blinked open. Had she fallen asleep? Amazingly, she thought she must have because one minute, she'd been standing with Titan as his body protectively surrounded hers and now...

Now they were on the floor of the shelter. His legs were beneath her. She sat on his lap, and his arms curled around her as he cradled her against him. His warm, strong chest pressed against her back, and she realized...

*I was sleeping on him.*

Her breath shuddered in even as her gaze frantically flew around. The shelter was in complete darkness. She remembered the lights flickering and then...

Then she'd just been afraid. For a very long time.

"When you stopped talking, I knew you'd gone to sleep."

Her head jerked, and she was pretty sure she clipped him on the chin.

"Fuck."

"Sorry!" Cassidy twisted against him as she turned to try and see his face. "I—" Useless. She couldn't make out his features. She could feel him, but not see him. No light at all down there, and the place felt way too much like some kind of tomb to her. "Is it over?"

"Not sure. Thought it might be a good idea to wait down here for a while, seeing as how you seemed determined to run into storms."

She swallowed. "I wasn't running *into* the storm."

"No. Just trying to run from me." A pause. "Both times."

Guilty as charged.

She shifted a little, and he groaned.

Cassidy froze. *I'm on the marshal's lap. Got to move. Now.* Except when she tried to jump up, the cuff on her wrist prevented her from going anywhere. Instead of a rushed exit, she just got yanked back against him. She tumbled down, and this time, she wound up with her front facing his chest. Her legs did a straddle around his hips, and...

Great. She'd just gone from bad to way worse. Way, way worse.

Her breasts pressed against him, and her hips arched when she tried to get away. So instead of putting space between them...she was now rubbing against his dick. In the dark. While cuffed to him.

And for the record, she'd discovered that he was big *everywhere*. Cassidy's breath shuddered out. "Are the cuffs necessary?"

"I was trying to stop you from running into a tornado."

"I think you were trying to stop me from stealing your car." Could she get up without rubbing against his dick again? She tried a little wiggle.

He growled.

Uh, oh. She'd done a definite rub.

"Let me help you," he said. His breath seemed to feather over her cheek. Hearing that deep, rumbly voice in the dark...

*No, don't you dare do it. Do not go getting turned on by a guy who handcuffed you.* What was wrong with her? Was she just wired wrong?

*Or is it that I like fear? Is something just off with me? Am I as bad as—*Cassidy stopped the thought. She'd gone down that road too many times in her head, and she never liked where the path took her.

He reached for her wrist. The one with the cuff. *Snick*. It popped open. Before she could lunge off his lap, his hands had wrapped around her waist. He lifted her and rose at the same time. And in a fast moment, she was on her feet and no longer rubbing against a particularly prominent part of his anatomy.

But his hands remained around her waist, chaining her just as good as a handcuff.

"Do you always walk around with handcuffs in your pocket?" she blurted.

"Yeah, I do. I keep my ID and cuffs at the ready, and, just so you know, on my right foot, I've got my gun in an ankle holster. I never go anywhere without being armed."

Of course, he didn't. "I know what you want."

"I don't think you have a clue." His hold tightened on her.

"I went to the cops before. I took them right to that kitchen. I told them everything. You know what happened?"

"They sent you to a psych ward."

She could still hear her own screams. "It was my word against his. He was calm and charming. So seemingly confused by my wild accusations. And he had this whole story ready. About how I'd had a psychotic break years ago when my parents died. How I had been sent to a treatment facility back then." A bitter laugh broke from her. "That was true, damn him. But only because I had nowhere else to go. I had *no one* else. I couldn't stop crying. Couldn't stop hurting. The court didn't know what to do with me—a seventeen-year-old who'd been the only survivor of a robbery gone so wrong—and they locked me up. He *knew* that, even though I'd never told him. He knew so much about me and I..."

Too much. She was talking too much again.

It was dark all around her, but she still closed her eyes. Cassidy tried to pull in a deep breath. "I wasn't psychotic at seventeen. I was consumed with pain. I missed my parents. Didn't understand why I had made it and they hadn't." It had just been a normal night. *A normal night.* They'd gone out to dinner. They'd been laughing when they headed to their car. Her mom had been talking about college plans and—

Gone. All of it. Gone so fast.

*I have the worst luck in the world.* "Some people are cursed." She believed that. After all, she was one of those people.

"Cassidy."

Her eyes opened. If she strained hard enough, she could almost make out his shadowy features. "I sounded crazy when I talked to the cops in Florida. I know that, now. I was screaming about a woman's body. About how he'd cut her up—" No. Cassidy stopped. She *could not* remember that scene. Or how she'd watched every moment from that damn pantry. "There was no blood when I brought the cops back. There was just me screaming about a woman who wasn't there. There was my boyfriend, being sad and concerned, and the cops believing *him*. Then I was being sent into an involuntary psychiatric commitment for seventy-two hours."

"Cassidy..."

"They strapped me down because I was trying to get away. I can remember what it felt like when they slid a needle into my arm. 'Giving you something to help you calm down.' That's what the nurse said. But whatever they gave me only made my body feel numb. My mind was still screaming."

His hands remained around her waist. "I know you weren't crazy."

"I wasn't crazy then. Can't really say too much about how things are going these days."

*"You aren't crazy."*

Right. Not like crazy was a clinical term, anyway. Except...her ex?

*He was fucking crazy.* "Before I was wheeled away in that facility, he smiled at me. He told me that he'd be waiting for me when the seventy-two hours were over. Said for me not to worry. He'd be there for me. Always."

"Fuck."

"Actually, I believe my thought at the time was 'Fuck, no.'" Blake's tender promise hadn't been the last thing her ex had said to her. Hadn't been the last time he'd seen her. Because later, when the ward had been quiet and dark, when everyone else had been sleeping, he'd snuck into her room.

She shivered.

"Do you know who the Ice Breakers are?" Titan asked her.

"What?"

"The Ice Breakers. Have you heard of them?"

No, she hadn't. "What the hell is that? Like a hockey team or something?" She looked upward. "Can we get out of here? I need to *breathe."* Okay, fine, she was breathing. But she also had zero idea how much time had passed, and she needed to check on the building. She owed it to the manager-slash-owner who'd given her the job—and the apartment.

"We can get out, but you have to promise not to run again."

She would make zero promises on that score. "Running is a way of life," she muttered and stepped back from him. She turned and promptly walked into what felt like a stack of boxes. Dammit.

Once more, his hand curled around her waist. "I think my eyes have adjusted better. Let me help." He eased her to the side. "The Ice Breakers solve cold cases. They started online. Came from all kinds of different backgrounds. A reporter. A former bounty hunter. A bastard with more money than God."

Her brows climbed at that last description. "How wonderful for him."

Titan grunted. "Some of the team comes from law enforcement. The doctor of the dead is part of the group, too, and let me tell you, there isn't a body that Tony and her dog Banshee can't find. Hell, they are the reason I came after you in the first place." He guided her up the stairs and kept his grip on her the whole time.

Maybe she was grateful for that grip.

Maybe she was grateful for him. *What if I'd been on the road when that tornado hit?*

There were no lights in the bar area, but at least there were windows. One was broken, and rainwater had poured inside. Rainwater...and a bit of sunlight.

Because dawn was coming.

*We were down there all night long?*

He let her go. "Tony was working a case in Florida when she came upon some human remains. Not the vic she thought, but someone else. Someone who had been...well, the body was in pieces."

Cassidy had just taken a step back from him, but at his chilling words, she froze.

"Tony retrieved all the severed remains."

Cassidy stared at him, waiting for more.

The faint lines around his mouth deepened, but he got the hint and growlingly continued, "She was able to ID the victim. She is quite amazing when it comes to ID'ing the dead. Turns out, Tony had found a woman who'd gone missing about thirteen months before. Tracy Eldridge, twenty-seven. A woman who'd been vacationing in Florida but was actually from Graham, Tennessee. A woman who, according to her driver's license, was five feet five inches tall, one hundred thirty-five pounds, with dark brown hair and brown eyes." A pause. "Were they brown? Or were they really dark gold, like yours?"

"H-how would I know?"

"Because Tony believes she was the woman you found in your boyfriend's kitchen."

She did not move. Still too rooted to the spot.

"You were telling the truth that night. He'd ditched the body before the cops could get back to the house with you. Hidden it so well in the woods that no one *would* have found it, if Tony hadn't been working another case about a missing teenager. That case took her there. Only instead of the teen, Tony found Tracy. Not too long after that gruesome discovery, another body was located...also in the woods, but in South Carolina, not Florida. A woman in her late twenties, approximately five feet five inches tall, a slender build, with dark hair and dark—"

*They all look like me.*

"The body had been dismembered, too. This vic was taken and killed *after* you left Florida."

Her hand flew to her mouth. *Don't be sick. Do not be sick right here.*

"The Ice Breakers believe a serial killer is hunting."

Those Ice Breakers were right. He'd been hunting for a long time, and he had no intention of stopping.

"They've been creating victim profiles." Titan's rough voice told her, "Pulling up all reports of missing persons and comparing them with the killer's preferred target."

She knew all about his preferred target. *It's me.* "How many victims have they found?" Soft. Hoarse.

"They've found two bodies that match the MO that's been crafted. The one in Florida and the one in South Carolina. But they have matched two other potential victims from the missing persons reports. Just haven't found them yet, but Tony is working on it. That means that the Ice Breakers suspect four victims."

She shook her head.

His jaw tightened, stretching the white line that marked him. "They don't have conclusive proof that the man you knew as Blake Normandy was behind the crimes, but they suspect—"

"There were more than four."

His incredible eyes widened. "How do you know that?"

"Because he told me."

Titan took a slow step toward her. It was a gliding, stalking movement. The way a predator would close in on prey. Her shoulders stiffened. She was so tired of being prey.

"When." Not a question. A demand. And suddenly, his blue eyes looked hard and cold. He stared at her with suspicion.

"I'm not his partner." Was that what he thought? Hadn't he even asked—hadn't he asked before if she was still in contact with her boyfriend?

*"When."*

"I was never involved. I went straight to the police. I tried to stop him." The guilt burned through her. "They didn't listen. They locked me up."

"*When* did he tell you about the other victims?"

"I haven't been talking to him!" Why could he not understand her? "If that's the reason you hunted me down and cuffed me...if it's because you think I can lead you to him, you're dead wrong—"

"I'm dead right. You're the key to finding him. To stopping him. It's all about *you.*"

Her stomach twisted. She'd heard those words before. *It's all about you.* Those exact words. A tear slid down her cheek. "Don't."

"You can stop him. You have the power to do it. As far as the Ice Breakers know, you are the only witness to his crimes. Blake Normandy doesn't exist. That was a bogus name, but the cops never even bothered to check beneath the surface to find that shit out. The man is a ghost."

No, the man was a killer.

"You're the only one who knows him."

She shook her head.

"You can help the Ice Breakers. You can lead us to him."

No, she couldn't.

"Don't you want him stopped?"

More than anything, she did. Another tear slid down her cheek.

His hand rose and brushed it away. "I tracked you down because I want you to help us."

"You want to use me." She wasn't stupid. She knew where this was going. "You think if you have me, if I stop hiding, he'll come for me."

She had to give him credit. For what it was worth, Titan didn't lie to her. He stared straight into her eyes and said, "Yes. I want to use you."

She blinked away more tears that she *would* not let fall.

"I found you," Titan told her. "You've left town after town. You did that because you knew he was hunting you, didn't you, Cassidy?"

*Yes.*

"If I found you, then you have to know that he will, too. Sooner or later, your luck will run out."

"Fuck luck," she breathed. "It's never helped me any."

"I can protect you," he vowed.

Those words sent chills racing up and down her spine. The cops hadn't believed her before. The people at the hospital? The psych ward?

They'd ignored her pleas and just pumped a sedative into her system. Then, when Blake had broken into her room that night, she'd been helpless. Still strapped to the bed. A total prisoner for him.

If he'd wanted, he could have killed her right then and there. They both knew that. But death wasn't what he wanted from her. Or at least, that was what he claimed. But how long before he changed his mind? How long before he realized she just wasn't what he believed her to be?

"Cassidy?"

"No one has offered to protect me before."

"You haven't met anyone like me before."

She wasn't sure there was anyone else quite like Titan out there. Cassidy licked her lips. "No one believed me. They didn't think he was a monster."

"I believe you." Simple.

She knew he did. If she went with him, what would happen? She'd be the lure to try drawing out Blake?

"Aren't you tired of being afraid?" Titan pushed.

Yes, she was. Bone and soul tired of it. Cassidy nodded.

"Then why don't you agree to help me—"

"I was nodding because my answer is yes." Her spine straightened. "I'm in. You stay with me. You really protect me." Because no way did she want to be on her own if Blake was closing in. "And I'll help you. I'll do whatever I can to stop him." Cassidy lifted her hand toward Titan. "Deal?"

His hand closed around hers. The rough calluses brushed across her skin, but, despite the massive size of his hand, his touch was very, very careful. “Deal.” His blue eyes glittered. “Let’s go catch ourselves a killer.”

God, that sounded...absolutely terrifying.

# CHAPTER FOUR

"I have rules," Cassidy announced as he drove them out of Nowhere. There were downed trees around the road. A power line that had crashed to the pavement. Titan made sure to steer clear of it. The storm had been a nightmare, and he was damn glad the weather was clear this morning.

Cassidy had taken some time to clean the bar and left a note for her boss. She'd said she wanted him to know that she was okay. Apparently, leaving a "thank you" note was part of her MO because he knew she'd done the same routine several times before. As he'd ushered her from the bar, he'd questioned her about the tactic, and she'd told him that she always had to thank a kindness.

So she had.

The woman hadn't left any detail about where she was going in the note, though. Just told her boss that it was time to move on. That she'd been grateful for the opportunity. That she wished him the best.

She'd also insisted on calling and checking out Titan's identity. He wasn't sure why that call had reassured her. It would have been easy enough to get any Joe off the street to back up his claim of being a marshal. But...

She was in the SUV. They were on the road. They were a team. And he had a killer who needed to be taken out.

"Titan? Did you hear me?"

She was right beside him, so, yes, he had. But his gaze had turned to the right. An ambulance's lights flashed near the side of the road. Several patrol cars were there, along with a rather beaten-up-looking truck. One of the patrol cars had parked directly behind the truck.

"Oh, God." Cassidy grabbed his shoulder. "I hope everyone is okay!"

Titan slowed the SUV and rolled down his window. A tall, thin deputy stood near the edge of the accident, and he waved them onward.

But Titan still hesitated. "Everyone all right?" he called. He didn't like just driving past a scene without trying to help.

"Got an injured deputy. Was caught in the storm last night."

The ambulance's siren wailed as the driver pulled onto the road behind Titan's vehicle—then drove the opposite way.

"Keep moving," the man ordered Titan. "Watch out for the power line."

Titan eased slowly forward, but his gaze kept straying to the rearview mirror. The ambulance grew smaller and smaller.

"I didn't see Maverick." Cassidy had let go of his shoulder. "That was his patrol car right behind the truck, but Maverick wasn't on scene." She twisted in her seat. "You think he was the one who got hurt?"

Certainly a possibility. "Want to follow the ambulance?"

Still twisted, she stared behind them. "No one at the hospital will let me near him. I'm not family. We're just...barely acquaintances."

But she was worried.

"Do you mind if I call...when we get to wherever it is we're going?" A rough laugh. "Just a check-in at the station. I figure he'll be examined by a doctor and maybe I can get an update from someone I know at the sheriff's station."

"You close with all the deputies?" Because the tall guy that had just ushered her on hadn't seemed particularly friendly with her. He hadn't acknowledged her at all. *Maybe he didn't see her.*

"I'm not *close* with anyone." She settled back against her seat. "But the deputies and even the sheriff will come in the bar from time to time, so I've talked to most of them before. It would be good to just know everything is okay. Maverick might not even be the one who's hurt, but I'd like to check."

The ambulance was long gone. "We'll call." He'd find out exactly what had happened because something about that scene had set off an alarm bell in his head.

*The truck had been a rental.* He'd seen the tell-tale barcode on the back windshield that rental companies used to scan the vehicles at check-in and check-out. And the deputy hadn't said anything about the truck's driver. Had he been injured, too?

"We're going back to Florida, aren't we?" Cassidy suddenly asked. "You didn't exactly give me a travel plan when you threw me into the SUV. I rather think it's important for partners to *share* details like that."

He hadn't thrown her. He'd lifted her up. Boosted her.

"You're back to not talking much." A sigh. "I'm guessing you exhausted yourself with all that conversation back at the bar?"

He slanted a glance her way. Was she mocking him? Sure felt that way. "Do you think your ex is still in Florida?"

"No, I think he's been tracking me." Another long sigh. Though this one was sadder. "Why else would I have switched towns so much?"

This was exactly what Titan had suspected. "Did he make contact with you?"

"I...a few times, I could swear I felt someone watching me. Back at the beginning, the first place I stopped...I came home one night, and there was a nightgown spread out on the bed for me." Her voice sharpened. "Scared the hell out of me. I left that gown and ran as fast as I could."

*Sonofabitch.*

"I don't leave anything behind that says where I'm going." A pause. Cassidy cleared her throat. "Something I've been wondering. How, exactly, did you find me?"

"I'm good at hunting."

"That's wonderful and all. Bravo to you."

His lips twitched.

"But it's not really an answer. Want to add a few more words?"

They were away from the tornado damage. “One of my jobs is to apprehend federal fugitives.”

“That sounds incredibly fierce and official.”

Again, he almost smiled. What the fuck? Titan cleared his throat. “Those fugitives switch identities a whole lot, too. I learned to watch patterns. That helped me find them. And you.”

“So…you’re saying you treated me like your garden-variety fugitive and hunted me down because I left patterns behind?” Suspicious now, she pushed, “What patterns?”

“You preferred jobs where you would be paid in cash. Or at least where you could get a whole lot of tip money in straight cash.”

“Cash is harder to trace.”

Yes.

“Uh, Titan? Can you give me a little more to go on? I’d really like to *not* make the same mistakes in the future. I thought I was doing a pretty good job of staying low.”

She had been doing a “pretty good job” but pretty good wasn’t good enough. “You try to save money because cash is important to you. So you don’t fly. Flying would be too easy to track, anyway. You ride the bus whenever you can.”

“Guilty.”

“You’re hard to forget.”

“What? What in the hell does that mean?”

“When I went to the bus terminals, I always found someone who remembered you.”

“That’s not possible.” She huffed out a breath. “I changed my hair color. In Biloxi, I was blond. I was a redhead in Tennessee. Even had pink hair for a time in Colorado. I *just* went back to this color because I...dammit, I thought I was safe. Then you had to march into my life."

*You weren't safe.* "Different hair wasn't good enough."

"I changed the cut, too. And my clothes. And I'd wear glasses or—"

"You can't get rid of your dimples. Or change the shape of your face. You're fucking beautiful, and people noticed."

Silence.

From her? Now that was odd. He glanced her way.

Her wide eyes were on him.

Shit. He cleared his throat. *I called her beautiful.* He had not meant to do that. Even if she...was. "You were entirely too friendly."

"Excuse me?"

"At each stop, in each town, you made friends."

"I did not." Now she seemed disgruntled.

"Yes, you did," he returned without missing a beat. "Because I talked to the people you worked with. Met your old customers. You were always chatty and warm, and they did *not* forget you. Even the people at the bus terminals remembered you because you were—"

"Chatty?" she filled in, voice flat.

He rolled one shoulder. "If you want to blend, don't try making friends everywhere you go."

"Thanks so much, but I *don't* make friends. I "

"That deputy from last night—"

"Maverick Thomas."

"He drove all the way to the bar to make sure you were okay. That's not making friends?"

She sniffed. "I am polite. Sorry that I tend to not always be an asshole. I can assure you, I will work on that tendency."

"Doubt it." From what he'd been able to tell, her bubbly personality was just as much a part of Cassidy as her dimples. For her, being friendly was probably as natural as breathing. He was actually glad she hadn't lost it after everything that had gone down with Blake. The fact that she hadn't? It told him Cassidy was one hell of a lot stronger than she looked.

"Listen up, marshal," Cassidy began angrily. "I am going to—"

"Vegas is our destination."

"What?"

"Vegas. Figured I should tell you that."

Her fingers tapped against her jean-clad thigh. "I thought we were going to Florida."

"Eventually, yes. But first, I've got an FBI buddy in Vegas who wants to talk with you. He's been working on the profile for your boyfriend—"

"Don't call him that." Low. "Please."

Fine. Titan didn't like thinking of the sonofabitch as her boyfriend, anyway. "Oliver wants to interview you and get more intel." Fair warning... "I'm sure he has plenty of questions for you."

Silence. Something that he knew meant trouble coming from her.

He glanced in the rearview mirror. Far down the road, he could just make out the shape of a distant vehicle.

"You're...you're not just going to dump me off on this Oliver person and leave, are you?" Cassidy questioned, voice careful. "That's not going to be how we work?"

Dump her?

"Because like I said before, I have rules."

His gaze slid from the rearview mirror. "What rules would those be?"

"Rule one is that you *don't* dump me. At least, not until I say it's okay. I-I don't know your buddy Oliver. Not like I rode out a tornado with him."

No, not like she had.

"Rule two is that you don't keep secrets from me. If something bad is happening, you tell me about it. I don't care how scary it is, don't keep secrets." Pain whispered beneath those words. "I hate secrets."

Considering how things had gone down with Blake, he could see where she wouldn't be a fan of secrets, so he nodded.

"Rule three," she continued as her tone turned crisp, "no handcuffs. You don't get to slap those on me anytime you want. I'm your *partner*, not your prisoner. Get the difference?"

"You were running."

"Uh, huh, and you were *imprisoning me*. Something that probably isn't legal."

"If I'm making an arrest, it's completely legal to cuff the criminal."

"I'm not a criminal!"

"You were stealing my ride," he reminded her. "Vehicular theft is a crime."

"I was *borrowing* your keys. If I had been stealing the ride, we wouldn't be on this magical road trip now, would we? I'd be far away from you."

"The tornado stopped you." Would she deny it? He waited, curious.

"My own fear stopped me. You can only go to so many towns and start over so many times." She reached out and turned on some music. "No more cuffs, Titan. Not unless we are doing something fun and very kinky."

*What?*

His head whipped toward her.

"A joke," she said. Her eyes had closed as she leaned back against the seat. "Get your eyes back on the road."

*Her* eyes were closed, so how did she know he was looking at her? And, why, *why* did he suddenly have the image of them doing something fun and kinky in his head?

***

He'd always been lucky.

The tornado hadn't taken him. It had ripped the deputy from his arms and sent the man flying into a nearby fence. If his luck held—he was sure it would—the deputy's injuries would be attributed to the storm.

Not to his knife.

He'd gone back to the scene when the weather cleared, wondering if the deputy had been found. Wondering if he was dead or alive. *I left him pretty close to dead.* He would have finished up the job but...

*Tornado.*

And just as he'd returned to the scene, what had he seen?

The big SUV. With his Cassidy sitting in the passenger seat. She'd stopped—along with the asshole driving—to check on the deputy. He'd wanted to rush to her. To yank her out of that vehicle and into his arms. To run the hell away with her.

But too many deputies had been buzzing at the scene.

So he'd stayed back. Waited in his newly "borrowed" ride. Then slowly tailed them. He'd been tailing them for much of the day. He knew better than to get too close. Not like it was his first time to hunt. If you went in too fast, you'd spook your prey.

You had to time things just right. You had to wait for your perfect moment.

He had Cassidy in his sights.

He would wait.

The moment *would* be perfect.

And before he claimed her again, he would slice apart the "boyfriend" with her.

***

"Rise and shine."

Her neck hurt.

"Time for lunch, sunshine. Or dinner. Whatever you want to call it."

She cracked open her left eye and peered at the man beside her. "You seem awfully...chipper." And she'd been sleeping like the dead. Rather odd considering that she usually barely slept at all.

Maybe a few moments here or there. Only to wake up from a nightmare with her whole body covered in sweat.

Except...

She'd slept during the storm, held in his arms. And she hadn't woken until morning.

And she'd just slept in his car. A deep, dreamless sleep that had her feeling more refreshed than she had in...forever.

*Or in about thirteen months. Since I found out the man I was planning to marry was a killer.*

Her right eye opened, too. "No way we're in Vegas already."

"Nope. Just stopped at a diner outside of Casper, Wyoming. You didn't have breakfast, so I figured we'd better grab you something."

That was awfully...nice of him. After unhooking her seat belt, Cassidy glanced around. She could see why he'd said the diner was *outside* of Casper. There was literally nothing else there. Just an old-fashioned—if somewhat rundown—diner. Big, glowing letters of DINER were on top of the restaurant, but the I in "diner" wasn't working. Windows filled the front of the place, letting her clearly peer inside to see that the restaurant was as deserted on the interior as it was in the parking area. From what she could tell, there was only one other car in the lot. A faded, yellow station wagon.

"Cassidy?"

Her stomach growled. Truth be told, she could not remember exactly when she'd had her last meal. Maybe yesterday, around three?

"Starving," she declared as she shoved open her door and hopped out. It was all she could do not to run up to the restaurant, but she tried to wait for Titan.

Titan slammed the driver's side door and met her on the sidewalk in front of the diner. She noticed that he paused to glance around, as if he was looking for trouble. Automatically, she glanced around, too. *No one* was there. "I'm sure you'll see trouble coming," she told him and impulsively grabbed his arm. "Come on, marshal, let's go."

"Titan." He didn't go.

"What?"

"You should call me Titan." His gaze swept over her, then he looked toward the door. He reached out his left hand and hauled it open. "After all, you've slept with me twice now."

Oh, damn. He had *not* just said that to her. Eyes narrowing and chin rising, she marched ahead, tugging on his arm. "*Sleeping* is all we did and we—" She stopped.

Mostly because a woman with long, dark brown hair and wearing a white waitress uniform had bustled forward. The woman's welcoming smile froze on her lips, and her eyes seemed to bulge as she looked at Titan.

Or...actually...

Cassidy's stomach tightened.

*She's looking at his scars.* Because when she followed the woman's line of sight, that was where the waitress's horrified stare had fixated. Anger burned in Cassidy's gut, and before she could even think to hesitate, she blurted, "It's super rude to stare. I know he's crazy hot, but he's taken. So how about stop that, would you?"

The waitress flushed a dark red as she pulled her gaze off Titan's scars and hauled it to Cassidy.

"Thanks so much," Cassidy told her sweetly. "Because I am incredibly jealous and possessive." *And don't stare at him that way. He's not some freak.* She kept one hand on Titan's arm while her other hand plucked the menus from the waitress's hold. "Guessing we can sit anywhere, hmm?" Because she just saw one other couple inside. An elderly man with a fishing cap on his head and his lovely wife who had pearls around her neck.

"Ah...yes. Anywhere." The flustered waitress waved vaguely in the air.

"Back corner," Titan rumbled.

The waitress flinched.

Cassidy ignored her and headed for the back corner. Why he wanted to sit all the way back there when they'd be passing about twenty empty booths before getting to the back corner was beyond her, but...whatever. He'd been driving for hours, so she figured the least she could do was let the man pick their seats.

She slid onto one side of the booth, the side that let her get a view of the door, and she figured he would slide onto the seat opposite her but...

Nope, someone got cozy. Titan sidled up right beside her.

Her head angled toward him. "People don't do this." Wasn't it some unspoken rule? "I sit on one side, you sit on the other." That was how it worked.

"Not when you're so incredibly possessive and jealous," he returned, deadpan. "When you're that way, you like to be as close to me as possible."

Her eyes narrowed. "Cute."

"I believe the word you used to describe me was 'hot.' But do correct me if I'm wrong."

She started to fire off a correction—even though, yes, fine, that had been her word—then she realized he sounded almost...cheerful. Or as cheerful as she imagined that sexy, rumbling voice of his could get.

One of his shoulders rolled in a lazy shrug. "I like to watch the doors when I'm in a place. Want to see everyone who enters."

Of course, he did. Probably some marshal thing.

"It's not anything personal that I'm sitting so close," he added. "Not like *I'm* getting possessive of you."

Cassidy slapped down the menus. "You get that a lot?" Because Maverick had done it, too. Gaped at the scars. "The staring BS at your scars?"

A shrug from Titan.

"Don't know why," she said, gazing right at him. Pretty much unable to look anywhere but into his amazing eyes. "The scars are nothing. They don't matter."

Already close, he eased even *closer*. His mouth came toward her ear as he said, "They're everywhere, Cassidy. The ones you see are only the tip of the iceberg. Trust me, I'm as much of a monster as people think."

Her breath caught. *Everywhere?* Sympathy flashed through her. "Titan—"

"When the waitress comes around, order me a coffee, would you? Strong and black. I'll be right back." And with that, he was gone. He'd slipped from the booth and headed for the restroom that was just a few feet away.

As she sat in the booth, her shoulders slumped. Cassidy couldn't help but wonder how Titan had gotten his scars. He must have gone through so much pain to get them. *And he needs to stop calling himself a monster.* She knew monsters. Titan wasn't one. He was the exact opposite.

He was the guy who slayed the monsters. Or at least, that was what she was really, really hoping.

"Uh...can I get you started with something to drink?" The waitress sidled closer. Her gaze darted a bit nervously toward the bathrooms.

"Water for me. Coffee—black and as strong as you've got—for him."

The waitress's head bobbed as she backed up a step. She wore a gold name badge with *Tisha* embossed on the surface. "Be right back with that."

Tisha spun around and hurried toward the counter and the coffee pot. And as she reached for the pot—

The diner's front doors flew open. A man in a black ball cap and a black face mask—one that covered the lower portion of his face—burst inside. He clutched a gun in his right hand. "Don't anyone move!" he bellowed.

The coffee pot fell from Tisha's fingers and shattered.

And a bullet exploded from the masked man's gun.

# CHAPTER FIVE

Titan was drying off his hands when he heard the thunder of a gunshot, and everything inside of Titan seemed to ice.

*No! Cassidy!* A roar filled his head even as he grabbed for the bathroom door. He caught himself right before he ran out. *What the fuck are you doing? You know better than this.*

His breath shuddered as he bent and yanked his weapon from the holster on his ankle. The gun was a familiar weight, and he carefully cracked the door so he could peer outside.

Someone was screaming.

*Don't be Cassidy. Don't be Cassidy.* She'd better not be hurt.

He eased the door open a little more and realized that the screams were coming from the woman with the white hair and the string of pearls around her neck.

A grating voice snarled at her, "Shut the fuck up!"

Titan crept out of the bathroom on silent steps just as a man in a black mask and a black ball cap rushed forward and aimed his gun at the screaming woman.

*"Shut. The. Fuck. Up!* Or I will shut—"

"*Don't!*" Cassidy's cry. Because that was Cassidy who'd just put herself between the screaming woman and the gunman.

Sonofabitch.

Cassidy lifted her hands into the air. "She's just scared," Cassidy explained as her voice trembled. "You don't need to shoot her. You don't need to shoot anyone."

Titan's gaze took in everything. The lone gunman. Cassidy—right in the line of fire. The waitress who'd dropped to her knees on the floor and was huddling near a broken coffee pot.

The gunman boomed, "I want money!" His gun trembled in his grip.

Not a good sign. A nervous, twitchy gunman could fire off a shot at any moment. And as close as the bastard was to Cassidy, he could kill her.

*Not on my watch.*

Titan rushed forward on silent steps. His gaze never strayed from his target, and when that SOB lurched toward Cassidy and grabbed her arm—

*That's your last mistake. You don't touch her.*

Titan was on him. He jerked the bastard's wrist—the one holding the gun—and yanked it to the side so any stray bullets wouldn't hit anyone. Then he swept his foot under the prick and took him down with a hard crash. As the fool lunged up, yelling, Titan drove his left fist into his face. The blow had the guy's head cracking into the old linoleum.

The man blinked blearily, and his cap fell off to reveal long, thin red hair. The would-be robber gasped, "You can't—"

"You're under arrest, asshole." Titan put his gun in the man's face. "You really picked the wrong fucking diner."

"Titan." Cassidy cleared her throat.

"Baby, tell me you don't have so much as a bruise on you." The *baby* part slipped out. Heat of the moment.

He didn't take his attention from his prey. If she had a bruise...

*Wait. What the hell am I doing?* He should take a breath. Calm the hell down. He should—

"I'm fine," she assured him.

The woman behind her was still screaming.

"He's a marshal," Cassidy told her. "He's got this." Another delicate throat clearing. "Titan, I think this would be a perfect time for you to use those cuffs you love so much."

The guy on the floor had started *crying*.

He'd really be crying when his ass was in jail. Titan hauled out his cuffs. "You have the right to remain silent." *You fucking bastard. You ever put a gun on her again...* "You have the right to an attorney." *I will destroy you.* "If you cannot afford one..." *No one hurts her.* "Then I'm sure some asshole will be appointed for you."

***

"Your boyfriend is hot."

Cassidy glanced over at Tisha's words. She'd been watching Titan as he chatted with the local cops—and as the perp was shoved into the back of a patrol car. Cassidy nodded in response to Tisha. "I think I told you that when we first arrived."

Tisha tucked a lock of brown hair behind her ear as she edged a little closer. "I've never seen someone do that...just—just lunge at a guy with a gun. It was like he had no fear."

Her attention slid back to Titan.

Only to find him staring at her.

"I, uh, my manager said you can have anything you want from the menu."

"Where exactly *was* your manager during all the action?" She'd only seen the man come rushing out when the sirens started screaming.

"In the back."

Sure. *Safely* in the back.

Titan began heading toward her. Tisha let out a little sigh. "He's so...big."

*Seriously, Tisha? Seriously?* She needed to stop that dreamy-sigh crap. "I think we'll be taking our food to go," she told the other woman, voice sugary sweet. "Just grab us some burgers, will you?"

But Tisha wasn't listening. She'd headed straight for Titan, and as Cassidy's mouth gaped open, Tisha threw herself against Titan and held him tightly.

*Seriously, Tisha?*

And damn if what could have been a bit of *real* jealousy flared inside of Cassidy. Perhaps more than a bit. That was just weird.

Titan awkwardly patted Tisha on her shoulder before disentangling himself. He headed straight for Cassidy, and as he did, his gaze swept from her head to her sneaker-clad feet, then back up again. He didn't stop walking, not until he was right in front of her. Then he did the head-to-feet sweep again with his electric eyes. "You're sure that you weren't hurt?"

He kept dwelling on that point. Unnecessary. "Not so much as a scratch."

"That's good, I—"

The lady with the pearls made a beeline for them. She nearly elbowed Cassidy as she surged toward Titan. The hug she gave him was just as tight as Tisha's had been.

"Young man, you saved my life!"

Um. Okay. Cassidy didn't point out that *she* had stepped between the woman and the gun. Clearly, the focus was on Titan.

Cassidy crossed her arms over her chest and watched Titan give this woman an awkward pat on the shoulder, too. The man did not look like a natural hugger.

"I knew you were an officer of the law the minute I saw you." This didn't come from the woman, but from her husband who'd bustled forward. "It was in the way you moved." He nodded knowledgably as he joined their little group. "You picked that booth specifically, didn't you? So you could keep watch on everyone. Saw a guy do something like that in a movie once."

Again, Titan disentangled himself. "Just glad everyone is all right."

Tisha rushed back to them. Her hands clutched a big, white bag. One filled with Styrofoam containers. Her manager stood right behind her. His hands gripped drinks. Bottled waters. Nice.

"Can't thank you enough," the manager said.

Titan sent her a helpless look. He clearly feared he was about to get another hug.

She took pity on him. “All in a day’s work. Now, we really need to get going. The car just doesn’t drive itself.” Had they already had the hamburgers ready and just waiting inside or what? Talk about *fast*. She took the food. Titan grabbed the drinks, and they made a dash for their SUV. Once they were inside…

“That happen a lot?” Cassidy asked casually as she put the drinks in the nearby holders.

“People giving me free food?”

Her eyes rolled. “No, you being the hero and effortlessly taking out men with guns. That a typical occurrence for you? Like a normal Friday or something? If so, not to tell you your business or anything…” Cassidy thought she was doing a pretty good job of bluffing out this scene, but her fingers did tremble as she fiddled with the drinks. And her stomach would not stop twisting. “But that is a seriously dangerous way of life.”

He’d shifted in the driver’s seat. Her words seemed to make him pause, just for a moment, before he hauled the door shut. He cranked the SUV. Cool air blasted on them before he shoved a hand into the bag and handed her a burger.

Their fingers brushed. Dammit. Had he noticed the tremble? And why was that surge of heat rushing through her? Every time they touched, it seemed to happen. She’d never felt that little electric spark just from touching someone before.

"You were the one standing in front of the gunman." A distinct edge entered his voice. "Don't do that shit again."

Her mouth opened. Then closed. Granted, standing in front of a person with a gun was clearly not the best choice. But... "I was afraid he was going to shoot her! What was I supposed to do? Stay huddled in my booth and do nothing?"

And that horrible memory rushed back. The memory from Florida. Of that night.

*Standing there...for so long...the sounds, the sights. Doing nothing but watching.* She pushed the burger back at him. "I think I'll wait a bit on eating. Not so hungry right now." Her hand yanked her seat belt into place.

"Cassidy."

"I don't want someone dying right in front of me, okay? She was scared, and I just rushed over there, in front of her, before I could think about what I was doing. Trust me, I get it was dangerous." And she was sweaty and shaken from the events in that diner. "Luckily, you were there to save the day." Through the windshield, she could see more cars pulling into the parking lot. Not so empty any longer. "And it was hot, dammit. You were hot. Saving the day and taking him out like it was nothing." Talk about an impressive sight. Her own action hero. "Tisha was right. I knew when I saw you rushing up behind him that the jerk in the mask had no chance." She'd actually known that all along, and how crazy was that? Even as she'd stepped between the masked man and the woman with her pearls,

Cassidy had thought...*I just have to distract him for a little while. Titan will come.*

And he had.

"Do me a favor?" Titan asked in the voice that made her toes curl.

"Want me to drive?" Cassidy nodded. "I can do that. My turn, after all. You can eat, then sleep for a bit, and I'll—"

"Don't ever fucking stand in front of a man with a gun again."

She flashed him a bright smile and hoped to sound flippant as she asked, "Worried about me? Aw, Titan that makes me feel all—"

"Yes." Flat. "I was worried."

Her breath caught. Her fake smile started to become real—

"If something happens to you," he continued doggedly, "then how the hell are we supposed to pull in Blake Normandy?"

Her smile died. "You say the sweetest things."

His brow furrowed.

"Eyes on the prize, am I right?" She flipped on the radio. Turned up the volume as high as it would go. And over the blasting music, she assured him, "Don't worry. I'll try not to do anything inconvenient like *die* before my serial-killing ex finds me."

Then she started to sing along to the radio. Loudly.

***

He'd watched the drama at the diner with intense curiosity. When the patrol cars had rushed to the scene—their sirens screaming and their lights flashing—he'd felt vague alarm. For a moment, he'd worried that something had happened to Cassidy.

But then the young guy with red hair had been led out of the diner. Cuffed, sullen. The big bruiser with Cassidy had shoved the man toward the cops.

And then he'd talked to those cops. Acted as if he was one of them.

While everyone else had been distracted, he'd taken the time to tag the SUV that the jerk had driven to the diner. He'd slid under the ride and nestled his little black device in a sweet crevice. Highly doubtful it would be found. With the added security of the GPS tracker, he didn't have to immediately follow Cassidy.

He could take his time. Learn more about his prey.

So when the cops finally rolled away, he left his vantage point and sauntered toward the diner. He opened the door, and the waitress immediately whirled toward him. A flush of excitement still stained her cheeks red, and her blue eyes gleamed. As she headed toward him, her brown hair tumbled over her shoulders.

"Table for one?"

"I'll just sit at the counter." He didn't need a table. Maybe some coffee. A quick bite. And a whole lot of intel.

After he'd slid onto a barstool, she eased behind the counter and pushed a menu toward him.

"Looks like you had some excitement here earlier..." Deliberately, he leaned back and let his gaze track toward the front door. "Saw a whole lot of police cars leaving."

"We had an attempted robbery."

His head jerked back toward her. Rather dramatically, just the way he expected normal people would react to her news. "You don't say?"

A quick nod. She leaned forward. Her voice dropped as she said, "Luckily, we had a US marshal inside."

A fucking US marshal. "You don't say." Hell. He should have given another response that time.

"Oh, he was amazing. Took the guy down like that." She snapped her fingers. "And it's a good thing he did." A hard nod. "The creep with the gun was about to shoot the marshal's girlfriend. But he rushed to the rescue. Took the jerk's gun and cuffed his ass before the robber could even scream."

*About to shoot the marshal's girlfriend.* His hand fisted. "The woman wasn't hurt?"

"Nah. Like I said, the marshal saved her."

His smile hurt his face. "How wonderful for her."

She blinked. "Uh, you want some coffee? One of our pots broke, but, ah, we have another in the back."

"Coffee would be great."

*Tisha.* That was her name. She turned away, but he kept his eyes on her. "You remind me of someone, Tisha," he said. His stare had locked on her hair. From this angle, she reminded him of—

She looked back at him, blue eyes wide and surprised. "I do?"

The eyes were the wrong color. She was the right age, though. Right size. The hair was very, very similar to Cassidy's.

Close...enough. "If only I could stay longer," he murmured.

But, wait, he *did* have the tracker on the SUV.

Maybe he could linger, just a bit. "You've got a gorgeous smile," he told her.

Her smile flashed. The usual response to that particular compliment. He'd found if you complimented your prey, they tended to lower their guard faster. It was a pity she didn't have dimples. He liked dimples. But she did have a nice smile.

Tisha stepped closer to the counter once more. "How long are you in town?"

He unfisted his hands and put them on the worn surface of the counter. "I guess that depends on you." *How long will it take me to get you alone, Tisha? How long will it take you to die?*

Usually, he had a system. Rules. But it had been too fucking long. Cassidy's fault. Everything was going wrong.

She bit her lower lip, hesitating. "I—"

"*Tisha!*" A woman's voice. High. Cracking. Coming from the doorway.

His head whipped toward the door.

"Tisha, I just heard the news!" The woman's hair was short, close-cropped, and sprinkled with gray. She rushed toward Tisha and held her tightly. "My God, you could have been killed."

"It's all right, Mom." Tisha hugged her back. "I'm fine."

Fuck. Now he had family to deal with. Screw this. He dropped cash down on the counter and slid off the stool. His steps shuffled for the door.

"Sir?" Tisha called after him. "Sir, are you—"

"Got places to be," he said curtly without looking back. *It's your lucky day, sweet thing. You get to keep living.* As for the marshal...he might not be so lucky.

# CHAPTER SIX

"It's not the Ritz," Titan told her gruffly. His eyes were grainy, his neck stiff with tension, and he needed to crash. Hard. During the storm, he'd barely gotten any sleep. He'd been too afraid the building would get ripped off around them. Then he'd driven them all day, until the sun had dipped beneath the sky. Darkness surrounded them, and he figured they'd been lucky to stumble across this little motel off I-15 in Utah. Nestled off the road, the motel's sign promised clean beds and a vacancy. Who could ask for more?

"Not really interested in the Ritz," she assured him. "But a comfy bed does sound like heaven right about now."

She'd stopped singing sometime after they'd crossed into Utah. The radio had kept blasting, and he'd been able to feel the tension pouring off her. She hadn't spoken a whole lot to him, and damn if he'd known what to say to her.

Apparently, he'd said the *wrong* thing to her at the diner. But at the time, he'd been struggling with a vicious adrenaline rush, a furious rage, and a strange, biting fear.

*I thought he would shoot her before I could stop him.*

She reached for the car's door handle.

He leaned over and grabbed her hand. "Promise me you won't jump in front of any other guns."

Cassidy sucked in a breath. Her hair fell forward as she looked at his hand...then her head lifted and turned as she looked right at him. "Is that supposed to be funny?"

No, it was supposed to be a way for him to keep his sanity.

"I doubt we are going to encounter any gun-toting bad guys in the lobby of this little motel, but you know what? If we do, I will let you take them out, and I'll stand to the side. Happy?" she asked sweetly.

No, he was not.

But he let her go. She climbed out of the vehicle first, and he grabbed their bags before meeting her in front of the little office.

"It is going to be so good to stretch out in bed," she murmured. "What's the plan? You gonna get us side-by-side rooms? Maybe with a connecting door in case of any emergency?"

"Ah, Cassidy..." She was clearly not understanding things.

"Let's see what they've got," she said brightly. "Maybe the bed will vibrate. I could use a vibrating bed about now."

He blinked. *A vibrating bed?* What kind of motels had she been staying in during the last year? Did motels still have vibrating beds? He sure hadn't encountered any. But Cassidy and a vibrating bed would be...interesting.

Cassidy hauled open the door, and the bell overhead gave a quick jingle. She led the way inside, and he followed on her heels with the bags. When they entered the small lobby, he realized they weren't the only guests trying to find shelter for the night. A family of four waited. A harried-looking dad had his credit card on the counter as he gripped his wallet. A mom held a tired toddler in her arms, swaying back and forth in that constant-movement thing he'd seen other mothers do. Beside the mom, a small girl with freckles on her nose and pigtails watched him with wide eyes.

He knew that wide-eyed look. Especially when it focused on his scars...

The little girl inched closer to her mother. Her eyes never left Titan.

"We have one room with double beds left," the desk clerk said to the dad. "Gonna be two-oh-eight for the night."

The dad grumbled but shoved his card forward.

*Uh, oh. One room with double beds left.* Had Cassidy heard that part? Had she—

She elbowed him.

"Nothing I can do about it," he told her flatly. "It's the last one." As usual, his voice came out deep and hard and—

The little girl's mouth dropped open. Her eyes got even wider.

"I was trying to get you to *smile,*" Cassidy muttered. "To look friendly for the girl."

Look friendly? "How the fuck am I supposed to do that?"

Shit. Those words had come out like a snarl.

"Bad word." The girl pointed at him. "Bad man."

The dad whirled around, a glare on his face, but then he saw Titan...

"Oh, fuck," the dad breathed.

"Bad word," the girl pointed out again. But it looked like she was about to cry.

Titan sighed. He hadn't even been *trying* this time. He'd just been standing there, minding his own business. And bam. A kid was crying.

Cassidy stepped in front of him. "What a lovely family." Her voice was bright. He could imagine that she was flashing her dimples. "You must be in the middle of a wonderful vacation. That's what my, ah, friend and I are doing, too. Seeing the world. Nothing like an epic road trip, am I right?"

The mom said something back. About going to visit family or some shit like that. The dad swiped back his card and they hightailed it out of the office.

Cassidy watched them go and crooked a brow at Titan. "That happen a lot?"

He nodded. "Kids hate me."

"You're like...six-foot-three—"

"Four," he corrected her.

"And built along *massive* lines everywhere. Kids are tiny. They get scared of things that are bigger than they are. That's why you should have tried to look friendly."

"Can't."

Her other eyebrow crooked up, too.

"My looking friendly just makes me look extra scary." True story.

Shaking her head at him, she made her way to the counter. He dropped the bags and moved to her side. From the corner of his eye, he saw her flash her mega-watt smile to the desk clerk.

"We'd like two rooms, please," Cassidy declared, her voice all bright and warm.

"One," Titan corrected, his voice flat and curt and growly.

Her head jerked toward him. Her mouth opened. "But—"

"One." On this, there was no debate.

Before she could argue, the balding clerk cut in to say, "We only have one room left."

Both of their heads swung toward him.

He winced. "Sorry, ma'am. But we're doing some remodeling. Only one room left."

Titan had to give her credit, she rallied quickly, and her smile came again. Dimples in full force. "That's fine," Cassidy assured the man. "We just need two beds—"

Whoops. She'd apparently not overheard the clerk's conversation with the tired dad.

The guy grimaced. "Got a king I can offer you, but that's it."

Her short nails tapped across the counter. "I'm sorry, say again?"

"Got a king I can offer you and your *friend,*" the man told her. "Two-oh-eight for the night."

Her nails stopped tapping. Her whole body swung toward Titan.

He tried to be helpful. "Not like it's the first time we've slept together."

She smiled at him. There were no dimples. He knew she hadn't taken his comment to be particularly helpful. Her hand rose, grabbed his shirt, and she tugged him toward her. Curious to see where this would go, he leaned close even as she pressed onto her toes.

"I'm calling dibs on the bed," she told him, voice husky.

Of course, she was.

"Two-oh-eight," the clerk said again.

***

The bed looked clean. That was a bonus. And it was big. Probably big enough for two. Okay, *maybe* big enough for two given Titan's dimensions, and she was feeling all kinds of guilty for calling dibs. After all, the man had saved her life that day.

If the gunman had fired in the diner... *Would I be dead right now? Or just spread out on some doc's operating table?*

Her spine snapped straight. "We can put pillows between us."

The bags hit the floor. The distinct thud had her spinning around.

Titan closed the door. Flipped all the flimsy locks. Then looked over at her.

"To share the bed, I mean." Her breath shuddered out because his blue eyes had gone all extra intense on her, and they'd been exceedingly intense to begin with. "We can put some of the pillows between us. I'll stay on the left side. You stay on the right. We can be professional about this." Was professional even the right word when you were in a one-bed-with-a-stranger-situation?

And *how* had she wound up like this? One freaking bed. In the movies, that was romantic. Saucy. Sexy.

In reality...

"I should warn you that I will probably wake up screaming. I may try to throw some punches. Just be prepared," Cassidy advised him.

He blinked. Then he stalked toward her. Unable to help herself, Cassidy tensed. Especially when he stopped right in front of her. Towered over her. His crisp scent—still miraculously so good after a whole day of travel—teased her nose. And she could have sworn she felt warmth coming from his body.

She caught herself leaning toward him.

"You're telling me that you're going to attack me during the night?"

She pressed her lips into a line. That was *maybe* what she was telling him. She hadn't actually slept with any other men since the horror in Florida, so Cassidy didn't exactly know what she'd do to someone who was in the bed with her. "I have night terrors." Was that even what they were? Not like she'd seen a counselor or anything who could tell her. "Flashbacks." Maybe that was a better term. "Never had anyone in the room with me when they occurred, so I'm not sure what I will do to someone who might be sleeping right next to me. Honestly, that's the whole reason I called dibs. But it's a witch thing to do because you drove us all day and you have to be exhausted and there's plenty of room."

His stare held hers.

Uncomfortable silence had her almost twitching.

"I—" Cassidy began when she couldn't take the silence for another second.

"Not really a lot of room for someone like me. Even with pillows, I'll come into your space." A shake of his head. "Better for me to bunk on the floor."

That sounded horribly uncomfortable. And who knew *what* had been on the motel room floor. "But—"

"I'll be between you and the door. Those locks aren't worth shit."

Way to make her even more afraid.

"Want to take the shower first?" he offered. "I need to make some phone calls."

A shower sounded heavenly. But before she gave in to that particular brand of bliss... "Can one of those calls be to Nowhere? Because when I tried to get info on Maverick earlier," during that endless drive, "I was stonewalled. Maybe if you, I don't know, tell them you're a marshal, they'll cooperate with you?"

His head dipped. "I'll try."

Her shoulders sagged. "Thank you." She could have hugged him. Almost did. And that was certainly a sign she was way, way too tired. Before she gave into any other hugging or touching impulses, Cassidy made a dash for the bathroom and the promise of that sweet, sweet shower.

***

"Critical condition?" Titan glanced back over his shoulder at the closed bathroom door. The pipes had groaned loudly moments before, then he'd heard the spray of the shower rushing out. "Any other news?"

The sheriff sighed. "Sorry, Marshal Everett. It's just not looking good. Maverick suffered some really severe lacerations. Slices deep into his stomach and even across his throat. Surgeon said he lost a ton of blood out there. I just...we're all praying for him. That's pretty much the only thing we can do." A pause. "Exactly *why* were you working with my deputy in Nowhere? He didn't brief me on any task force work, and that typically goes through my command."

Sure, it would. If there had been any task force work occurring with the sheriff's office. "Just met him in passing."

They talked briefly. Titan asked about the driver of the truck he'd seen, but the sheriff had no info on him. When they were done, Titan put in another call, this one to his FBI buddy in Vegas. Special Agent Oliver Foxx answered on the second ring.

"Yo, Titan. About time. You're supposed to update me regularly—and a regular update means—"

The shower water had stopped rushing out. He turned fully toward the door. "Don't have long to talk."

"You never talk long. That's sort of your thing," Oliver groused.

"I've got her."

"What?"

His eyes remained focused on the closed bathroom door. "I've got her."

"Are you shitting me right now?" Oliver demanded. Excitement sprang into his voice. "Do not be shitting me. My heart can't take it."

Titan didn't speak.

"I'll take that to mean you are not shitting me," Oliver stormed on without missing a beat. "That's fantastic. You found her? You seriously found her?"

He'd already said as much.

"I will never doubt you again. Never."

Bull.

"I want to see her. Talk to her."

"I know." He'd already told Cassidy they'd be heading to meet the Fed.

"Has she told you anything useful? Has she perhaps revealed anything that can help us to hunt—"

The door creaked open, and he didn't catch the last part of Oliver's question because Cassidy had pretty much just blown every thought from his head.

*Fucking fuck me.*

She stood in the doorway with a white towel wrapped around her body. The curves of her breasts pushed against the top of the towel as she clutched it to her body with one hand. Faint water droplets clung to her flushed skin, and her wet hair curled over her shoulders. "Sorry." She bit her lower lip. "I rushed in the bathroom so quickly that I forgot to get any fresh clothes."

"You're naked." A growl.

"I'm technically wearing a towel."

*"Who the fuck is naked?"* Oliver blasted in his ear. "*Is it her? Is our star witness naked with you right now? What is happening?"*

"I need my bag." Her nervous gaze darted to said bag, then back to Titan. "Could you hand it to me? Or I suppose I could get it." A hard breath. "No big deal." She started to walk out of the bathroom in her towel.

Very big deal.

Because he was drinking her in like a man dying of thirst. His dick shoved hard against the front of his jeans, and all he wanted...

*Towel, please fall.*

"Hold on," he barked to Oliver.

"*What? No, tell me what is—"*

Titan tossed the phone onto the bed. He grabbed for her bag and practically lunged toward her as he extended the bag.

The towel dipped a wee bit as she took the bag from his grasp. "Thank you."

She stared at him.

He wanted to put his hands all over her.

*No. Stop it. You're protecting her. She just forgot her bag. This is not some elaborate seduction routine.*

He stepped back. She shut the door.

His dick kept saluting her. And he remembered to *breathe.*

He also remembered that he'd left the FBI agent hanging. Grudgingly, Titan went back for the phone. After scooping it off the bed, he put the device to his ear. "I'm back."

"Where the hell did you go?"

"She needed clothes."

"*She. Needed. Clothes.*" Oliver seemed to be strangling. "Where are you, just, you know, out of curiosity?"

"Motel."

"And you're...ah...in the same room with our witness?"

Obviously. "How else am I gonna keep my eye on her?"

"Sure. How else?"

"She likes to run." But he thought they might be past that point. Hopefully. "Can't handcuff her again."

"For fuck's sake. *What is happening with you two?* Are you terrifying this poor woman or what?"

That gave him pause. Just as the door creaked again. He didn't have to whirl toward it this time. Funny thing, he'd already turned to look at it. As if he'd been waiting for her.

*Because I was.*

No towel wrapped around her this time. She wore a tank top with tiny little straps and a pair of faded jogging shorts. A flush still coated her skin, and her wet hair trailed over her shoulders.

She sent him a quick smile. "Your turn." The smile dimmed a little. "Oh. Sorry. You're on the phone."

"She's not scared of me," he told Oliver. The absolute truth. Other people might be afraid when they saw him, but not her.

"But—" Oliver began.

"We'll be there tomorrow. Probably tomorrow night." Given all the miles they had to cover. "I'll call you when we're close." For now... "I need to take a cold shower." He hung up on Oliver's rapid fire of questions.

He stepped forward.

Just as Cassidy stepped forward.

He stepped to the right.

So did she.

Her breath fluttered out.

His hands rose to curl around her shoulders.

"Titan..." Her breathless voice. Her head tipped back. Her lips parted more.

"Don't leave this room."

She blinked.

"Not under any circumstances, understand? I will take a fast shower and be right back out. Do not leave." Were his fingers flexing lightly on her? They were. He should stop that. So he stopped.

And then his fingers slid down her arms.

Titan snatched them back. Holy hell, her skin was like silk. "Shower. Cold shower." He brushed past her and shut the bathroom door.

Then he turned on the iciest damn water in the world.

***

Lots of people took cold showers. There were supposed to be tons of health benefits from them. Improved circulation. Increased metabolism rates. She'd even read a study once that said a cold shower could help fight depression.

Cassidy slid under the covers. Her head turned on the pillow as she gazed at the closed bathroom door. She'd left the light on beside the bed, so she could see that door quite clearly.

Yes, there were lots and lots of benefits to be had from a cold shower. You didn't just take one if you were trying to fight an erection.

*But was he? Does Titan want me?* Because she could have sworn that she'd seen lust flash on his face and in his eyes. And when she'd seen it...

*I wanted him, too.* She'd actually thought he was getting ready to kiss her when those big, strong hands had curled around her shoulders. She'd gotten all breathy as she said his name...

Only for him to tell her to keep her ass in the motel room.

Fabulous.

It was a bad idea for her to be lusting after the marshal. Bad, bad, bad. The last time she'd fallen for a hot stranger, he'd turned out to be a killer.

*But Titan isn't the bad guy. He's a marshal. He wants to catch the killer.*

And she had no reason to believe Titan wanted her. She'd probably imagined what she'd seen in his face. Or maybe she'd done some projecting because, dammit, she *was* attracted to him. Had been from the first moment she'd seen him. And the longer they were together, yes, he infuriated her, but...

*Maybe it's just been too long.* Maybe that was it. Maybe—

The door creaked as it opened. She was staring right at that door and...

*Oh, wow.*

Titan stood in the doorway. Titan, with just a white towel wrapped around his hips. With muscles and *so many muscles* flexing. His abs of freaking *steel* and his powerful shoulders were wet with gleaming drops of moisture because he hadn't dried off well.

She jerked upright in bed. "Titan!" She could not drag her gaze off him. That was not a six pack. Not in any universe. Way, way more.

"Sorry." Gruff. "Forgot my bag, too." He strode forward, holding the towel at his hip with one hand. He reached for the bag.

And that was when she finally stopped noticing all of his muscles and instead realized that his powerful body was lined with scars. Some thin, white lines. Some thick. But there were so, so many of them. "Oh, Titan." She shoved the covers aside and ran to him. Cassidy grabbed him before she could think better of the move. "What happened to you?"

# CHAPTER SEVEN

A man hated it when a beautiful woman pitied him.

He'd stirred lots of emotions in women since the attack. Some looked at him with horror. His ex had stared at him with pure revulsion on her face. And, sure, sometimes, he'd seen pity.

But he hadn't wanted to see it from her. Not from Cassidy.

Titan stretched out on the hard floor and drove a fist into the pillow beneath his head. The few feathers in the old thing provided no cushion for him at all, and the thin blanket over him didn't do anything to—

"Titan?"

Of course, she wasn't asleep.

Faint light trickled through the blinds on the lone window in the room. Just enough light for him to see—

Cassidy popped her head over the side of the bed. "Did you get any news on Maverick?"

Nothing good. "He's in the ICU."

A swift inhalation from her. "He's going to make it, though? Right? He'll be okay?"

Titan had no idea.

"Do you know what happened?" she pushed. "Did you get more information?"

Some. "Sheriff said it seems like he stopped to check that abandoned truck and another tornado rushed down in front of him. It's...the sheriff said his injuries were pretty bad." He wouldn't lie. "I'll check in again tomorrow and see if there are any updates."

"Thank you." A pause. She didn't ease back into bed. Instead, she kept leaning over and staring down at him.

Titan found he couldn't move a muscle.

Her hair slid down, almost touching him as she leaned ever closer. "I'm sorry for prying about your scars."

"Forget it."

"No, I'm not going to forget it. I shouldn't have pried, so I'm apologizing. You don't need to tell me what happened. I get what it's like to have a dark secret. Your past is yours, and again, I'm sorry I pushed you for more than you wanted to give me."

It wouldn't be hard to touch her face. He could just stretch out his hand and touch the silk of her cheek—

"And I get that I was gawking at you, but it wasn't because of the scars. Don't think that it was. I was gawking because you're dead sexy, and I was trying to count your six pack, only it wasn't a six pack, it was way more and that was why I was counting for so long." A huff of breath. "I wasn't staring because of the scars. I was staring because you're hot. And then I did notice the scars, and I just hated that you'd gone through so much pain.

That's why I asked about them. But I shouldn't have. I won't do it again."

Her head popped back. She'd finally returned to a normal position on the bed.

He stared up at the ceiling. The air conditioning hummed faintly in the room. A little vibration that he knew wouldn't be stopping all night.

But he didn't mind the hum. And her words kept rolling through his head. *I was staring because you're hot.* Hadn't he done the same thing to her when she'd opened the bathroom door? Only she'd had the guts to actually say the words to him. He hadn't told her a damn thing. "You're fucking gorgeous."

He heard the sheets rustle on the bed.

"Too gorgeous for a scarred, surly bastard of a guy like me, and I know it." This attraction that burned through him? Fuck it, this white-hot lust he felt for her? He got that it was going nowhere. "You want the truth?"

"Ah...yes?"

"I think I wanted you from the first moment I saw your photo. Your smile was like a punch to my gut."

"Titan...that's...that's..."

Stalkery? Weird? Yeah, he got that. *Tell me something I don't know.*

"Kinda sweet of you."

No, it wasn't. There was nothing sweet about him. She shouldn't make that mistake. "Even before the scars, I was a bastard. I like danger. I like violence."

"I'm...not sure how to respond to that."

Probably because he wasn't explaining himself well. Story of his life. "I'm good at it." Dammit. Was he trying to get her so scared she ran out of the door screaming? "I'm big. Always been stronger and bigger than everyone else. Fighting was natural for me." He'd been earning extra cash in fights since he was sixteen years old. "I worked special ops for a time." With a team he'd valued like family. "When I was done, I knew I needed more." No way could he have just slipped into some bullshit nine-to-five routine. That hadn't been him.

"So you became a marshal."

"Did you know that when it comes to power, marshals have the biggest authority to arrest criminals? More authority than the Feds? The most of any federal enforcement agency?" A mocking smile twisted his lips. "We're the badasses." Supposedly. "The boogeymen who come after the most violent fugitives out there. But we do *more* than that. We..." He stopped.

"You protect witnesses...like me." Halting.

There had never been anyone quite like her in his history. "Witness security is one of our main jobs. I helped relocate one witness a few years ago, a woman who was running from her husband. Guy wasn't just any domestic abusing dick. Turned out, he was second in command for a sex trafficking and drug running ring. Her testimony was gonna take him down and rip apart the whole organization."

Once more, her head popped over the side of the bed as Cassidy peered down at him. "That sounds like you were making a big difference. Not just feeding some crazy need for danger or violence."

She didn't get how the story was going to end.

"Her husband found out that I was the one to give her the new identity. That *I* knew where she was being held. So he and his goons jumped me. Should never have let my guard down that way." The fact that he had still burned. "Truth is, one of my own men turned on me. Sold me out. Helped them get the drop on me." *Be careful who you trust.* The guy had worn a badge, but he'd been as corrupt as they came. "I woke up tied to a chair, with the woman's husband right in front of me. He wanted to know where she was. Told me he'd ask me the question, and each time I didn't answer or if I lied to him, he was gonna cut me."

*"Titan."* Shock filled his name.

"I never told him."

"OhmyGod."

The knife had come at him again and again. "After a while, I stopped feeling the cuts. I think the fact that I wasn't reacting just made him even angrier."

"That's terrible! I'm so sorry, I—"

Why was she sorry? "Not your fault. My job. My choice."

"Uh, no," Cassidy told him fiercely. "It wasn't your *choice* to get tied to a chair and sliced open. I doubt anyone would make that choice. And I'm sorry because that is a horrible, horrible nightmare. I'm sorry you went through so much pain."

"He thought I was dying." He'd already told her more about that night than he'd told anyone else. Even the shrink he'd been forced to see for a time. His boss had insisted on those visits before Titan had been allowed back to normal duty.

"Wh-what?"

"There was so much blood. He thought I was done. That was when he lowered his guard. His mistake. I'd managed to work one wrist so it was almost free of the ropes. When I saw my opening, when he told the bastards who worked for him to get out of that room and go dig a hole for me—"

*"Titan."*

"When they left, I took my moment. I jerked out of that rope." All of the blood had made his hands and wrists slippery. He'd actually been able to get out of *both* ropes that held his wrists. "I grabbed him. Took the knife from him. And I buried it in his throat before he could even get out a scream."

She made a choking sound.

He stared up at her. "Then I cut free from the rest of my ropes and went after his men." Truth be told, he'd fallen on his ass three times as he'd tried to get out of that room. The blood loss had made him dizzy, and Titan had been sure he was dying. But he'd intended to take as many of those SOBs out with him as he could. "When I got outside, cops had swarmed." He'd been rushed to the hospital. Though he didn't remember riding in any ambulance. Titan just recalled waking up in a hospital room. His girlfriend had been beside the bed, and the first thing he'd seen had been the horror in her eyes.

Just what a guy wanted to find waiting for him when he woke up from a nightmare.

Cassidy wasn't talking. Odd, for her. He'd shocked her into silence. Or scared her into silence. Not his intent. "I told you the story so you'd understand that I will *never* give you up."

"Wh-what?"

Shit. He'd phrased that wrong, hadn't he? It had come out sounding all hard and possessive and he'd meant...

*What did I mean?* "I won't turn on you. I protect my witnesses, no matter the cost."

Her hair moved in a soft slither as she shook her head. "I don't want you getting hurt for me."

"I can heal. Been hurt before." What would more scars be? Nothing new.

"I *don't* want you getting hurt for me," she said again, voice sharper. "You need to give me up to save yourself? Then you do it. I have enough blood on my hands. I don't want more."

An odd statement. "Why would you have blood on your hands?"

"I—" She stopped. Yanked her head back. Settled in the bed once more as the covers rustled. "Don't do anything crazy like take a knife or bullet for me. And absolutely, under no circumstances are you to *die* for me. Got that? I would never, ever forgive you if you pulled some martyr crap like that."

He stared at the ceiling. "I hear your words." *I just intend to do whatever the hell I want.*

"Look, you're Mr. Big, Bad, and Scary. Can't you just, I don't know, promise to knock out any threats that come our way? That is a million times better than you getting hurt."

"I'll take out any threats that come your way," he vowed. Easy enough promise to give.

"Thank you. And in return, I will never put you in a position where you have to get tortured in order to protect me." He could practically hear the shudder in her voice.

The moments slipped past. His eyes began to close.

"Titan?" Soft.

He grunted.

"When you woke up in the hospital, you weren't alone, were you? I, uh…you had family with you, right?"

"Parents are dead. No siblings." *Don't say it. Don't.* "Girlfriend was there." Why in the hell had he just overshared that shit? Why, for the first time in his life, was he having trouble talking too much?

Maybe he was too tired. That was it. And being tired was making him say crap he shouldn't.

"You have a girlfriend." An odd note entered her voice. "Of course, you do. You have—"

"She couldn't even look at me. Tried to stay for a few days, but then cut out. Told me I was a nightmare." That was it. He was not going to say another word. He was not… "Night, Cassidy." Okay, now he was done. *Done.*

His eyes closed. He tried not to think about how close she was to him.

But he could hear her gentle breathing.

And…

"Titan?"

"Go to sleep, Cassidy."

"I will, I just...she sounds like a real bitch. Just so you know."

His eyes opened.

"You're not a nightmare. I know about nightmares. I have them all the time." The bed squeaked, and he knew she'd probably turned onto her side. "You're not a nightmare," she said again. "In fact, I'm pretty sure you're the closest thing to a *good* dream that I've had in ages."

He blinked. He was no dream. Certainly not a *good*—

"Good night, Titan."

***

*"I can stop for you."*

*Her hands strained desperately at the straps around her wrists. She pulled as hard as she could, but the straps held. Straps around her wrists. Straps around her ankles. Her body arched against the hard mattress.*

*His fingers slid over her cheek. "You're different."*

*Her head shook. She wasn't. She was not—*

*"You're like me, aren't you? On the inside. I knew it when we met. I could feel it. They say like calls to like."*

*No. "Help!" A gasp that tore from her lips. But the gasp seemed so quiet. Why was it quiet?*

*"I think you broke your voice with all that screaming earlier. I heard they had to sedate you. Poor Cassidy. You can't talk. Trapped in silence."*

*Like she'd been trapped in that pantry. She hated silence. "Help," she tried to croak again.*

*He leaned closer to her. "The nurse is on a break. She went outside for a cigarette. How do you think I got in? Even if someone heard your weak cry, it would just be another patient who caught the sound. You really think someone from the psych ward will rush to your rescue?"*

*He was going to kill her. She knew it.*

*His fingers slid over her cheek. Down to her throat. His grip tightened around her neck. "Your pulse is racing so fast. Why are you so afraid of me?"*

*Uh, because he was a killer? Because she'd seen what he'd done to that poor woman...the woman who looked just like—*

*"The woman you saw? She was number six. I had originally planned for you to be broken by me, too, but then I saw the truth with you. Like to like. I realized you could change everything for me. You watched, didn't you?"*

*Her pulse raced even more. She knew he'd feel it beneath his touch.*

*"You enjoyed it."*

*No. Never. Her head shook—*

*His hold tightened, cutting off her breath. Her mouth opened wide, but she couldn't even croak out a sound this time.*

*"Don't lie to me, Cass. I know you too well." He lowered toward her even as his fingers kept squeezing.*

*He was killing her. Spots danced before her eyes. She strained against the straps, but she couldn't get out. Couldn't—*

*He let her go.*

*Cassidy sucked in desperate gulps of air.*

*"I'm going to leave you here so you can think about what you did. It's the punishment you deserve. You should never, ever have gone to the cops. That's not what partners do."*

*They were not partners.*

*"You were going to move in with me. That was step one. You were always so skittish."*

*Skittish? She fought to breathe.*

*"Moving in, then marrying me. That was the goal. Staying with me forever. The goal has not changed."*

*Oh, yes, it had.*

*His hand lifted once more.*

*She tensed.*

*But his fingers just stroked tenderly over the now bruised and swollen skin of her throat. "She was the last one. Just ending unfinished business. I won't kill anyone else. Not if you're with me. When you stay with me, things will be different."*

*A tear slid down her cheek.*

*"You stay with me. You fill up my dark spaces. We'll be happy."*

*He was right above her. But all she could see was the woman who'd been on his kitchen floor. The plastic beneath her. The blood—*

*"Enjoy your time here, Cass. Think about what you've done. How you can make things up to me."*

*He was the psychotic one. Not her. He should be strapped down. Not her.*

*"See you when the seventy-two hours are up. Can't wait for you to come home. Home is where the heart is, am I right?"*

*No, home was where the murders were. She would never go home with him.*

*"You can make me stop, Cass. Only you. I can be different with you. I know it. But without you..." He reached into his coat. He was wearing one of his expensive suits. Looking debonair and handsome and so very much not like a twisted killer, even as he pulled a scalpel from the interior pocket of his suit coat. The bright light overhead—a light he'd turned on when he crept into her room—hit the scalpel. "Found this on my way to you." His head tilted as he stared down at her. "I don't want to hurt you."*

*Her throbbing neck said differently.*

*"But you try to leave me, and I will." He smiled at her, then his hand flew out, and he drove the scalpel right toward her chest—*

"No!" Cassidy screamed. She struggled against the straps that bound her. Her hands strained against their imprisonment. Her feet kicked at the restraints. She twisted and turned and—

"*Cassidy?*" A deep, growling voice penetrated through her terror.

Too late, she realized that covers were trapping her legs, not restraints. Covers were around her arms, not straps.

Too late...because she'd heaved her body too far and she was falling off the bed.

She tumbled down, down...and landed right on top of Titan.

***

The motel was a total dump. "Should have stayed with me, Cass," he murmured as he stared at the glowing MOTEL sign near the road. A sign that tilted a little too far and hard to the right. "I never would have let you stay in a place like this." He guessed the marshal had different standards.

The SUV that the bastard had driven was in the lot, but not, conveniently, parked in front of a particular room. No, the SUV was right in front of the glass doors that led to the tiny lobby and main office area. Meaning that the prick could be in any room.

*With my Cass.*

He slammed his car door shut. A different ride than he'd had before. After leaving the diner, he'd helped himself to a new vehicle. Tisha's mom's ride. The woman definitely shouldn't have left her keys in it. She'd been too worried about her daughter. She'd rushed right in the diner...

And been ever so helpful to him because she'd left her keys *and* her purse in the vehicle.

His gaze slid over the motel. All of the doors were accessible from the outside. But which one belonged to the marshal? And was he in the same room as Cass? Or a different one?

Had to be a different one. They couldn't really be lovers. *She belongs to me.* Cass wouldn't dare turn to another. She knew that he owned every single inch of her.

That bit the hick deputy had told him about Cass being with her boyfriend? Just some BS cover story. The marshal had obviously forced

Cass to go with him. He was holding her against her will.

*Good thing I'm here to rescue her.*

Maybe the marshal had been the one taking Cass away all along. The whole time that he'd been searching for his Cass, maybe the marshal had been the one moving her. Hiding her. Over and over again.

The bastard would pay for that.

*Which room is he in?*

Pulling his cap low over his head, he made his way to the little office. A faint light glowed from inside, and he pushed on the door.

It didn't open.

What the fuck?

His hand lifted and his knuckles rapped against the door. No response. He pressed his face against the glass as he peered inside. Someone had to be at the front desk. You didn't just leave a motel unattended. There were *guests*—

But he saw no one inside.

Unbelievable. Talk about some fucking poor service. *See, Cass, I would never have brought you here.* He would have given her the five-star treatment. She must sure miss being with him.

He shoved against the door once more. Harder. Nothing happened. He started to kick the freaking thing in and—

*Camera.* From the corner of his eye, he caught sight of the little camera perched high and to the right of him. Immediately, he froze. Every place had freaking cameras these days. Made shit so much harder.

He backed away from the door. Tugged his cap down even more.

So the night desk clerk had stepped out. *Or maybe just left because he's a lazy ass who doesn't give a shit about anything.* That was all right. There were other ways to find Cass.

He wasn't just going to let her stay the night with the marshal. No, he'd been away from her long enough.

Time to get Cass to come back to him.

Turning away from the door, he began to walk in front of the rooms to the right. It was after one a.m. Everyone was quiet. No voices. No TVs. No...

He heard the sound of a child crying. Up ahead. The very last room.

And he got an idea.

Marshals were the heroes, weren't they? They were supposed to save the day?

*Come out, come out, marshal. I'm about to have someone for you to save.*

And while the marshal was busy...

*I'll take my Cass away.*

# CHAPTER EIGHT

Oh, no. No, *no*. Embarrassed, frantic, Cassidy immediately tried to haul herself *off* Titan. But her legs had straddled his hips and her hands were on either side of him and when she tried to shove up—

"Cassidy." *His* hands clamped around her waist to hold her in place. "What's wrong?"

Her breath heaved in and out. A thin blanket separated their bodies. Or at least, the blanket separated their lower bodies. Because when she'd fallen down, her chest had smashed onto his. Titan hadn't put on a shirt, and she could feel all of those rock-hard muscles pressing against her through her thin tank top.

And, um, he had to feel her tight, pebbled nipples pressing against him.

"Cassidy?"

Her racing heart thundered in her ears. "Sorry. Bad dream." She'd warned him about those, hadn't she? But, dammit, she'd slept with him before—twice—and been okay. Why couldn't she have been okay just once more? Would one more time have been too much to ask? "Sorry."

"It's okay." His hold tightened on her. "Want to talk about it?"

While she was straddling him? While her chest was crushed to his? And even if that hadn't been the case... "A million times, no." She should get off him. Now.

Her hands pushed down harder against the floor as she started to angle up—

Oh, bad plan. All she did was somehow angle her hips *down* against him, and as she did, Cassidy pretty much rode the very long and very erect dick that shoved against her.

Immediately, she froze.

"Sorry," he bit out. "My turn to apologize."

Her breath kept coming too fast. "Sure it's...ah...nothing personal." Maybe he'd been having a hot dream. Maybe he'd—

"Fuck that. It's very, very personal. Told you before, I wanted you from the first moment I saw you. I. Want. You." Guttural.

Her hips *might* have dipped against him a bit more. "I'm...sure there are rules about a marshal being with—" Cassidy stopped. She really didn't want to think about rules. "You make me feel safe," she blurted out the truth.

"You *are* safe with me." A grim promise. "But you should get back in the bed—"

"I haven't been with anyone in the last year. You make one epically bad choice, and you get scared as hell to trust someone else. I..." God, it was good that it was dark. Otherwise, he'd see her flaming cheeks. "I've been scared to want anyone." She was still scared. Only, not with him. "Part of me felt dead." As dead as all of Blake's other victims. “Then you kissed me in Nowhere, and it was like I was waking up again. Coming back. A stupid, pretend kiss that probably meant nothing to you—and it changed me.”

One of his hands rose to cup her jaw. “It meant something.”

“It was just for show. For Maverick—”

“No one is here now. Just us.”

Just them. No show. Just...*I want my life back.* So she was taking it. Her head jerked forward, and her mouth locked onto his. It was awkward. Her mouth kind of rammed onto his, and she knew there should have been some sort of finesse, but Cassidy had basically acted before she could allow her fear to hold her back and now...

Now he was growling softly. Rasping against her mouth, “Let me...”

Her lips parted.

And she let him in.

He had enough finesse for the both of them. Big, rough Titan kissed like some kind of connoisseur. Licking and tasting and sending her body melting against him. The man could work his tongue like a master, and she was all too eager to be taken by him.

He wasn’t dominating. Wasn’t pushing hard and fast. He was seducing. Didn’t he get it? She was already his for the taking. He didn’t need to waste energy on a careful seduction.

Because she wanted this—wanted him—so badly she could hardly breathe. The nightmare had come back in brutal force because she feared Blake was closing in on her. That he’d get her again.

*And I will never be his. Never.*

Titan kissed her deeper. Her hips lifted and fell against his, riding the heavy length of his cock even through that stupid blanket. Oh, the blanket needed to go. One of her hands wedged between their bodies, dipping over all of those hot, powerful muscles of his, and she managed to grab the blanket. She shoved it out of the way, or tried to, anyway. But in the process...

Her fingers touched him. His cock. He had on sweats that covered him. She had no idea when he'd put on those, but her hand stroked him through the soft fabric, and then...she started to dip her fingers beneath the top of his sweats.

In a flash, he rolled her onto her back. Pinned her to the floor with his body over hers.

Her breath sawed out.

"You need to be sure, Cassidy. Very, very sure."

"I'm not sure of many things." Her life was too crazy for certainty.

He started to lift off her.

*Don't leave me.* Her hands flew out and clamped around his shoulders. "But I'm sure I want you." This room—what was happening between them—it was almost like a dream. The good kind. Hadn't she told him that before? He was a good dream. She would hold this dream tight, and when morning came, it would vanish, and life would go back to being scary.

She wasn't scared in that moment.

She was turned on.

Her greedy hands flew over his chest. He felt so *good.* Her legs rose to wrap around his hips.

And he kissed her again. Deeper, harder. A kiss that drugged and tempted and had her whole body trembling beneath his because she didn't think anyone had ever kissed her the way he did. Total focus. Complete seduction.

Sex and pleasure. The promise of so much pleasure.

But then his mouth tore from hers. Why? Why had he done that? "Titan!" A cry of protest that burst from her lips.

He started kissing his way down her neck. Tender, careful kisses where another man had hurt her. Tears burned her eyes because he didn't know. Couldn't know. No one knew. But he was taking away the pain. Giving her a better memory. And there was pleasure. Pleasure where there had been horror.

Down, down he went. He kissed her collarbone. Eased a broad finger under the thin, tank top strap on her right shoulder. She opened her eyes because she wanted to *see* him.

But it was too dark to see clearly.

She just felt him when his mouth closed over her nipple. Cassidy nearly surged right off the floor. Okay, she *did* surge up a bit. Pushing against his mouth and that wicked, wicked tongue of his.

While he worked her nipple—licking and sucking and making her gasp his name—his other hand slid between her legs. Her legs had already been spread because his hips were between them. She was open for him. And his big hand went to the top of her shorts. He shoved his hand inside, not pushing the shorts down—but just getting the shorts and her thin cotton panties out of his way so that he could...

*Touch me.*

His fingers slid to her core. Pushed against her heat. Stroked her clit and she could only shudder and buck against his hand.

His mouth turned to her other breast. He yanked down that strap too, exposing both of her breasts to him now even as his other hand stayed between her legs. He took that nipple into his mouth just as one finger pushed into her.

"Fucking perfect." His voice was such a deep, dark growl. "You're so tight."

Her hips rose and pushed against his finger.

His thumb slid over her clit.

"Titan!"

"Take another." A second finger worked into her. Stretched her. She was wet for him. So eager. This hadn't happened to her before. Usually, it took longer but...

*I want this. Want him. Don't need to think about anything else. Not tomorrow. Not what could happen. Not—*

She stopped the thought. Or, rather, Titan did. His thumb dragged over her clit. Once more. Twice. But then his hand yanked away from her even as she was shoving her hips toward him with eager abandon.

Blinking quickly, she tried to understand why he was pulling back. Jerking to the side. Only...

He yanked down her shorts. Ripped her panties.

Okay. That was helpful.

"Not on the fucking floor. Not you." He lifted her up with that mad strength of his, the movement seeming effortless. Her tank top had shoved down around her abdomen. Her shorts and underwear were gone while her breasts thrust toward him. In a quick, rough move, he had her on the bed, but she was sideways, with her legs dangling over the edge. He grabbed her legs. Hauled her closer as he stood beside the bed and then he lowered down. Shoved her thighs even farther apart and put his mouth on her.

His tongue drove into her as his fingers began to rub and strum her clit. In and out, his tongue thrust, tasting and taking and his fingers were driving her crazy. She wanted to twist and turn, but one of his hands had locked around her hips. Held helplessly in place against his mouth, her hands flew out to grab the sheets. Her fingers fisted them even as her back arched and an avalanche of mind-numbing pleasure seemed to explode through her body as...

Alarm bells rang.

No, no, there was nothing about Titan that set off alarms for her. Her body trembled and shook, and her hips bucked as the pleasure continued but...

The alarm bells were ringing. Like, actually ringing.

"Why..." Panted from her. "Do I always hear alarms when we're...together?" First the wail of a tornado siren when they kissed the first time and now—

His head whipped up. "Fuck."

She had very much hoped that would be the next item on their to-do list.

Titan leapt to his feet. He ran toward the lone window and yanked on the blinds so he could create an opening and peer outside. “Fire.”

When he said fire, her body immediately iced. She lurched into a sitting position on the bed. “What?” Aftershocks of pleasure still quaked in her sex.

“Get dressed. *Now.*”

Cassidy was already pulling the shirt straps back into place on her shoulders. She jumped out of the bed and almost fell straight down when her jittery knees did a fast tremble. Her hand flew out and landed on the nightstand as she balanced herself.

“Here.” He had her shorts. He pushed them into her left hand right before he yanked open the nightstand drawer and hauled out a gun. “We need to move, now.”

She tugged on the shorts. No underwear. Great. Didn’t she have a vague memory of the underwear shredding? Even as she took a step toward her bag so that she could snag a fresh pair of panties—and maybe a bra because that would be awesome—Titan caught her hand in his and tugged her toward the door.

“Out,” he barked. “Now.”

He was just wearing sweats. Didn’t he want more clothes, too?

“Titan, I—”

He yanked open the door. The scent of smoke immediately hit her. The alarms were still ringing, and Cassidy realized she could hear voices rising and falling. There were cries and some screams and...

Titan hauled her from the room. Rushed her away from the motel and across the street where a small group of guests had formed a huddle. She saw a man with a ton of tats on his chest and with his hair sticking out in all directions as he stood there wearing just a pair of jeans. A woman in a cheap hotel robe clung to his arm. There were a few families, some with scared-looking teens, some with babies and there was—

"Where's the family from check-in?" Cassidy asked. Her gaze scanned the growing crowd. More people had arrived, but she still didn't see them.

Titan frowned as he looked around. She could see him taking stock of every face.

And then...

"It's going to be okay!" A cracking voice. Her gaze jerked to the left. It was the clerk who'd checked her in. He ran a shaking hand over his balding head. "The fire department is coming. Everything will be fine!"

Didn't look fine to her. Smoke billowed from the motel. Was everyone out? Shouldn't there be some kind of evacuation procedure that the motel staff followed? And where was the family from check-in?

"Mister..." A low whisper.

Cassidy's head snapped down. They stood beneath a streetlight, or, close to one, anyway, and she caught sight of the little girl tugging on Titan's sweatpants. The same girl with pigtails that she'd seen at check-in. Thanks to the light, Cassidy could almost see the freckles that trailed across the girl's nose. *When I had them as a kid, my mom used to tell me they were angel kisses. That angels would always look out for me.*

Relief had her feeling light-headed. The family had gotten out. That was good. But shouldn't someone be doing a room check on all the guests to make certain no one was trapped? Were they supposed to wait for the firefighters or—

"You're big, mister. Can you open a stuck window?" A careful question from the little girl as she squinted at Titan. "'Cause it wouldn't open enough for my mom and dad to get out...just me."

Oh, God.

Titan's head whipped toward the fire. "Fuck."

"Bad word," the little girl whispered. She sounded on the verge of tears.

Titan's attention swung to Cassidy. "Keep her here," he ordered flatly as he pointed to the little girl. He shoved the gun into Cassidy's hand. "And you stay safe."

No, hold up—

Titan ran back to the motel. He ran back to the smoke and the fire.

Cassidy took a lunging step forward.

The little girl grabbed her leg. "He's big."

Cassidy looked down at her.

"Can he get them out?" Tears poured from her eyes and streamed down the little girl's face.

***

The marshal was off to be the hero. He'd figured it would just be a matter of time before the bruiser ran back to help anyone who'd been trapped. And he'd made sure people were trapped.

The room with the crying kid had been an easy target, especially since it had been located at the far end of the motel. He'd started the fire right in front of their door. Let the flames flare and grow so big that they wouldn't be able to come out that way.

When the alarm had blared, he'd made sure escape from the lone window in the motel room hadn't been a possibility. He'd had to act fast there and had gotten lucky when he found a hammer, nails, and some random pieces of wood in the ramshackle maintenance room. The motel was undergoing some construction, and some helpful jackass had left the maintenance room unlocked for him.

The blaring of the alarm had hidden the quick strikes of the hammer on the nails. And since the family's room had been the last one on the little strip, their window was on the side of the building, not in the front. It had been so easy to hide on the side and get his job done.

Then he'd blended with the others when everyone else had come running out and rushed away from the fire.

He didn't stand beneath the streetlight. Instead, he watched from the shadows. Cassidy had tucked a gun into the waistband of her shorts, then tugged down her tank top in an attempt to hide it.

Silly Cassidy. Like she could even shoot that thing.

A little girl clung to her as Cassidy looked helplessly around. He knew exactly what she was doing. Now that the marshal was busy, this was Cassidy's chance to flee. *If* the marshal had been forcing her cooperation, that was. If he'd made Cassidy hide and go with him, this would be her perfect chance to escape. He'd given Cassidy that chance.

*You're welcome.*

So he waited for Cassidy to make her move.

She grabbed a thin, shaking guy who kept running his hand over his forehead and up to his gleaming, mostly bald head. "You're the desk clerk."

Her voice carried easily. There was a bit of bite in her words. He loved her bite.

The man nodded, seemingly numb.

"Aren't you going to *help?"* Cassidy blasted.

The man didn't move. Silly Cassidy. The desk clerk hadn't been at his post. There was nothing about the man that shouted *helper*.

"Dammit!" Cassidy erupted. She released the clerk's arm. "You keep the kid here, got me? You guard her like she is the most precious treasure in the world. If she gets so much as a bruise, I will come back and I will rip you open."

Ah, his Cassidy. She always had been soft when it came to kids. He could *almost* get it. Most kids were innocent. Cassidy saw that. But, unlike Cassidy, he didn't mind destroying some innocence if it let him get his job done.

Cassidy was making sure the kid would be okay before she made her big escape. Probably didn't want that guilt on her conscience. Typical Cassidy.

"You're leaving?" It was the little girl who'd asked that question.

He pulled his cap a little lower and edged closer. Some of the people in the crowd were on their phones. Calling for help. Crying. No one else had run back toward the fire.

They were waiting for the firefighters.

The marshal should have done the same. You didn't run *into* a fire, not without proper equipment. Not unless you had a death wish.

He guessed the marshal wanted to die.

"I'll be right back," Cassidy assured her.

Oh, Cassidy could be so good at lying. Something else they had in common.

"Watch her," Cassidy barked at the night clerk. She took a lunging step forward.

"Where are you going?" the little girl called, voice breaking.

*To me. Cassie is running from the marshal. She's coming to—*

"To help my friend and to get your parents out." Then she ran toward the smoke and flames.

*What. The. Fuck?* He glared after her. *Cassidy—no!*

But she wasn't escaping. Wasn't trying to get away from the marshal bastard. She was running straight into danger...*for him.*

He knew right then that he had to kill the fucking marshal. And he had to make the death *painful.*

# CHAPTER NINE

The flames were freaking huge. Crackling and racing along the exterior of the motel's right side. The snaking structure was ancient, and he knew that was probably helping the fire to spread.

*"Help! Please!"* Titan could hear the cries, and he raced around the side of the building, giving the flames a wide berth and covering his mouth and nose. The fire was right in front of that last room. The door and front wall were consumed by a twisting, heaving mound of flames.

The smoke billowed everywhere, turning the night even darker.

His feet pounded as he headed for the window on the side of that last room. And as he got closer, his feet crunched the broken glass on the ground. *That's how they got the little girl out. They broke the glass so she could fit.* It was a seriously weathered-looking window, perfectly in tune with the rest of the motel, and...

*What. The. Fuck?*

Long slats of wood had been nailed in a haphazard manner across part of the window. *No wonder only the kid could fit.* When he tried to wrench one of the slats out of the way, his fingers slid over nails that protruded from the wood. Several twisted nails that were partially inserted.

Someone had deliberately nailed the wood into place in order to trap the people inside. But...but how could that—

"*Help!*" Another frantic, feminine cry from inside the room.

"I'm here!" Titan bellowed back as he jerked out more chunks of glass. The wood wasn't giving, dammit, not with those nails inside. *I'll make it give. I'll try harder. I'll make it give.*

"Take her, please, take her!" The mom pushed the child through the broken chunks of glass, being careful not to let the toddler get cut on the sharp edges. "Just get my baby out!"

The kid was screaming her head off as long tears streaked down her cheeks. Titan took her, pulling her quickly away from the window, and tucking her against his body.

"Get her away!" The mom coughed. "Too much smoke! Get her out!"

"I'm getting you all out." He wasn't leaving them to die from smoke inhalation or from the flames. He just needed to put the kid—

"I'll take her." Cassidy.

Cassidy who should have been somewhere safe and not right there. "You were supposed to stay with the group—" Titan exploded.

"No. You said for the kid to stay. She stayed. I was just supposed to be safe. I am safe—and I'm helping you. Give her to me." She didn't wait. She took the screaming kid. "It's okay," Cassidy soothed. "Everyone's getting out."

He hoped they were. "The window was nailed shut." But he'd pry that sonofabitch open. He grabbed for another thick slat of wood and heaved with all of his strength. Cassidy needed to get the hell out of there because if she got too much smoke in her lungs—

The wood popped. Disintegrated in his hand. One slat. He grabbed the other. Ignored the sting of broken glass and the jab of wood splinters in his fingers. He heaved and that bitch broke, too. He used his fist to punch the rest of the wood out of his way. Slats that he didn't think had ever belonged on the window.

*Who boarded this up? Who trapped them?*

"Thank God!" Coughing from the mom. She started crawling out. He grabbed her arms and heaved her through. As soon as she was clear, she immediately grabbed her kid from Cassidy and clutched her daughter tightly. Then she spun back for the window. "My husband!"

"We'll get him," Cassidy said before Titan could. "Go across the street—your other daughter is waiting over there. Go! *Hurry!*"

"There's so much smoke in the room...I-I..." Coughing. "I think he passed out..."

Hell. Not good. Now Titan knew he had to get his ass in that room.

Cassidy had pushed the woman away with another order of "Go!" At least the lady and her kids were clear. One problem at a time. He sent Cassidy a hard glare. "Get the fuck out of here." She needed to get *clear*. Fires were too unpredictable. He was already coughing, his eyes were streaming, and Cassidy needed to get to safety.

"Love you, too," she shot back.

The words made him flinch.

"How about we drag the dad to safety, and *all* get the fuck out of here? Sound like a plan?" She coughed. Then tried to crawl through the window. He grabbed her around the waist and heaved her back.

*"I'll* get him." She wasn't going to be able to lift a grown-ass man. "You get with the group!"

He didn't wait to hear her argue. Cassidy seemed to love arguing too much. He began to go through the window but—

"You're too big!" Cassidy grabbed him around the waist and jerked him back. Or attempted to do so. She failed. "Your shoulders are too wide!" Cassidy snapped. "You won't fit."

The window area was too freaking small. That was the problem.

"I think the husband can get out because he looked a whole lot smaller than you when we saw him in the lobby, but you can't make it. I have to go in!" More coughing from Cassidy.

The woman actually thought he was going to let her go into a burning building? *Try again, baby.*

It was a tight fit, yeah, but he'd shoved out most of the wood in his way. He would get in. And he did. He drove his body through that window before Cassidy could try and get past him. Wood and broken glass scraped over his shoulders, and he wished that he'd taken the time to put on a freaking shirt. Oh, well. More cuts. He barely felt them.

He hurtled through the window and crashed onto the floor in the motel room.

*"Titan!"* Cassidy yelled his name.

The smoke was so thick in there. The whole room swirled around him, and he crawled forward, knowing he needed to stay low. Where the hell was the husband?

"Titan! Titan, the fire is spreading to the roof!"

Wonderful. Just what he needed—for the whole place to fall in on him. Cassidy had better keep that sweet ass of hers outside. He surged forward, moving with his hands spread out.

*The wife kept the kid close to the window so she could get fresh air. Smart. Or else they all would have been passed out in here.* Why hadn't the husband gone toward the window, too?

Where was the husband? The flames were burning too hot and—

"It's on the wall here, Titan! Come out! Come out before you're trapped!"

*Trapped.* The husband had been trying to look for another way out. The guy couldn't get the rest of his family out through the window, the front door had been blocked so...

*Adjoining rooms.* Titan whirled and headed toward where he thought an adjoining door might be. Sure the hell enough, he found the slumped figure of the dad right in front of that door. The door on the dad's side was open, but the door for the connecting room...

*It was locked and you couldn't get out.*

"Titan!" Terror echoed in Cassidy's scream. "The fire is at the window!"

She'd better have backed away, and yeah, he knew she was right. The fire was a fucking hungry monster, eating everything in its path. He and the dad weren't getting out of that window.

He grabbed something from the floor. Someone's shirt? Titan put it over his mouth and nose. Then he staggered upright. The room spun around him. He focused on the connecting door. He lifted his foot and kicked in the area of the lock. Once, twice, three times.

*"Titan!"* He could barely hear Cassidy's cry. The fire crackled too loudly.

Titan kicked the door and lock again. Then he just fucking drove his shoulder into the whole damn thing with as much strength as he had.

***

He was in the room, and he was going to burn, and she had to get him the hell out of there. Cassidy backed away from the side of the building, her horrified eyes on the flames that burned and stretched and *consumed*. "Titan!" He wasn't answering her. He hadn't answered any of her screamed calls. He was inside, and she was shaking apart.

The wail of a siren reached her. Help! Finally. She whirled, intending to run toward the siren. She'd grab the firefighters and drag them over. They'd get Titan out. They had to get him out.

A cough shook her body, and Cassidy covered her mouth as she rushed to—

*"Cass."*

She froze, then whirled back around. "Titan!" She'd heard him, hadn't she? Saying her name. He needed her help. Her feet shuffled forward. "Titan?"

The sirens wailed louder. The window—part of that wall seemed to heave with the flames. No, no Titan wasn't coming out through the window. He couldn't. He couldn't leap through fire.

*"He's dying in there."*

That voice again. But...coming from the woods near the motel. Again, she turned. This time, the turn was toward the right. The flames were hot, smoke still billowed, but a chill rose onto her arms. She knew that voice.

A dark figure stepped from the woods. Bulky coat. A cap pulled low over his head. He extended one hand toward her.

*OhmyGod, no.* She could not move.

Her gaze raked over him. That gloved hand reached out to her...but in his other hand, the hand that remained near his body, half-hidden, he...he was holding something.

"Did you miss me?" he asked her.

The sirens screamed. And maybe she did, too.

***

Titan burst out of the motel room. Not the room that had belonged to the family. He'd knocked down the connecting door and managed to drag the unconscious man out of there. "Need some..." *Cough. Cough.* The smoke seemed to strangle him. "*Help over here!*" Titan thought he bellowed but his voice sounded funny, even to his own ears. Rougher than normal. Scarier.

The flames had practically consumed the family's motel room. He kept his grip on the unconscious dad and staggered forward. The more forward he went, the better the air tasted on his tongue. Greedily, desperately, he tried to suck it in, but his lungs refused to take it at first, and he sputtered.

*Sonofabitch.*

But then the air seemed to sink into him, and he gulped it frantically. He saw firefighters running toward them. One guy was hauling a long, white hose. Another had an ax in his hands. Masks covered their faces.

Titan realized he'd fallen to his knees. When the hell had that happened?

A masked firefighter reached for him. Titan jerked away. "Get him help first!" The guy had a family waiting.

The firefighters grabbed the father. Hauled him up. Titan squinted against the smoke. "Cassidy?"

He didn't see her. Good. She'd gone back across the street with the others.

"Who else is here?"

The smoke was so thick and dark.

A firefighter bellowed, "*Who else?*"

Titan was being pulled away from the blaze. "No one...in those two rooms..." The ones behind him. But he didn't know about the rest of the motel. Had everyone escaped the fire? All the other guests? Were they all safe?

"Get a search going!" An order he heard distantly. Water sprayed at the twisting flames. The siren kept screaming, and as the firefighters took him toward safety, he saw that an ambulance had braked to a stop near the assembled crowd. The streetlight shone down on the ambulance.

"He needs oxygen!" Another bark before the firefighters who'd been dragging Titan finally let him go.

The dad Titan had saved was already receiving oxygen. His eyes were open above the small mask. His crying wife huddled near him, clutching his hand tightly. The kids were there. They'd crowded in close, too.

Someone slid an oxygen mask over Titan's face. He'd been shoved onto the back of an ambulance. Not fully *in* the ambulance. More like just sitting on the edge of the thing as the doors hung open beside him. For a moment, he just took in that sweet, sweet oxygen.

"You've got lacerations." It was a female EMT talking. "Not too deep. I don't think you'll need stitches, but we're taking you to the hospital to make sure..."

She said something else, but he didn't catch the words. He was too busy scanning the crowd and looking for Cassidy. *Only I don't see her.* Titan checked again. *Again.* But Cassidy wasn't in the whispering crowd.

Titan jerked the mask off his face and surged away from the ambulance. "Where is she?"

"Sir, sir, put the mask back on! We need you inside the ambulance so that we can—"

The little girl ran to him. The one who'd been so afraid in the lobby. Pigtails and freckles. The girl who'd been so brave as she tried to get help for her parents. She ran to him and threw her arms around Titan's right leg and held on tightly. He frowned down at her.

She tilted her head up. "I love you."

Okay, he did not have time to—

"The pretty lady went to help you. I stayed where she told me—"

Yes, yes, Cassidy had come. But he'd told her to go back. He'd *told her.*

Except...*Cassidy doesn't listen for shit.* Terror knifed right through his heart. If Cassidy wasn't there, then she had to be back...with the flames. "Cassidy—"

A gunshot pierced the night. The blast boomed over the screaming sirens and the crackle of the flames.

Titan disentangled himself from the girl, pushed her toward the hovering EMT, and he ran straight toward that echoing sound. Firefighters rushed to the left and right. Water poured from the hose. Smoke surrounded him. "*Cassidy!*" The only thing that mattered to him was finding her.

Where the hell was she? His heart seemed to burst right from his chest as it raced faster and faster. And—

She seemed to run right from the flames. The gun was still gripped in her hand and her hair flew around her face. She ran straight to him.

Fuck that, he ran straight to *her.* Titan grabbed her and yanked her against him, and his whole body shuddered. He held her so tightly that he was probably making breathing hard for her, and he should ease up. He definitely should, but first…

*"Baby, don't ever scare me like that again."* No way could he handle it. He eased his grip, just a little, because he didn't want to hurt her. Not her. Ever.

"He's here." A fast rush of words. "He's here and I shot at him…He's here. OhmyGod…*Blake is here."*

It took a beat for her words to register. And when they did…

Titan pulled the gun from her fingers.

*I shot at him.*

"Where." A savage demand.

"Near the woods. Titan, I—"

"Drop the gun!"

His head snapped back toward the parking lot. The cops had finally come rushing in, tailing the firefighters and EMTs by a good five minutes.

"Drop the gun!" The cop had his weapon aimed at Titan. A rather shaky grip on that gun, too, Titan noted.

Cassidy broke free of Titan's grip, but only so she could put herself between him and the cop. Oh, the fuck, no. Hadn't he warned her about doing that shit? *Don't stand in front of guns, baby.* She had not learned her lesson. Clearly.

"Dropping it," Titan said because what choice was there? He put the gun on the ground and raised his hands.

"He's a US marshal!" Cassidy shouted. "You've got this all wrong!" Except she was coughing when she said half of her words, so Titan wasn't sure the cop had caught everything.

"Need to see ID!" The cop motioned with his weapon even as his partner sidled forward and snatched up the gun Titan had just dropped. "Now!"

"Yeah, that's gonna be hard. My ID is in the motel. You know..." His voice was still way rougher than normal. "The one burning behind us."

"There's a killer here!" Cassidy yelled at the cops. "He's near the woods! A serial killer! You have to go and get him! *Go!*"

The cops looked at each other. They made no move to go anywhere.

*Sonofabitch.* "He's getting away," Titan snarled.

"You're bleeding, buddy." From the partner who'd been silent. "Let's get you patched up and figure out what the hell is happening. Come on, walk toward the ambulance."

Fucking fuck. They wanted to figure out what was happening? *Easy.* A killer was getting away. But he had two guns pointed at him, so Titan had to walk. He made sure, though, that he caught Cassidy's elbow, and he moved her *away* from the weapons. No more of that BS where she acted like a shield for someone. *Sure as hell not for me.*

As they neared the ambulance...

The little girl he'd left came barreling toward them.

The kid latched onto his leg again while the cops barked for her to get back.

She didn't.

"I love you," she told Titan.

***

The bitch had shot at him.

He thundered through the woods, his blood boiling in his veins and the hammer still gripped tightly in his hand. He'd thought that she was coming to him. Her steps had staggered as she'd advanced, and he'd been smiling because he had his Cassidy back...

Then she'd grabbed the gun from beneath her tank top and fired it at him.

If he hadn't already been leaping to the side—and if she still hadn't been such a shit shot—the bullet might have hit him.

The bitch. The *bitch.*

She was going to pay. He'd make sure of it. He'd planned to put her on a pedestal. To put the world at her feet.

Now he'd just put her ungrateful ass in the ground.

# CHAPTER TEN

"Marshal Everett?" It was the uniformed cop. The younger one. The guy who'd first ordered Titan to drop his gun. Kid's name was Dillon McKell. Dillon shuffled his feet. "I am so sorry, sir." An apology for about the fiftieth time. "I just...we didn't have your ID then and we couldn't take any chances and—"

"And Blake Normandy is long gone." The sun had risen into the sky. The firefighters had put out the blaze a few hours ago. Some of the firefighters had been cautious, assessing the risk of a reflash, but so far, there had been no sign of the flames reigniting.

Just as there had been no sign of Blake Normandy.

Titan's ID had been retrieved. The fire had never reached his room—that room had been on the opposite side of the complex. He and Cassidy had been able to change. To grab their bags. And he'd proven his identity.

Too late.

"We don't know for sure that he was ever here." Ah, now that slightly nasally voice belonged to Dillon's commanding officer. H.G. Small had arrived quickly to the scene once talk of a suspected serial killer had spread to him. H.G. put his hands on his ample hips. “My people are still searching the woods. So far, no sign of him. Might be that your friend...” His head dipped to the right toward Cassidy. She sat on the curb, with her hands curled around her updrawn knees. She’d changed into jeans and a blue T-shirt. Put sneakers on her small feet. She hunched forward and seemed to ignore the scene around her.

H.G. grunted. “Might be that she just got a little scared. A lot was happening last night. Sometimes, people jump at shadows.” His nasally voice had been pitched low, so Titan didn’t think Cassidy had caught those words.

But her head tilted back and then turned toward them. She stared at Titan.

“She doesn’t jump at shadows.” A simple statement of fact from him. If Cassidy said she’d seen the guy, he believed her.

*Fucking patterns.*

They’d come rushing together in his mind when he’d seen the nails jutting from the wood in that window. Someone had deliberately started that fire and then trapped the family. Someone who might have wanted everyone else to run *out* of the motel.

*You did that, didn’t you, you sonofabitch? What happened, you didn’t know which room Cassidy was in? So you thought you’d smoke her out?*

And he had. The plan had worked. Almost perfectly.

*Bet you felt real fear when she fired that gun at you. Didn't expect that, did you?*

But, in order for Blake Normandy to have been there, to have found the motel...

*He must have tracked us.*

And that was where another piece of the pattern puzzle had clicked for Titan. He remembered driving past the chaotic scene in Nowhere—with the worried deputies and uprooted tree and the truck with the rental barcode on the back window—as he and Cassidy left town. When he'd called to check on Maverick, the sheriff had said the cop had a whole lot of lacerations and that there had been no sign of the truck's driver. The sheriff had thought the guy rushed to safety somewhere, fearful of the storm. But...What if...

*What if...*

*What if Blake had been the one driving the truck? What if he had been out there, watching, and he saw me leave with Cassidy?* Titan liked to think he was good at spotting a tail, but no one was perfect. And, of course, if the piece of shit had gotten close enough to put any kind of GPS tracker on Titan's ride—

"We really can't be sure he was ever here," H.G. continued, voice grim. "I'll keep an APB out with the man's description. We will certainly remain vigilant, but there isn't a whole lot else we can do to locate—"

"I need a new car."

H.G. clamped his mouth shut. Nodded. "Sure, sure. Uh, we have some rental companies not too far away. We can help you out with that—"

"Can you get people to check my vehicle for a tracker?" He pointed toward his SUV. There was a barcode on the back of it, too. He'd make arrangements for the SUV to be returned to the rental agency, *after* it was checked.

Again, H.G.'s head moved in a quick nod. "Sure, but...why?"

"Because I think a killer has been stalking me." No, not him so much. Titan stared at Cassidy.

*Her*. Blake just could not let her go. Like a moth to the flame, he kept coming right back to the fire.

Titan's nostrils flared. *Fucking literal fire.*

"You sure you don't want to head over to the hospital?" Dillon asked as he rocked back on his heels. "The EMTs seemed pretty worried about you."

Titan's gaze returned to the young cop—just in time to see the kid's eyes dart to the scar that ran the length of Titan's jaw. H.G. wore a pair of dark sunglasses, but Titan was sure he'd spent time eyeing the marks on his face, too.

*Story of my life.*

"I'm fine." New cuts and bruises. No big deal. He'd stopped the bleeding. And he'd taken the oxygen offered on scene.

The father he'd saved had gone to the hospital. The whole family had packed up. This was gonna be one vacation they never forgot.

*At least he's okay. At least the dad survived.* Speaking of the dad... "Someone nailed that window shut." He forced his gaze away from Cassidy—because it had already drifted back to her, it kept doing that—and he pinned Dillon. "The dad might have seen something. I already asked the mom—she didn't remember anything, just her kids screaming and the alarm blaring. But when the dad was breaking the glass and trying to get them out, maybe he saw something."

"Like...like the Blake Normandy guy?" Dillon asked. His eyes had widened.

"Exactly like him." And Titan also wanted Maverick questioned when he woke up. *If* he woke up. Maybe he'd seen the bastard, too, before the second tornado came. Titan also intended to get his Fed buddy to check out the rental truck he'd seen in Nowhere. When you rented a vehicle, you had to provide ID and a credit card. *But if it's Normandy, he would have just used a fake ID and a stolen credit card.* Still, they would check every lead. Titan nodded as he considered options. "I want you to keep an eye out for any cars that might go missing in the area. Blake is gonna want to get out of here fast."

Well, now that wasn't exactly true...

Titan once again glanced toward Cassidy. She'd put her head on her updrawn knees. Her hair spilled forward. She looked beautiful and fragile at the same time. He wanted to scoop her into his arms and take her far, far away from there.

*But he's going to follow her.* Wherever she went, he thought that Blake would follow.

His jaw locked. *I need to keep her safe until we're ready for him.* He'd underestimated Blake. Had thought that he was too far ahead of the other man. This attack was on him. "I won't make the same mistake again."

"Uh, come again, Marshal Everett?" Dillon's voice cracked a little. "What mistake?"

Underestimating his enemy. "You have my number. You'll call me if you learn anything from the father? Or if you find anything else on scene?" Part of him wanted to prowl every inch of those woods himself. But he'd seen the maps already. *Miles and miles.* The local authorities were searching. They would keep searching long into the day and night, he knew that.

*But I also know the bastard got away.*

For now.

"Absolutely," H.G. assured him.

He couldn't stay away from her any longer. Titan skirted past the cops and the firefighters who lingered and made his way to Cassidy. She stiffened as he approached, but she didn't lift her head. Not even when he stopped right beside her.

"Let me guess..." Her voice came out flat. She was rarely flat. "They found no sign of him? They aren't sure he was ever here, and they think I just imagined the whole thing?"

Pretty much, yes. "They're going to keep looking. They'll talk to the dad, too. See if he saw anything useful."

Her shoulders sagged. Then she slowly raised her head and stared at him. Her eyes had never seemed darker. "I'm not crazy."

"Never thought you were."

"But do the cops? Did they look up my record and see that I was committed before? Do they think I'm making up a story about my ex following me? The same way those cops thought I had made up the story in Florida about that poor woman on the kitchen floor?" She licked her lips. "Do *you* think I'm making it up—me seeing him at the motel? You think I got confused by the smoke and I shot at nothing? Or I just shot at an old nightmare?"

Titan crouched beside her. "You weren't supposed to follow me toward the fire."

"You needed backup. Everyone else was just standing here."

Here. In the spot where she sat. Beneath the streetlight. Though most of the other motel guests had long since left. The cops had talked to them first, then the guests had fled as fast as possible.

No one else had seen the man that Cassidy knew as Blake Normandy. Or at least, no one remembered seeing him. But the scene had been pure chaos.

*By his design, I'm sure.*

"Everyone else was standing here," Titan responded slowly as he fought the urge to reach out and pull her into his arms, "because this is a safe spot. It's away from where the fire was blazing."

A wan smile curved her lips. "You don't say."

"Civilians stay away from fires unless they want to get burned."

"You're not some firefighting hero, you know. You ran toward the flames." A shrug of one shoulder. "It wasn't any safer for you to go toward the fire, but you did it."

His jaw hardened. "That was different."

“Why?” A lock of dark hair fell over the side of her face.

He had to brush back that lock. His hand lingered against her silken cheek. “Because it was my life on the line. Not yours.”

“I happen to think your life is pretty important.” She wet her lips. “I was afraid you were trapped in there. The fire stretched over the window. It was eating at the wall. Going up to the roof…” A ragged release of her breath. “I was rushing around to try and figure out another way to get in when I heard my name being called.”

“I found another way out. Broke down the connecting door and left via the other room.” But he wanted to hear her retell the scene with Blake once more. Yes, she’d told the cops. Twice, actually. He’d listened intently to every word. But he still wanted to hear the tale once more. “You went back when he called you?”

“I went back because I thought it was you. Then he came out of the woods. He was wearing a big coat, and I-I think he had a hammer in his hand.”

Right. Titan nodded. *He used the hammer to nail the wood over the window.*

“He was coming toward me. Reaching with one hand while the other held that hammer. He asked if I’d missed him.” Her voice was still too flat. Hollow. He wanted the emotion—the life—back in it. “He acted like I was just going to take his hand and run away with him. But I knew better. You take his hand, and the other could just as easily have slammed that hammer into your head. He’s evil, straight to his core. I don’t care what bullshit he's said before about loving me. About me being able to stop him from hurting others..."

*Fuck me.* This part was new. She'd never said this before. "Cassidy?"

Her lower lip trembled. "I was strapped to the bed in the psych ward, and he said I could change everything. That if I stayed with him, he wouldn't need to kill anyone else. That I was just like him." A tear slid down her cheek. Immediately, her fingers rose to swipe it away. "Then he brought a scalpel down. He drove it right at me, and it stopped at the last second. I thought he was going to stab me, kill me right there, but he stopped over my heart. And said...told me... *'See, I'm different with you.'*" Another tear. Another fast, rough swipe of her fingers. "But I didn't believe him. I thought it would only be a matter of time before he turned on me, too. And I didn't want to be like that woman in the kitchen..."

He wanted her in his arms. Her words were breaking him.

"I ran. Even though he warned me that he would hurt others. He *told* me that I could stop him." She blinked quickly. "Then he almost killed that family tonight. Would have, if you hadn't been able to get them out. That's because of me. I did that. I should have stayed with him and none of this would have ever—"

"Hell, no." A guttural growl. Then he let his control break. He grabbed her and hauled her into his arms, and he didn't care if the cops or firefighters saw him. Screw what they thought. Cassidy was in pain. He pulled her tightly against him and kept her in the cradle of his arms as his head bent over her. Against her ear, he rasped, "Nothing is on you. Not a damn thing, you understand that?"

She shuddered. She didn't hug him back. Just stood within his arms. Her pain seemed to live and breathe in her. He *hated* it.

So Titan said again, "Nothing is on you." She was warm and strong and alive against him. He kept hearing that booming gunshot blast in his mind. And thinking...

*What if that sound had been Blake, firing at her? What if I'd lost her?*

No, screw it, *no,* not happening. Cassidy was not dying.

"What if he'd stopped?" Such a low whisper from her. "What if I could have stopped him?"

"You will stop him. *We* will." A vow. Titan's head raised so he could look down at her.

She was staring straight at his chest. At his neck. But he thought she might just be seeing her own past. His fingers moved to curl around her chin so he could tilt her head back. "He's a manipulative bastard."

Tears still filled her eyes. "Did you see the kid the mom was holding? She was like...two years old. I could have stopped him...I should have stayed..."

"So you could have been chopped into pieces and left to rot?"

Cassidy flinched. Her face bleached of all remaining color.

"Shit. No, baby, I'm sorry. Dammit!" He didn't know what to say. Didn't know how to comfort. Couldn't. Yet another reason why he preferred not to talk too much. He said the wrong thing and screwed everything to hell and back. "*You can't trust anything he says.*" There. Was that better?

She was still as pale as death.

*Cassidy is not dying.*

"He was trying to guilt you into staying." When they got to Vegas, he'd get Oliver to talk to her. The FBI agent knew all about the manipulation strategies of serial killers. Serial killers were his specialty. A twisted as fuck specialty to have, but there you go. Twisted was a way of life for Oliver. "You can't control another person. Anything Blake does—that's on him."

Her expression didn't change.

He knew she didn't believe him. "Dammit, Cassidy, you are a *good* person."

"You don't know that." She pulled away from him. Wrapped her arms around her stomach. Stood looking lost and sad. "You don't know me." Her head tipped forward.

He hated her beaten posture. "Sweetheart, I damn well do."

Her head snapped up.

"How else do you think I found you in Nowhere?" He'd been tracking her for months. Taking time off from other cases. Using breaks and vacations. Never giving up. Continuing to hunt because she'd become an obsession for him. "I know you. Inside and out."

He fucking knew her intimately. Had put his mouth on her core and lapped her up like a starving man. He would have been *in* her, had it not been for that blasting fire alarm. But now wasn't the time to talk about that. Hell, it wasn't the time to think about it. They needed to get on the road. Her staying out in the open wasn't a good idea. She needed a safe place to crash. He'd give her one.

"You are good," he told her again.

Her chin lifted a little more. "As a marshal, you should know there is plenty of evil in this world."

He did. Absolutely, Titan knew that.

"Even evil in places that are supposed to be good. Blake thinks I'm just like him. The only person in the world he has ever loved. Why do you think that is?" A shake of her head. "Maybe it's because when he looks at me, he sees something that you don't."

"Screw that shit," he said brutally.

Cassidy blinked.

"I've got plenty of *evil* in me. I can see it. Recognize it. You don't have any, Cassidy." He extended his hand toward her. "Now, how about we get the hell on the road, go meet up with a cocky FBI agent who thrives on taking down the most sadistic pricks out there, and we all devise a plan to lock your ex away for the rest of his miserable life?"

Her right arm uncurled from her body. Her hand reached for his.

His fingers threaded with hers.

***

The miles passed in a blur. New ride, same blasting radio.

Cassidy wasn't talking to him. A sure sign of a problem. Not singing along to the tunes, either. She'd cranked up the volume to high, and her head tilted to the side as she stared out of the window at the passing scenery. Not that there was a whole lot to see on this particular stretch of I-15. The occasional billboard maybe. Not a whole lot else.

"We, uh, should be in Vegas probably around nine p.m." They'd grab a bite somewhere. "Provided, of course, that we don't stop at a diner and interrupt another robbery." He slanted a glance her way.

She didn't acknowledge his weak and shitty attempt at humor. Right. His hands tightened on the wheel. Automatically, he glanced behind them. No sign of any tail. And he'd randomly picked the car from the rental agency lot. No way could there be a tag on it.

Cassidy sat next to him in the rental, but she seemed a thousand miles away. He knew she was trapped in the hell of her own thoughts, and he fought desperately to come up with a way to bring her back.

His hand reached out, and he turned down the radio.

Cassidy flinched but didn't look his way.

"You want me to apologize?" The words felt rusty. His apologies usually were rusty. But this needed to be said. Maybe it was part of the reason why she was shutting him out.

"For running into the fire without a second thought to your safety?" A seemingly casual reply from her. "Sure, you can do that. I would ask you to promise not to do it again, but something tells me it's not a promise you can keep."

She'd just given him several sentences. After two hours of silence from her, Titan considered that a win. "I wasn't talking about that."

"No?"

"No."

"Then what were you talking about?"

"I'm talking about nearly fucking you on the motel room bed."

"Oh."

That was all he got? An *oh?* "I was out of line."

"Is that what you were?"

He slanted a fast glance at her. Cassidy still stared out the window. "Yes. You were upset."

"Was I?"

Okay, was this what it was like when people normally talked to him? Like pulling freaking teeth to get a full answer? "You...you had a nightmare."

"I have those all the time." A pause. "I'm scared to nap in the car right now because I'm afraid I'll wake up screaming."

"Have you talked to anyone about your dreams?"

"Who would I talk to?"

Well... "You could talk to me."

Her head turned toward him. He *felt* her stare. And he held his breath as he waited for her reply.

Then she told him, "You don't need to apologize for something I wanted."

*She wanted me.* "You sure you weren't just...um, riding some adrenaline rush from the diner? Or maybe you were scared from the nightmare, and you wanted—"

Her soft laughter stopped him. Didn't quite feel like real laughter, but he figured he'd take what he could get.

"Titan." A sigh. "Titan, Titan, Titan...I *was* scared."

He'd thought as much. *And I took advantage because I wanted her so badly.* He was such a dick. "I'll keep my hands off you. It won't happen again."

Another sigh. "I was also riding adrenaline."

*And all I wanted was to fuck you.* Yeah, he was a super dick.

"But adrenaline and fear had nothing to do with me wanting to rip those sweats off your body and touch every inch of you."

The vehicle swerved a bit to the right. He jerked it back on track. "Pothole," he lied.

"Sure."

She didn't buy his lie.

And he could not stop hearing...*Adrenaline and fear had nothing to do with me wanting to rip those sweats off your body and touch every inch of you.* He swallowed the lump in his throat and shifted a bit in his seat. This was going to be a painful ride to Vegas. Maybe he should have kept his mouth shut. Normally, that was such an easy task. So why on earth was he... "You wanted to fuck me?" Dammit. Why could he not stop talking?

"I wanted you more than I wanted to breathe."

He would keep the car on the road. He would. They would not die in a fiery crash because he couldn't maintain his focus on the freaking road.

"I haven't been with anyone...since I left Blake."

*Sonofabitch.* He concentrated on breathing. And driving. And breathing some more.

"I always thought I was a pretty good judge of character. Then, you know, I picked the guy who had hobbies that included torture and burying bodies. Something like that tends to make a woman second guess herself." Soft. Sad. "Actually, it makes her second guess everyone that she meets. It makes her think she can't trust anyone. That she can't ever get close to anyone, and the best way to stay safe? It's to keep everyone far, far away."

He exhaled. "Doesn't sound like a way to live."

"No? To me, it seemed like the only way."

He didn't know how to respond to those words.

"Then I met you," Cassidy said. "And you were different."

"Uh, you *ran* when we first met. Twice, in fact."

"And you cuffed me, showing off that kinky side you like to keep hidden."

He could feel heat rising in his cheeks.

"Relax, marshal. I'm just teasing." Her fingers brushed over his arm. "The last time I fell fast for someone, it was the worst mistake of my life. I got burned. Badly. And I didn't think I'd ever lower my guard with anyone else. But here we are...what, a little over twenty-four hours into our acquaintance? Thirty-six? And I'm throwing myself at you. Literally."

Titan cleared his throat. "You didn't throw yourself so much as you fell onto me."

"Is that a joke? From you? Be careful, Titan, I'll think you're starting to relax around me," she chided. "Lowering *your* guard."

There was no part of him that was relaxed.

"I don't do that," she declared suddenly. "Throw myself at men I've just met. Even with Bl-Blake..." Cassidy stumbled over the name. "It was several months in before I..."

She stopped. He was glad. He did *not* want to ever think about that bastard having his hands on Cassidy.

"Sometimes I just want to shower and shower. I want to wipe everything away." If possible, her voice went softer. And became sadder.

He knew she was going to reach for the radio and crank up the music even before her hand extended.

So he caught her wrist. His fingers flew out and locked around hers before she could blast him out again. "You don't have anything to wipe away." Not a damn thing.

"I do. I feel like he marked me, and I can't get that mark off."

Screw this. He glanced in the rearview mirror again. No one for miles and miles. So Titan pulled them off the road.

"Titan?" Alarm flared. "What's wrong? Do we have a flat? What's happening?"

He shifted to park, unhooked his seat belt, and twisted to face her. "There is no mark on you."

Her eyes were so deep.

"He didn't change who you are. You're still *you*. And you don't belong to him. Not one single, tiny part of you belongs to him."

"He thinks I do. He thinks I'm his."

"Yeah, well, from where I stand, he's just some psychotic prick so what he thinks holds zero weight with me." Titan wanted to touch her. "He's a guy who will be in a cage soon, and then all he will be to you is a memory that fades more and more over time. You'll move on. You'll live your life, and he will be that occasional bad dream that you have. The bad dream that fades when you wake up."

Cassidy shook her head. Dark shadows lined her beautiful eyes. "I don't know if it will be that easy."

Probably not. But fuck it. "When you were coming for me, coming against *my* mouth, did you think about him?"

Her lips fell open. "What?"

"When you were coming for me, did you think about him?" A savage question.

"No, no, of course not!"

Damn straight. Because when he had his mouth on her, when he had his dick in her, there would be room for no one else. "Then you use me, got it?"

Once more, she shook her head. A bit more frantically this time. "I'm not following. And we should...probably drive..."

"You use me whenever you feel him getting too close in your head. When his memory is hurting you, you turn to me. I will fucking wipe him away. I will give you so much pleasure that the pain you knew will vanish." A vow he meant to carry to his grave. "He didn't mark you, but I will. I will mark you so deep that you will feel me inside and out. There will be no place for him. There fucking never was. You aren't his, and you never will be."

Her expression was stunned. Yeah, no big surprise. She probably thought he'd just lost his ever-loving mind. Maybe he had. He'd definitely lost his control. His mouth had started running and everything he felt had just come pouring out.

But wasn't it the truth? Hadn't he felt that consuming desire...that strange possessiveness for months now as he tracked her? He'd traced the picture of her, memorized the curve of her lips. And when he'd met her...

*She came back through the smoke and faced the fire to help me. She looks at me, and Cassidy doesn't care about any scars.*

He was out of control, hell, yes, and Titan didn't care.

The only thing that worried him was if...if he'd gone too far...if he'd scared her, if he'd...

She surged forward. Her hands flew behind his head as she yanked him toward her. Her mouth crashed onto his.

# CHAPTER ELEVEN

She shouldn't be kissing him.

But she couldn't remember wanting anyone more.

The need that had ripped through her in the motel room was back. It shouldn't be. This wasn't the right place. It was a *car*. She hadn't made out in a car since her high school days. But here she was. Here they were. Her hands were sinking into his incredibly thick, dark hair, and her mouth had opened wide for him, and if the annoying seat belt wasn't holding her back, she would have been on top of him. Definitely in his lap.

She moaned when his hands stroked over her. He kissed her even deeper. Even harder. So much passion. Her hands jerked away from him, but just long enough for her to grab the seat belt and unhook it and then she was nearly climbing over the console and her knee hit part of the radio and sent the music blasting again.

The blast of music jerked her back to reality.

Her eyes flew open. The gasp of her breathing seemed to fill the car.

Lust covered Titan's face and blazed in those incredible eyes of his. "Fuck me," he rumbled.

"Shouldn't have done that here." He lifted her. Put her back in her seat.

Kissed her once more. Fast, though. Not nearly long enough.

And he hooked her seat belt again. Then he put his own seat belt on. He turned down the radio's volume before his hands clamped around the wheel.

Her heart thudded so hard she thought it might jump out of her chest at any moment. This little pitstop had certainly been unexpected. "So you don't regret what happened between us at the motel?" In the harsh light of day, things could have been different. He could have regretted crossing any lines with her.

She'd dreaded his regret. The last thing she wanted to be was Titan's mistake.

"I regret that we didn't finish." Those blue eyes of his seemed to eat her alive. "We will. At the first available opportunity."

"Oh." She fanned herself a little. Jeez. Had they steamed up the windows? Or maybe she was just the one feeling hot.

"This is not that opportunity." He glanced in the rearview mirror. "Not fucking safe." And he shifted and pulled them back onto the road. "But when I get you alone...in a hotel room with a bed..." A muscle flexed along his jaw. "You will be mine."

*Drive faster.* She almost said those words. Almost.

"I'm a bastard," he growled.

No, she didn't think so—

"You need care and patience, and I'm supposed to be protecting you." Each word was bitten off. True Titan style. "You can tell me to back the fuck off."

She could? What was he doing? Helpfully laying out options for her? If so, he could stop. She'd already picked the option that worked best for her.

"And I will," he added, voice all grim and hard. "I will protect you no matter what."

Good to know. She believed him, one hundred percent.

"But I don't have to touch you. You say the word—"

"No."

A jerky nod. "I understand." His knuckles whitened. "I will keep my hands off you."

"I don't think you understand at all." She licked her lips and could still taste him. "I was telling you, 'No' as in, I won't be saying any magic word to stop you. I want you to touch me." For so many reasons.

*Because I don't want Blake to think he owns me.*

*Because if that bastard gets his hands on me, I want to know I had a good memory first. I want to have a moment to hold close even when the world falls apart.*

*Because I want something for me.*

And Titan was that something. A man she wanted so much that it maybe scared her a little bit. But, in a good way.

Unlike the dark, horrifying way that Blake terrified her.

She wanted Titan. She wanted to take control of her life. To stop running. To reach out and take the man she desired.

This wasn't some forever deal. She got that. It was lust in the middle of chaos. Probably a situation driven to some fever pitch by the circumstances around them. But she didn't really care about the reasons why. What she cared about...

*I feel safe with him. I feel good with him. I want him.*

Her hand reached out, and she turned the radio up a little more. She needed a distraction from the lust coursing through her veins. Lust was better than fear any day of the week. But she knew they weren't going to have a quickie in the car. The way Titan kept glancing in the rearview mirror, she suspected he feared a tail might be following them.

Automatically, she glanced back. No one was there.

She settled back against her seat. And Cassidy started to softly sing along to the lyrics.

From the corner of her eye, she saw Titan smile.

***

She'd never been to Sin City. Cassidy practically had her nose pressed to the car window as they drove down the strip. They'd been in the dark, on that stretching road for seemingly forever, and then...

Light.

So much light.

Everywhere. Flashing signs. Neon images. And a water fountain that danced and swirled in time with a whole insane light show. She smiled at the sights. "This is incredible. I mean, I worked at a casino in Biloxi, Mississippi, for a while, but that was nothing like this." So many people filled the streets. Energy seemed to buzz in the air. She could even make out a replica of the Eiffel Tower in the distance. Her head craned as Cassidy attempted to take in everything at once. Unbelievable. So. Much. Stuff.

While she was busy gawking, Titan drove easily, as if he'd been to the city dozens of times. Didn't even use any GPS from the car. Suspicious, Cassidy glanced over at him. "Just how many times have you been in Sin City?"

"Enough."

That wasn't a very good reply. No quantifiable number. It was, rather, back to basic Titan-talk. "Is that like, five times? Seven?"

"More than a dozen. I've tracked plenty of deadly fugitives here."

Oh, well, that certainly made things seem less bright and shiny, didn't it?

He slowed the car and she realized he was, in fact, pulling into the place with all the swirling fountains. "Aren't we supposed to meet your FBI buddy?" She knew Titan had called the special agent. He'd made the call while standing guard in front of the women's restroom in a random gas station. Titan had barely let her out of his sight at all during the last portion of their road trip.

Considering she was afraid Blake would jump out like a boogeyman from some scary movie, Cassidy hadn't exactly been fighting the overprotective routine. More like she'd been full-fledgedly supporting it.

"We are meeting him. Here." He eased the vehicle toward the valet section. "Oliver has a room waiting for us."

Feds normally met witnesses at super fancy hotels? Good to know.

"Place has great security." He parked the car and then took out the key. A fast movement of his fingers, and he had a tip ready to hand off with the key. "I'll carry our bags. Don't want my weapons out of my sight."

She did wonder about how many weapons he had in his bag.

"When we go to the front desk, we'll be registered as Mr. and Mrs. Robert Price." His lips twisted. "Oliver freaking loves horror movies. He's always pulling shit like this."

"I don't follow." The valet was coming.

Titan didn't answer her. He climbed from the car even as the valet moved toward Cassidy's side of the vehicle. The uniformed man smiled at her as he swung open the door. She stepped out, feeling way too travel-worn and bedraggled for this place with its amazing, dancing fountains. After all the madness at the motel, she hadn't exactly stopped to apply makeup. Her hair was in a ratty ponytail, and the jeans she wore were so old they were practically faded straight through.

*And Titan paused for a make-out session with me?* Jeez. She felt horrible and, meanwhile he sauntered around the vehicle looking all muscled and dangerous with a thin line of sexy stubble covering his jaw. That five o'clock shadow worked for him. Though, technically, it was more like nine o'clock. Or two days' worth of shadows...or, who cared?

He passed off the key and the tip to the valet but waved away the man's attempt to help with the bags. Titan just carried them easily and looked toward her with an expectant stare. "Ready, darling?"

Her stomach did a little flip. She didn't know if the flip was from the way his raspy voice had almost *purred* the endearment or because she was scared to meet the federal agent. Either way, she wasn't ready. Nope, not at all. But she was still doing this thing.

Cassidy nodded. After straightening her shoulders, she led the way into the hotel with as much grace as she could muster. *Mr. and Mrs. Robert Price.* Right. She could do this. Not like it was the first time she'd used a fake identity. She'd play it cool and stay in character. Except when she stepped inside...*Wow.* Her gaze flew up to the ceiling, and she knew her mouth had to have dropped open. So much beauty.

"Ah, I see you like our glass ceiling." A man stepped forward from the concierge desk. A shiny gold name tag on his lapel indicated his name was Kurt. "Quite a masterpiece, isn't it?"

She couldn't stop gaping.

"Want to guess how many hand-blown flowers are included up there?"

Cassidy's gaze slid over them. Titan had stopped behind her as she took in that fabulous ceiling. So many colors. The flowers seemed to stretch down toward her. She found herself actually starting to count them.

"Over two thousand," Titan said.

Oh. Well, that would have taken some time to count. Her gaze darted back to the concierge guy.

Kurt nodded, apparently pleased that Titan knew the answer. "And they weigh over forty thousand pounds. Quite stunning, isn't it?"

Yes.

"Are you joining us for business or pleasure?" Kurt asked.

"Both," Titan replied.

Cassidy caught Kurt's gaze darting over Titan's face. Kurt swallowed with a faint, nervous click.

She edged a bit in front of Titan.

But he just stepped to her side. "My wife and I have a suite reserved. Mr. and Mrs. Robert Price."

Kurt beamed. "Yes, yes, of course. Your assistant called just moments before to say you would be arriving soon."

Wait, his assistant?

"And you are, in fact, in the honeymoon suite." His smile stretched even more. "Congratulations to you both!"

She hid her left hand behind her back so he wouldn't notice that she wasn't wearing a ring. "The honeymoon suite?"

"Perfect," Titan said at the same time.

"Here, let me take your bags for you," Kurt offered. He reached for the bags Titan held.

Titan didn't let go. "I don't think so."

Sweat dotted Kurt's forehead. "Ah, of course." His stare jumped to Cassidy. "I have your keys." He took them off the concierge desk and offered them to her. "And there is champagne chilling for you. Along with chocolate-covered strawberries. It's our romance package, and I am sure you will find it to be just what you need for an..." His slightly worried stare darted back to Titan. "Unforgettable night?" The last came out as a question.

"I'm sure it will be quite unforgettable," Cassidy agreed. She flashed Kurt a sunny smile. "There a specific elevator we should take?"

Rattling off their room number, he pointed toward the bank of elevators on the left. "You have an amazing view of the fountains. Truly lovely at night."

"Let's go," Titan muttered.

Kurt's worried stare got worse. Probably because Titan wasn't acting like the besotted groom. She doubted he knew how to do besotted.

Luckily, she could help him out a bit. Cassidy patted Titan's chest. "He is in such a hurry to get me naked."

Kurt's mouth dropped open.

"You know how it is." She worked her dimples for all they were worth. "Newlyweds."

But Kurt's stare had dropped to her patting hand. Her left hand. The one without a wedding ring.

Crap. She leaned toward him conspiratorially. “If you want the truth, we’re not married.”

She felt Titan stiffen beneath her hand.

“But that’s why we’re in Vegas, am I right?” A soft laugh rolled from her. “We *will* be wed by tomorrow night.” She gave what she hoped looked like a delighted shiver. “I saw the cutest little chapel when we drove into town. And the sign said it’s open twenty-four hours.”

“I...yes,” Kurt rallied quickly. “There are several wonderful chapels in the area. I’m more than happy to recommend a few for you. I can even book the services, if you’d like.”

*Slow down there, Kurt.* “Recommendations would be great.” Time to get in that elevator. “Maybe you can get a list sent to our room first thing tomorrow? Right now, I’m dying to see that promised fountain view from our window.”

Helpful Kurt followed them to the bank of elevators. Cassidy had to use one of the key cards in order to access their floor, but, blessedly, those elevator doors soon closed on Kurt’s smiling face, and she was alone with Titan once more.

Her breath shuddered out. “You need to provide me with a bit more of an advanced cover story next time.” Soft music played from overhead, and the elevator smelled like flowers. Her nose twitched. Mirrors made up the walls of the elevator, so everywhere Cassidy looked, she just saw her bedraggled reflection staring back at her. She winced. The shadows under her eyes... “Super scary.”

"Never in a million years." Gruff. "You're always beautiful."

She sent him a real smile. "Titan, has anyone ever told you that you can say the nicest things?" And some of the dirtiest, but she didn't think now was the time to bring up that point. *When his memory is hurting you, you turn to me. I will fucking wipe him away. I will give you so much pleasure that the pain you knew will vanish...I will mark you so deep that you will feel me inside and out. There will be no place for him. There fucking never was. You aren't his, and you never will be.*

Promises, promises.

"No one has ever said that," Titan rasped.

"No? Well, you have clearly been hanging around the wrong people." She certainly had. But things were changing. She hoped.

*I'm not in this nightmare alone. I have Titan now.* And even though she'd only known him for such a brief time, Cassidy trusted him with her life. How could she not? In the short period that she'd known him, Titan kept proving himself to be a hero over and over again.

In her book, heroes were seriously hot.

Psychotic, serial killer exes? Not so much.

The elevator dinged. The doors opened. Titan stepped out first, and she noticed he looked both to the left and the right before inclining his head in a move that she took to mean everything was all clear.

Nibbling on her lower lip, she followed him down the hallway. The lush carpeting swallowed the sound of their footsteps. "So...are you going to be like...a bodyguard for me now?" It already felt like that was what he was, especially with the way he seemed to look for danger everywhere.

Titan grunted.

Behind his back, Cassidy grinned. "Is it one grunt for yes and two for no?"

He swung to look at her. And frowned.

After a brief hesitation, Cassidy confided, "I should probably tell you that I find your grunts and your growls and your whole intensely deep voice to be incredibly sexy."

He didn't smile at her. She'd hoped he would. Titan's smiles were entirely too rare.

If anything, though, his face became grimmer.

Automatically, Cassidy reached up and touched his arm. "What is it?" *I said something wrong*. She hadn't meant to. She'd been trying to compliment Titan because it had come to her attention that people gawked at him far too much and that he received far too few compliments. Her goal was to change that situation.

"My voice...it was always rough. Big body, growly voice. Made people steer clear of me." His chin lifted. "When I was...held by that prick, his goons decided to put a noose around my neck while he was slicing me open. They'd tighten it and squeeze as hard as they could. Kept doing it until they got tired of their game."

Ice seemed to cover her cheeks. Little pinpricks of ice that stretched slowly over her skin.

"When I woke up in the hospital, my voice was even worse than normal. It got a little better.

Not much. Docs explained what had been damaged and it just…" He turned away. "Hell, it is what it is."

Her breath shuddered in. Out. She had to blink away the tears that wanted to fill her eyes.

He stiffened. "Cassidy—"

A tear leaked out. "Don't you dare turn and look at me right now."

But, damn him, he did. He swung around and stared at her with horror growing in his eyes. "Why are you crying?"

*Because my heart breaks when I think about what those people did to you.* "Because I wish I could kill someone right now, but you already beat me to it."

He blinked.

Her palm slashed over her face as she shoved the tear away. "I like your voice. I like your face. I like your body. I just hate you went through so much pain. I really, really hate that for you." She was getting way too emotional. Too little sleep. Too much traveling. Too long having a killer on her trail.

*But I just casually told Titan I wanted to kill someone. Like it's just a normal thing.*

God, sometimes, she feared that Blake might have been right about her.

No. *No.* She shoved past Titan. "This our room?" Yep, it was. She checked the suite number, nodded, and didn't wait for him. She used her key to unlock the door. As soon as the little light flashed green over the keypad, she twisted the golden handle and shoved open the door. Cassidy practically stumbled inside the lush suite. Her steps staggered forward as she tried to put some much-needed distance between herself and Titan even as she swiped at her cheeks again.

And maybe her tear-filled vision was the reason why it took her a little too long to process the fact that a man was waiting inside the suite.

The tears made her eyes blurry. She blinked quickly. She didn't see him clearly at first, and when she did—

A terrified scream broke from Cassidy.

In the next instant, Titan shoved her behind him, yanked a gun from one of his bags, and he aimed it at the stranger. "Don't *move,*" Titan snarled. "I've got a gun pointed at your head, asshole."

The man stood in front of a massive floor-to-ceiling window. One that looked out at the dancing fountains. Cassidy hadn't turned on any lights in the room. She'd just walked into darkness. The man had been *standing* in the dark, like that didn't scream trouble. Standing there and what—watching the fountains?

He didn't move his body, but a long sigh slipped from him. His back was to her and Titan as he continued to watch the water dance.

"Titan, Titan, Titan..." Another sigh. "Is that any way to treat the man who got you this awesome suite?"

Titan swore. She inched a little closer to Titan as she tried to peer around him and get a better view of the man who'd been lying in wait for them.

But, hold up, if he'd gotten this suite for them...

The man turned. Very, very slowly.

Titan's hand flew out and hit the nearby light switch.

Illumination flooded the room. The man blinked. Squinted. He wore what looked like a super expensive, perfectly cut, gray suit. His brown hair shoved away from his forehead, and his narrowed eyes took in first the gun that was still pointed at him, and then the man holding said gun.

"You can lower that, you know," the guy told Titan.

"I know." Titan didn't. "*You* should know better than to break into someone's room. I could have shot first and asked questions later."

The man laughed. "If you'd done that, you would be a piss poor marshal." His stare slid to Cassidy. "Well, well, well...Cassidy Jacobs. In the flesh."

"You're the Fed." She would have pegged him as such based on just the fancy gray suit. But then, with the casual way he spoke to Titan—well, that familiarity had sealed the deal.

"I'm the Fed." He dipped his head forward. "How about you shut the door, lock it, and then we can get down to business? Provided, of course, that your scream doesn't get hotel security rushing in on us."

She shut the door. Locked it. And ignored the tremble of her fingers.

When she glanced at Titan, she saw that he'd lowered his gun. Her breath whispered out. Her whole body felt jittery, so she told the agent, "Thanks for scaring the hell out of me."

He rolled one shoulder. "It's a gift I have."

Some gift.

He sauntered toward her and extended his hand. "I'm Special Agent Oliver Foxx. That's with two *X*'s at the end."

She looked at his hand. Took it.

Oliver's hand tightened around her. "I'm Oliver, and you're Cassidy Jacobs, the serial killer's girlfriend."

# CHAPTER TWELVE

"There are two *X*'s at the end of Foxx," Titan announced as he strode a few feet to the right and dropped the bags onto the narrow couch. "Some say that's because he's an extra asshole."

Oliver's brows climbed. "I do not think that some—"

"Ex," Cassidy said, voice tight and grim. "I am Blake's *ex*-girlfriend. And you know it. I have been through an extremely exhausting twenty-four, forty-eight...*whatever* hours, so I am really not in the mood to deal with some *extra* asshole who is going to judge me. Trust me, I do enough judging without needing anyone else to pile on." Her nostrils flared as she yanked her hand away from Oliver's grip and fought the anger rising in her. "I was hoping you'd be more like Titan. I should have known not to put my expectations so high." Then she crossed to stand next to Titan as he lingered beside the couch.

Titan glared at Oliver. So did she. She'd truly reached her jerk quota for a lifetime.

"What?" Oliver blinked. "Why are you staring at me like that, Titan? She *was* his girlfriend. Jeez.

Sorry if my pointing out an actual fact has pissed you off. I won't say that shit again."

"Don't play your mind games with her," Titan snapped. He put his arm around her shoulders and hauled Cassidy close to his side. "Don't play them *ever,* understand?"

Oliver took in the way Titan had put his arm around Cassidy's shoulder. The way their bodies slid together, and his mouth dropped. Then snapped closed. "No."

"Yes," Titan corrected him grimly. "You're done, got me?"

"No, I mean..." Oliver drove his hand through his hair. "You two—is there something going on here?"

Sort of. Yes. One fabulous orgasm and the promise of more to come, only that "more" had been sidetracked because the Fed had been waiting in their suite. Then the jerk had started pushing her buttons.

But in the next beat, Oliver's expression completely changed. "Oh, I get it. I see what you're doing."

She didn't think that he did. The man was looking all approvingly at Titan now.

"That could work." A nod from Oliver. "Good plan. I like it. No, I *love* it." Another nod. Cunning lit his gaze. "Titan, it's brilliant. When you asked for the newlywed cover, I should have seen this coming. I just thought you'd taken inspiration from Smith since he used a honeymoon suite with Madelyn, and it had good security features. But I get the plan now, and absolutely, it's great. It will drive Blake Normandy crazy, and he will come out to attack." He began to pace. "But you can't stay holed up in here for it to work. You have to go out in the city. You have to be seen. If he followed you to the motel in Utah, then we can bet that he's going to show up in Vegas. It's just a matter of time. I'll get some Feds to blend in their plainclothes and keep eyes on you. We'll wait, we'll push him to the absolute edge, and then..." His hands slapped together as he stopped. "We close our trap."

Cassidy's head turned toward Titan. A sinking sensation filled her stomach. The feeling you got when a roller coaster raced down too far and too fast on a dangerous dip. "Do you know what he's talking about?" She didn't like roller coasters. Never had. They made her feel like she was seconds away from being ripped out of her seat.

"I—"

"Of course, he does. You do, too." Oliver sighed. "I'm obviously talking about you and Titan being lovers in order to draw out Blake."

Her head snapped back toward Oliver.

"Using the man's possessiveness and rage against him. Great idea. Though, it's not without risk." Once more, Oliver headed toward the window and peered at the dancing fountains. "It will put both of you in the crosshairs. I wish I could offer some grand insight on the perp to help you trap him, but I just...Honestly, I can't get a good handle on why Blake didn't kill you like he did the others. He certainly had the opportunity. He dated you for several months. His MO is usually that he kills a target within days of meeting her, but not you..." He turned back to face her as the water seemed to explode in a blast of motion behind him. "Not you."

Her heart pounded too fast. She slid from beneath Titan's arm. Put some distance between them. That distance made her feel chilled, so she wrapped her arms around her stomach. "Is that what you're doing?" Cassidy asked Titan because she needed to hear the words come straight from him. "Being my lover as a way to...to push Blake's buttons?"

"Oliver talks too fucking much."

That wasn't a denial. She backed up another step.

"I don't play games with killers." Grim. "That's more your style, Oliver." Titan sent a glare toward the Fed. "Didn't you learn from your last fucking mistake? Would have thought so."

Oliver's gaze cut to the floor.

Cassidy shook her head. There was a whole lot she wasn't following. Too many undercurrents in the suite between the two men. The one thing she was getting? That Titan wanted to sleep with her as some sort of strategy aimed at pulling Blake out of the shadows. She whirled away from Titan and found herself walking toward a small dining table.

The suite was quite huge. And the promised champagne was chilling on that table. The champagne nestled in an elaborate, silver bucket, with ice surrounding it. Chocolate-covered strawberries waited to the side.

Her hand grabbed for the champagne.

"I didn't make a mistake. I took a killer off the streets. The world is safer." Oliver's voice was measured as he responded to Titan. A little halting.

Cassidy popped the cork and sent it flying. Champagne bubbled from the bottle. She grabbed a glass—accidentally clinked it against the bottle, some bartender she was—before pouring herself a healthy portion.

"No regrets?" Titan asked behind her. The question seemed directed at Oliver.

She stared at the bubbles in her glass.

Oliver didn't respond. She took that to mean that the agent did have regrets. *Don't we all?* "Don't feel so bad," she told the Fed, not looking back. "Pretty sure regrets eat us all alive in the middle of the night." Her gaze fell on the manilla folder that rested near the strawberries. Cassidy brought the glass to her lips, took a sip of the champagne, and her left hand flipped open the folder.

Immediately, she spewed out the champagne.

"Christ, Oliver. What have you done now?" Titan was there at once. His arm brushed against her as he slammed the folder shut. "Cassidy."

She stared at the closed folder.

"Cassidy." His callused fingertips slid under her chin. "Look at me, sweetheart." Gently, he tilted her chin up.

Her chin rose, but her eyes remained on the folder. She put the champagne down. It was either put it down or spill it everywhere.

"That's his latest victim." The Fed had closed in with silent steps. His close voice had her jumping. "Judith Trace—Judy to her friends and what little family she had left—was found in the woods of South Carolina. She was discovered four months after you vanished from Florida. At first, when Dr. Rossi located the remains, I figured it *was* you."

Cassidy couldn't pry her gaze from the closed folder.

"Breathe," Titan urged her. "A slow, deep breath. It's not on you. Understand me? *Her death is not on you.*"

Her gaze jerked to him. The blue caught her. Held her.

"You seem to have gotten chatty, Titan," Oliver noted. "Something new?"

"Fuck off." His bright stare never left her. "Breathe. In and out. You're too pale. I'm worried you're going to pass out on me."

"Maybe she needs to eat." Oliver picked up a strawberry. "Want one?"

Her gaze flickered to him. The last thing she wanted was food. "I could have stopped him."

One of Oliver's eyebrows rose as he craned his head and studied her with renewed interest.

"I could have," Cassidy said again. "He killed her after I left. I..." Her eyes squeezed shut. "Titan, you told me a woman was found in South Carolina. I asked you if he'd killed again...you said yes...I *knew* all this. I knew it but—" But seeing those pictures made it real. Seeing those pictures made it all sickeningly real. "That poor woman. I should have stayed with him. She could still be alive."

"And you would be dead." He still cradled her chin between his thumb and forefinger. "You would be the one discovered in the woods. You had to run away. You had to protect yourself. Dammit, you did everything right! You went to the cops. You told them what happened—"

He was wrong. "I didn't do anything right. I didn't see what he was. And when I did, I *stood there.* I hid in the pantry, and I watched him as he...he cut her up."

"If you'd left that pantry," Oliver spoke with no emotion in his voice, "he probably would have cut you up, too."

She stepped back from Titan. "Blake wanted me to stay with him." The FBI agent didn't know all her secrets. "He said that he'd stop killing if I stayed."

Oliver pursed his lips. Nodded. "A control lie."

"Excuse me?" What was he talking about?

"Or maybe Blake actually thought what he was saying was true." Oliver's tone turned pensive. "Hard to know for sure without actually interviewing him, but I figure you have two options. Option one is that the man you knew as Blake Normandy told you that he'd stop as a way to control you. He wanted you to feel guilty enough that you were afraid to leave him. By saying that only you could stop him, he was exercising a truly skillful manipulation. If you left, you were the villain who didn't care about others. If you stayed, well, you would have to put up with every sadistic game he played, wouldn't you? Because there would be no choice. If you didn't dance to his tune, others would die."

Her stomach twisted. "I left. Someone died."

"Someone will keep dying until he's stopped." Oliver bit into a strawberry. Chewed a moment, then said, "Option two is that maybe he wanted the words to be true. Something is different about you. Has to be or else you would have been dead a few weeks after he met you."

She flinched.

Titan whirled to glare at Oliver. "Use some fucking tact, man!"

"Why?" Oliver appeared genuinely confused as he blinked at Titan. "You rarely use tact. And I'm just being honest. She knows this stuff. She must. Something had to be different or else she would not be standing here." He finished the strawberry and edged closer to her. "What was it? Did he tell you? Why did he think you were different? I suspect that is the key to figuring him out. You did something *right,* at least in his mind. Something the other women didn't do. They became victims. You became something entirely different."

She hated the way he watched her. Like she was some insect under a microscope.

"What was it?" Oliver pushed her. "Why are you the one left standing? Why weren't you a victim?"

*Like to like.*

She could not force those words out. Not right then. "I am really tired. We didn't sleep much last night. Not with the fire and me shooting at Blake."

"He thought you would go with him." Oliver nodded. "He created the fire as a distraction. He stood there, and he offered his hand to you."

Of course, Titan had told the Fed all about the events at the motel.

*Is Titan planning to sleep with me just to lure out Blake?* No, no, she wouldn't believe that. Things were different with her and Titan. The Fed was wrong.

"But you didn't take his hand. You shot at him instead." Oliver whistled. "Bet that scared the ever-loving-hell out of our perp. I suspect he's always been the predator, never the prey. Quite different when things are switched up on you." He rocked back on his heels. "Could be problematic for you. Instead of wanting you back, he may just want you dead now. Especially if you and Titan are keeping up some pretense of being lovers."

"No pretense," Titan snapped.

Oliver's eyes widened. "Are you serious right now? You *just* met her." He pointed at her. "You just met him!"

Cassidy rolled one shoulder. "What can I say? Guess it's like the song goes. I was holding out for a hero." She was about to crash in front of them. "I'm going to bed. Can we pick up our grand-plan scheming in the morning? When I'm not about to fall on my face?"

"Yes." Titan's instant reply. "Rest."

Cassidy nodded even as she turned away from them. Her gaze darted to the door on the right. "Guessing that's the bedroom?" She didn't wait for an answer. Cassidy put one foot in front of the other. Sort of the way she'd been surviving for the last year. *One foot in front of the other.* She made her way to the door and peered inside. Huh.

"Good news, Titan. That heart-shaped bed is definitely big enough for two."

Then she crossed the threshold. Shut the door behind her.

And Cassidy squeezed her eyes shut as the image of that poor dead woman flashed through her mind once more.

***

"Big enough for two?" Oliver cleared his throat. Twice. "This...I thought maybe you two were pretending to be involved."

"I don't do fake relationships." Had he just heard a muffled cry from the bedroom? Titan took a step toward the door.

Only to have Oliver move into his path. "You don't do relationships at all. In the time I've known you, you have never, ever been involved with anyone. Well, yeah, I know that you were with Tonya a million years ago."

It had not been a million years.

"But after that superficial witch cut out, you went all lone wolf on the world. You don't let anyone get close." He jerked his thumb over his shoulder. "But suddenly it's game on with her? *Her?* The serial killer's—"

"Ex."

"Uh, no, Blake Normandy is definitely not an ex-serial killer. He's continuing that twisted life choice of his. In my experience, killers like him rarely stop. They can't. It's a compulsion for them. They keep going until they *are* stopped."

Titan opened his mouth to reply but then he could have sworn he caught another muffled cry. Screw this. "Out of the way."

"But—"

He lurched around Oliver and made his way to the closed door. His hand lifted, and his knuckles rapped on the wood. "Cassidy."

"Fine!" A strangled cry. "Everything's fine in here..."

But he'd distinctly caught the sound of a sniffle. His eyes narrowed on the door.

"There's no danger," Oliver assured him. "I checked the suite thoroughly. There is no threat to her in that room."

"I'm coming in," Titan said flatly to Cassidy. "Step away from the door." Because he knew she was on the other side.

"Jeez. Not very heroic," Oliver muttered. "Give the woman some privacy. She was—"

The door cracked open.

He saw one beautiful eye staring at him.

"Cassidy."

It opened a few more inches. He hated the way tears swirled in her eyes, and he wished like hell that she had never seen the photo of Judith Trace.

"I was hiding," she whispered.

*No, sweetheart, you were crying.* And he couldn't have her huddled up and crying somewhere alone. Not on his watch.

"I do that," she confessed. "Hide. Run." Her shoulders squared as she released a shuddering breath. "But I'm trying to be better."

*You are perfect.* He wanted to haul her into his arms and never let go.

She slipped from the bedroom. "There really is a heart-shaped bed in there," she mumbled. "And lots of rose petals, too. I hate rose petals, so maybe we can get rid of them?"

He'd trash every single one.

"Used to love them. But the first day I met Blake, he was at the flower shop. He came out and bumped into me. He was carrying white roses. That's what I was there to buy, too. White roses. I always get them on the anniversary of my parents' death and take them to their grave. Or at least, that's what I used to do. I missed this year's anniversary."

"You *always* did that?" Oliver questioned.

There was something about the tone of his voice.

Titan slanted him a frown.

"Always. And that was when I met Blake. He told me that his parents had passed away, too. White flowers can mean peace. And I wanted my mom and dad to be at peace. Blake and I started talking and..." She shook her head. "Probably just another lie, wasn't it? A way to get close to me?"

Titan suspected it had been.

Her body brushed past Titan's as she headed back to the small dining area. "You have questions for me. I'll try to give you whatever answers I can. Me hiding and crying isn't going to help. The sooner you get answers, then the sooner you get a better profile of him, yes?"

Oliver watched her carefully. "That's the idea. But no profile is perfect."

She pulled out a chair at the table. "And no person is, either. Blake wanted me to believe he was perfect, but my instincts kept warning me away from him. I should have listened to those instincts."

Titan crossed to stand behind Cassidy. His hands slid down to curl over her shoulders.

The narrowing of Oliver's eyes said he caught the movement, but he didn't comment as he took a seat near Cassidy. Oliver pulled a laptop computer from the battered, leather messenger bag on the floor, booted it up, and then his gaze slowly swept over Cassidy. "The questions will be personal. Perhaps you'd like for Titan to wait in the other room?"

Screw that, he wasn't leaving.

Cassidy's right hand flew up and clamped around his wrist. "Titan stays."

Hell, yes.

Oliver nodded. "Then let's get started. Tell me about the first day you met the man you know as Blake Normandy."

"I just did." Her voice turned wooden. "I was going to Beach Flowers, the florist I use every year. He was coming out of their glass doors. Nearly ran right into me because he was looking down at the white roses in his hands."

"And you were there for roses, too?"

"Yes."

"Because it was the anniversary of your parents' death."

"Yes."

Oliver tapped quickly on his keyboard.

***

“He seemed to know what I wanted before I did. The first time we went out to dinner, we went to this Greek restaurant right on the beach.” There was still no emotion in Cassidy’s voice.

“By any chance…” Oliver stared at the screen of his computer. “Was that your favorite restaurant?”

“It was.” Faint surprise. “How did you know?”

Oliver’s gaze darted toward Titan. “A hunch.”

No, it damn well hadn’t been a hunch.

“What did you order?” Oliver asked her.

“Pastitsio. It’s, um, this Greek lasagna that I love. Blake loved it, too. Actually, I was surprised, because even before I put in my order, he told the waitress it was his favorite, too. At the time, I just thought it was something we had in common.”

A muscle jerked along Oliver’s jaw.

Titan knew that jerking muscle wasn’t a good sign.

***

“On our second date, he surprised me with tickets to see my favorite band.”

Titan didn’t think it was possible for Oliver’s jaw to clench more, but at those words from Cassidy, it did.

“The show had been sold out for months, so I kept asking him how he’d done it, but Blake just told me he had connections.”

“Sonofabitch,” Oliver muttered.

Beneath Titan's hands—because they still curled over her shoulders—Cassidy stiffened. "Is there a problem?"

"Lots of them." Oliver rubbed the nape of his neck. "Keep going..."

***

"My parents were killed in a robbery."

She'd been talking for over forty minutes straight. Titan could hear a faint strain in her voice. He'd moved to sit beside her, pulling a chair up close. He held one of her hands in his because it just felt right. Like she needed someone to hold her.

*Or maybe I just need to be touching her.*

"The man who killed them was never caught. I...I didn't deal with their death well. But I'm sure all of that is in your files. I got sent away for a time. There wasn't any other family to take me in, and I think it was easier for me to just vanish."

Oliver's fingers hovered over the keyboard. "Did you ever read the police reports on their attack?"

"I...no." A furrow appeared between her delicate brows.

Oliver cleared his throat. "Did you ever realize that you were suspected of possibly being involved in their murders?"

His question had shock rolling through Titan. *What. The. Actual. F—*

Cassidy jumped to her feet. "What?"

"I'll take that as a no." Oliver tapped on his keyboard.

"How could I be suspected? I would never—I could *never—*" Her wide, stunned eyes—so very dark—locked onto Titan. "I could never," she said again.

His fingers stroked along her inner wrist. "I know, baby."

He *felt* Oliver's stare on him. A disapproving stare. With his free hand, Titan casually flipped Oliver the bird.

Once more, Oliver cleared his throat. "Your parents were both shot at close range. You were standing with them, but the shooter never so much as touched you. It made the investigating officers suspicious. Suspicious enough that they arranged for you to be *held* in a facility because they were afraid that you might flee town with the shooter."

She yanked away from Titan. "That's absurd!"

Oliver nodded. "Yes, they eventually realized you weren't running. That you were just a grief-stricken girl who—"

"I didn't have a mark on me because my father stepped *in front of me.* In front of me and my mother. They shot him first. Then my mother. And when she fell, I did, too. I-I think they believed they'd shot me, too. I *told* the officers that—"

"The officers said you barely spoke at all when they arrived. That you just kept staring at the blood on the pavement."

She blinked quickly. Rubbed her temple. "I told the doctors. I know I told people. But it seemed like no one was listening."

He lowered the laptop lid. “Please let me be clear. I don’t think you had anything to with the murder of your parents.”

*Neither the hell do I.*

“But I believe that Blake suspected you did. More than that, I believe he thought you’d arranged it.”

She sucked in a breath. “Like to like.”

Oliver’s brows flew up.

“That’s what he told me. Why he was drawn to me.”

He pushed back the lid. Typed more. “Were you ever in danger when you were with him?”

A choked laugh escaped her as she slowly lowered back into her seat. And she reached for Titan’s hand.

Once again, he felt Oliver’s stare.

Titan scratched his cheek with his middle finger.

“Danger?” Cassidy repeated. “You mean *other* than when I found Blake in the kitchen with his victim? Or maybe when the cops wouldn’t believe me, and I got sent in for a psych hold—and Blake came in later that night while I was strapped down, and he pulled out a scalpel?”

Oliver’s lips pursed. “Tell me about that.”

She did.

***

Her shoulders slumped. Titan glanced at his watch. Nearly one a.m. “Enough,” he growled.

Oliver rolled his neck, popping it, and shut the laptop. "Yeah, yeah, that's enough for tonight. My vision is blurry."

Cassidy leaned forward. "Did I help any?"

Oliver's expression softened as he stared at her. "You helped plenty. Thank you, Ms. Jacobs."

"Cassidy."

"Thank you, Cassidy."

"I'm the one who should thank you. And Titan. You're helping me."

Titan wondered if she realized her words were slurring from tiredness.

She stood up, but then grabbed the table when her balance wobbled. "Sorry!" A weak smile. "I think my legs fell asleep." A big yawn slipped from her. "And maybe I'm about to, as well."

Titan rose and scooped her into his arms.

"Titan!" A sleepy grumble. "Totally unnecessary. I can walk." But she looped one arm over his neck and snuggled close. Her mouth fluttered near his skin. "God, how do you always smell so good? Your scent reminds me of the ocean. You make me remember running along the beach when I was a kid and everything was so much better."

He pulled her closer and carried her into the bedroom. He knew Oliver was watching them, but Titan didn't care.

He'd left her earlier while she talked with Oliver, but just long enough to ditch the damn rose petals in the bedroom. Then he'd gone back as she was recounting as much as she could remember about Blake and his habits. The things he liked. The things he didn't.

Titan had pulled the covers back and gotten the bed ready when he'd ditched those rose petals. So it was easy to slide her under the silk sheets and tuck her in. But his hand lingered on her cheek after he brushed back a lock of her hair.

Her eyes were already closing. "Probably gonna wake up screaming again," she mumbled.

"That's okay. I can handle some screams."

Her lips curved. "Course you can." She pulled the covers up to her cheek and turned toward him. "Bet you can handle anything, can't you?"

*No. I'm not sure that I can handle you.*

He eased away from her. Headed for the door.

"It's big enough for two."

Titan stilled.

"You don't need to sleep on the floor."

He hadn't planned to.

Titan turned off the lights and pulled the door shut behind him. He wasn't the least bit surprised to find Oliver waiting on him. Oliver had packed up the laptop, and he stood in front of the little table, with his arms crossed over his chest. His expression appeared unnaturally grim and, despite the work that he did, Oliver wasn't usually the grim type.

"May I offer you a word of advice?" Oliver asked pleasantly.

Titan grunted. "Is there any way I can stop you?"

"You're fucking up."

"Tell me how you really feel."

Oliver's hands dropped to his sides as he surged forward. "I want to catch this sonofabitch. Trust me, I do. I don't particularly like it when men chop up women and hide their remains in the woods."

*"Lower* your voice."

"Why? She knows what he did. She just *recounted* what he did—"

"I want you to lower it because she's either sleeping or about to sleep and I don't want her having more nightmares!"

Surprise flashed on Oliver's face. "You know about her nightmares?"

"I know pretty much everything about her. I made it a point to know. That's how I found her. Studied everything I could so that I could know what she'd do. Where she'd be most likely to work. How she'd travel and hide. I became pretty much her fucking *stalker...*"

"Just like him," Oliver finished.

Oh, hell, no. That was too damn much. Titan was too tired. The charge was too much. And he'd had enough. "I am *nothing* like him!" Titan lunged toward the man he'd thought was his friend.

# CHAPTER THIRTEEN

"No! I get it! You are not some sadistic prick who enjoys hurting women!" Oliver threw his hands up in surrender. "That's not what I'm saying. Take a breath, would you?"

He was more inclined to take a punch, and what the hell did that say about his control? Not a lot because there wasn't much freaking control left. Having to hear Cassidy's story. The pain and fear in her voice...

Rage had built and twisted within Titan.

*I will stop him. He will not hurt her.*

"What I was trying to explain," Oliver clarified quickly, "is that I believe our killer researched Cassidy quite extensively, the same way you did. The same way you do every single time that you go after your prey."

His shoulders rolled back. "Cassidy isn't prey."

"Not to you. She was—is—to him. Come on. There is no way he just coincidentally showed up at the flower shop when they first met. She was a target to him back then." He headed toward the small dining table. Oliver reached for the manila file. During Cassidy's recounting of events, the file had remained closed, but Oliver opened it now.

And he spread out the pictures of the women inside. Not the brutal photos that showed what the two vics had looked like *after* Dr. Rossi found them. But before—before the killer had ever entered their lives. Two smiling photos of the victims they'd recovered. And two smiling photos of the victims they suspected were still out there—the victims who'd matched the profiles Oliver had created.

"They all look too similar," Oliver noted. "Two of them even have dimples, just like Cassidy."

Not quite like hers. Her dimples were deeper. They flashed more.

"Same eyes."

Automatically, Titan shook his head. Yes, the eyes were dark, but Cassidy's were golden. Deep, deep gold.

"Same hair."

Cassidy's hair was thicker. It fell looser. She was—

"You're seeing her differently. I'm telling you...it's the same vic type. Same age, build, and same general appearance. Cassidy was meant to be a victim, too. I think that's why he waited on her at the flower shop. I suspect that was his MO. No way he just did that with Cassidy. He stalked her beforehand. Learned everything he could. Then when he was ready to close in, he did it in a non-threatening way."

"Shared grief," Titan said. *Sonofabitch.*

"He knew what flowers she bought—even though she bought them *only* once a year. That's concerning because it tells me he does a very, very deep dive on his prey."

"Stop calling her that."

Oliver waved toward the photos. "They were all prey to him. I'm betting he learned all of their favorite things, just like he did with Cassidy. Favorite food. Favorite band. He made himself seem perfect, and then...well, then he was a perfect nightmare."

Titan's stare swept over the women.

"Something changed with Cassidy," Oliver added. "He saw her less as prey and more as...a mate."

Titan's eyes flew to Oliver.

Oliver took a step back. "Don't shoot the messenger."

"She's not his fucking mate."

"Nope, one hundred percent, she is not. Not. But this guy isn't exactly what you'd call sane. You get that sane men don't cut beautiful women into pieces, right? He's not sane. He's seeing what he wants to see with Cassidy. In his eyes, she was different. Maybe he thought she was a killer, just like him, but..." Oliver's hands sawed over his jaw. "Something tells me it's more. Just can't put my finger on it. There is something else at play, and I need you to figure out what it is." His gaze turned considering as he studied Titan.

"What?"

Oliver's hand fell. "She trusts you. She will tell you more than she tells me."

"She just told you everything." What "more" did Oliver possibly want?

"We're missing a piece of the puzzle."

Talk about vague. And annoying. "So you want me to abuse her trust, you want me to use her the way you used—"

*"Do not say it."* Suddenly, Oliver's face had gone hard and cold. "I didn't use her."

*Her.* Titan knew exactly who the her in question was.

"I got close to her, yes, that was necessary, but I..." Oliver inhaled. "It's fucking late. We'll pick this up tomorrow." He shoved the pictures back into the file. "I'm trying to help, dammit. Sometimes, my methods might not be what you like, but I'm trying to get killers off the street." The file disappeared into his messenger bag. "I want your Cassidy protected. The way to do that? Get Blake Normandy—or whatever the hell his real name is—into a cage. Because he's not going to be all lovey and enamored with her any longer. You realize that, don't you?" He gripped the messenger bag and took a step toward Titan. "She *shot* at him. He probably watched her at that motel. He saw her run to help you, and then when he tried to get her attention, she fired at him. In his mind, that will mean she is choosing you over him. There is no world in which that guy will take rejection well."

Tension slithered down Titan's spine. "You think he will come to kill her."

An immediate nod. "There is no doubt in my mind that he will come to eliminate her. First, she ran from him in Florida. Hid. Then when he finally got close to her again, she chose another man. Cassidy is no longer his perfect mate."

Titan bristled. "Stop saying that. She's not his. Never was."

"If she's not a mate..."

Titan's hands fisted.

"Then she's just prey. We both know what he does to prey."

*Not on my watch.* "He will not hurt her." And just so they were completely clear..."There is no world in which I would allow that bastard to put his hands on her again."

Oliver's stare flickered toward the closed bedroom door, then back to Titan. "I was afraid it was like that." Soft. A little sad. "You get...you get that you can walk away now?"

Titan's brows lowered.

"You've been working this case on your own time. I know that. Taking vacation hours. Most folks go to the beach on vacation, but you—you hunted down a missing witness."

"I don't like getting sand in my ass." No, he didn't like all the stares at his scars. When you were at the beach, you were just in swim trunks. He didn't need his scars blazing in the sun.

"You tracked her on weekends. On holidays. You devoted every spare moment you had to Cassidy." He pulled the thick strap of his messenger bag over his shoulder and eyed Titan. "I know what it's like to get in too deep. You hunt for so long that maybe the obsession becomes real. It becomes personal. And that's dangerous."

"I am not dangerous to Cassidy." Never in a million years would he be.

"Yeah. I didn't mean her." A twisted smile curved his lips even as shadows came and went in

Oliver's eyes. "I meant it could be dangerous to you. You're tangled up in her. When the case ends—it will end, they always do—there isn't going to be a happy ending waiting. Take that from someone who knows."

Titan forced his hands to unclench. "Our situations are different."

"Oh?"

"Cassidy isn't Lark."

Oliver took a step back.

Yeah, he'd known saying the other woman's name would get a reaction. But Titan wasn't done. "And I'm not lying to Cassidy. She knows exactly who I am. She knows about my past." He waited a beat. "I'm also not trying to use her in order to take her brother down for murder, so...there's that."

A muscle flexed along Oliver's jaw. "Low blow."

He could go lower. But he'd caught the flash of pain in Oliver's eyes. Titan was one of the few people who knew exactly what had gone down between Oliver and Lark, and it had not been pretty. In fact, things had gone from great to absolutely brutal.

"You aren't going to walk away from her?" Oliver asked as the faint lines around his mouth tightened.

They needed to be crystal clear on this. "I promised Cassidy that I wasn't just going to dump her with you in Vegas. You were right when you said she trusts me, and I'm not going to abuse that trust. If he's looking to hurt her, he'll have to go through me."

Titan waited for an argument.

But Oliver gave a nod. "Then I'll talk to your boss. See if we can't get some task force situation going so you can come on officially. We're going to need more manpower on this one. It will get worse before it gets better." He headed for the door. "I'm in the room right next door. Wanted to be close. If you need me, I'll be here in moments."

"Why do you think he won't just run away?" The question was pulled from him. "Blake saw that Cassidy was willing to shoot him. Why won't the bastard just give up on her?" *And leave her the hell alone?*

With his hand extending toward the door handle, Oliver paused. Then he looked back. "He can't," he said simply. "The same compulsion that drove him to track her for months won't let him give up. He'll feel betrayed now. He'll have to punish her." His expression hardened. "It won't be pretty."

What part of the prick's crimes had ever been pretty?

"If he ever gets his hands on Cassidy again... if he manages to separate her from us...he will make her beg for death."

"That's not going to happen," Titan vowed.

"I just..." Oliver's nostrils flared. "I need you to understand what could happen on this one. I don't think our perp cares who he has to eliminate in order to get Cassidy. The attack at the motel proved that. If you're in his way, he will hurt you."

"Been hurt before."

"I know." Again. Softer. Sadder. "And I don't want to see it happen again. You went through that hell once, when you weren't emotionally involved—"

"It was my job. I was protecting a witness—" He broke off because the rest of Oliver's words had just registered. "Emotionally involved? Are you fucking serious right now?"

Oliver's grim expression said he was. "I swear, man, you've gotten downright chatty. That was the first sign. The second was the way you look at her. You can barely take your eyes off her. The third? It was the way you like to keep touching her."

"I was *comforting* her."

"You carried her to bed. Was that comforting her, too? Because when you lifted her into your arms, my jaw nearly hit the floor."

"Fuck off." A growl. "She was tired."

"Ah, now there is the Titan I know and love. All growly and fierce. Watch yourself, my friend. From someone who got burned, *watch yourself.*" He hauled open the door and stepped into the hallway.

Titan stalked toward the door. Made sure to secure the extra locks. This place was far, far removed from the lax security of the motel in Utah, but he still wasn't taking any chances.

*Emotionally involved.* Titan turned out the lights and pulled the heavy curtains to block out the lighted fountains. Taking his time, he headed toward the bedroom. He cracked open the door. Oliver was good at profiling people, but in this instance...

Titan kicked off his shoes. Ditched his socks. Tossed away his shirt.

And made his way toward the bed.

His eyes adjusted to the darkness. He could make out Cassidy's form as she turned on one side. She'd drawn her legs up close, curling in on herself. As if she was still afraid, even in sleep. The woman hadn't even taken the time to remove her tennis shoes.

He did it for her. Quickly, carefully. Just so she'd be more comfortable.

Cassidy had been right. The bed was definitely big enough for two. But if he crawled in that bed with her...

*Emotionally involved.*

It was annoying when Oliver was right.

Titan reached over her. Grabbed a pillow from the other side, and he knew that he was going to be bunking on the floor again. Was just safer that way.

For her.

For him.

His control was too weak where Cassidy was concerned. She thought he was a hero. Cute. She didn't get that when it came to her...

*I am obsessed.* And obsession could be a dangerous thing.

Better to stay away. To not get too close...

Even if close was the only place he wanted to be with her.

***

She woke with her throat parched and a scream on her lips. Cassidy surged up in bed, her hand rising to cover her own mouth in a jerky, automatic reflex.

The nightmare vanished.

Same old terror. Only this time, there had been a new highlight.

*Titan had been dead on the floor of my psych ward.*

Titan.

Her head whipped to the side. He wasn't in bed with her. Why not? What time was it? Where was he? The man needed sleep. Not like he was superhuman.

Cassidy shoved the covers out of her way and swung her legs to the side of the bed. She could use some water. And she could use some Titan.

It was so damn dark in that room.

She jumped from the bed.

And promptly rammed her foot into *him*.

"Ooof!"

That *ooof* had better be coming from Titan. Her hand flew out and slammed into the bedside lamp. After a bit of fumbling—why was it so hard to figure out how to turn on lamps in hotel rooms?—she had a flood of illumination spilling onto the bed. And down onto Titan.

He blinked up at her. She was sort of straddling him. Standing up, but with one of her legs across his body so that her foot touched down near his right hip. Her other foot pressed to the carpet near the bed, just beside his left hip.

"You aren't supposed to be down there," she chided him. "You have got to get over this weird habit of sleeping on the floor. No way can that be good for your back."

He stared up at her. "Bad dream?"

"The worst. You were in it." She hopped over him. Hopped. Swung her leg so she wasn't straddling him. Whatever. "I was...uh, going to get some water."

Titan sat up. No shirt. Just muscles. All those abs.

Cassidy turned away from him. She had a hard time looking at him, and not just because of his abs. Because he'd listened to every word she'd said to Oliver Foxx. And Cassidy was afraid Titan didn't want her any longer.

*The man is on the floor. I think that says what he wants.* It certainly wasn't to share a bed with her. And she wasn't going to beg Titan.

He'd heard all about how she'd foolishly fallen for Blake. How she'd believed his lies.

How she'd stood there, hiding in the pantry the day her world turned into hell.

"Your nightmares are worse because of me?"

His deep, dark voice sent a shiver chasing over her body. "The nightmare was worse because you were hurt in it. He came after you because of me." She was almost at the door. "You were bleeding on the floor, and I think you were dead, and I was trying to scream for you." A shuddering breath. "Lots worse than my usual highlight reel." She knew why, too. Because her new fear was that Titan would put himself in jeopardy for her.

And wasn't that what she'd asked him to do? When they'd struck their deal, hadn't she wanted his protection? But not at the price of something happening to him.

The covers rustled behind her. She didn't look back. She did hurry through the doorway and head to the little kitchenette area. Her hand pressed against the switch for the lights. Earlier, she'd noticed the mini-fridge. That sweet baby hummed softly as Cassidy opened the door and grabbed a bottle of water. She guzzled it quickly and became aware that Titan had followed her.

And was silently watching her.

Cassidy lowered the water bottle. Put it on the counter. "There's plenty in here, if you want a drink."

"Don't need a drink."

Her fingers curled around the edge of the counter. The curtains had been closed to block the fountain area. When had Titan done that? When had he even come to bed? Or, uh, to the floor? "Guess I should get back to sleep." Definitely felt like the middle of the night. But she doubted sleep would come immediately. No, she'd probably be staring at the ceiling and remembering what it was like to see Titan as he bled out. *A nightmare I won't forget anytime soon.*

Her stare flew to him.

He stood close, shoulders braced against the wall, with his powerful arms crossed over his chest. Jeans clung to his hips, dipping down low. No shoes. No shirt. Just those jeans. So freaking sexy.

As she started to edge around him, he took a step to the right. That step brought him right into her path.

Cassidy stilled.

"Do you ever have good dreams?" he asked.

*I wish.* "If I do, I don't remember them." She counted herself lucky if she didn't wake up covered in sweat. Even dreams that started well tended to end with fear. "What about you?"

"Not usually."

"Guess that's something we have in common." She was entirely too aware of him. At least she still wore regular clothes, that was a good thing. Jeans and a T-shirt. Bra and panties. Her tennis shoes were gone. Had Titan removed them? If so, when?

She remembered him carrying her to the bedroom. Remembered—embarrassingly—her saying he should get in bed with her.

But he hadn't.

*Because he heard too much. Because he knows my last lover was a psychotic killer. What does that say about me?*

She stepped to the side.

He was so big that he still blocked her path.

Cassidy started to take another side step.

"When I do get lucky and have good dreams, you're in them."

She froze in the middle of her step. "Say that again?"

"I dreamed about you before I met you. Oliver thinks I'm obsessed. That should probably be one big red flag for you. The man knows his obsessions."

Cassidy shook her head. "Maybe I'm just sleep confused, but it sounded like you said that I was in your good dreams."

"Yes."

She waited for more elaboration. But, this was Titan. There was no more elaboration. "What are we doing in your dreams?"

"Cassidy..." He lifted his hand and trailed his fingers down her arm.

Another shiver slid over her. It wasn't cold in the honeymoon suite. Not cold at all.

"Sweetheart, you missed the part about my obsession."

"I didn't miss it."

"Then why aren't you running to the bedroom? Shutting the door? And telling me to stay away?"

"Because I don't want you away from me. You're the one who keeps bunking on the floor. I want you with me. I thought—I thought you didn't want *me* anymore."

"I'll want you until I die."

The horrible image from her nightmare flashed through Cassidy's mind. "No. No dying. That's a deal breaker. Got it?"

"And why the fuck would I not want you?"

"Because...of him." Because she'd been with Blake, because she'd fallen—

"He's never touching you again. He doesn't get any part of you." Now both of his hands were on her. They curled around her waist as he tugged her closer. "Tell me to stop."

He couldn't be serious. "Not going to happen."

"Tell me to get my hands off you."

Why in the world would she do that? "I like them on me." She put her hands on him. Curled them around his shoulders. "And I like having my hands on you."

"Cassidy..."

"You think I'm going to be scared because you want me? Because you dreamed about me?" *Good dreams.* Oh, she would love a good dream.

"I dreamed about you before I even met you."

"You're not one of the bad guys, Titan. I'm not scared of you. I won't be." Enough of this. "Kiss me."

"I'll want every part of you."

"Do I get every part of you in return?"

"You get anything you want from me."

Seemed like a fair exchange to her. "Deal."

"Cassidy..." She could see a struggle in the depths of his bright blue eyes. And then... "*Fuck it.*" He kissed her.

# CHAPTER FOURTEEN

Mistake. Mistake. Mistake. He should be tucking her back into bed. Getting his ass on the floor. Not kissing her like he was desperate and needed her to keep living.

But, screw it.

She'd pressed her body tightly to his. Risen up onto her tiptoes, and she was kissing him back with wild abandon. He'd warned her. Told her he wasn't the man she needed.

But she still seemed to want him, and he had never, ever wanted anyone more.

Using his grip on her waist, he lifted her up. Immediately, her legs locked around his hips, and her core pushed hard against his eager cock.

*Not going to last long. Want in her. Need in her.*

But he had to make this good for her. Cassidy deserved pleasure. He wanted to give her so much pleasure that there wasn't room for anything or anyone else in her mind.

*Only me.*

Because he could think of no one but her.

He turned with her and caged her between the wall and his body. He kept kissing her. Hungrily.

Desperately. Possessively. A little moan rose in her throat and that was the sexiest sound he'd ever heard.

But too many clothes were between them. Far too many. He wanted her naked.

And he wanted her crying out his name as she came.

His mouth tore from hers, but only so he could kiss a fiery trail down her neck. He felt her pulse racing beneath his lips.

Her legs tightened around him. "Titan. We need a bed. *Now.*" Her nails bit into his shoulders. "Lucky for you, I know where a giant, heart-shaped one happens to be."

He was beyond speech. In a normal conversation, he struggled. But now, this moment, with need blasting past every remnant of sanity, there would be no more speech.

Just need.

Keeping his grip on her hips, he stepped away from the wall. He carried her back to the bedroom.

"God, your strength is so sexy." Her hips rocked against his dick. His cock was thick and eager for her. "Actually," Cassidy told him, "pretty much everything is sexy about you."

He felt that way about her. Her smile. Her dimples. Her perfect breasts. Her flared hips. Her sweet, sweet pus—

"But I love your eyes the most," she breathed. Her hips rocked against his dick again.

They were in the bedroom. He lowered her onto the bed and started to reach for the light.

Cassidy caught his hand. "I want to be able to see you."

He shook his head. No, she didn't. She was already seeing too much.

"I do." Definite. "Lie down." She scrambled to her knees on the mattress.

Titan's eyes narrowed. The light needed to go. The last thing he wanted was for Cassidy to freak out over the mass of scars on his body.

"Please?" Cassidy asked him.

Dammit. Well, she'd already seen most of them, anyway. And if she decided this was too much, he'd man the hell up and get out. Or, get back on the floor. Because he needed to stay close to her. When it came to her safety, he would do whatever was necessary. *Even stay in hell—or on the floor—while she is so very close to me.*

But he wasn't in hell. Not yet. He was close to heaven. And she wanted him in the light. *Such a bad plan.*

Yet Titan lowered onto the bed.

"We both have on entirely too many clothes for this to work." Cassidy grabbed the hem of her shirt and yanked it up. Then she was tossing the shirt over the side of the bed. She did a quick, twisting shimmy, and her jeans were off, too. "Better."

He could not agree more. But she still had on her panties and bra so...

Cassidy climbed on top of him.

Titan blinked.

She smiled tremulously at him. "Hi."

He stared back at her.

"So, I haven't been with anyone in a while. Not since I left Florida. And before that, it wasn't as if I had a ton of partners." She had straddled him. Her knees hit the mattress on either side of his body, and her hands pressed to his chest. "You probably have a whole lot more experience than I do. If I…if there is something you don't like, stop me. Tell me. I want to make you feel good."

Was she serious? He peered into her eyes. Fuck. She was. He unclenched his jaw. "Everything about you…feels good."

Her smile stretched. The dimples he loved came out to wink at him. "That's how I feel about you, too." Her fingers stroked over his chest.

Did she know that she was touching his scars? She must. She had to feel the ridges beneath her fingers. And she—

Cassidy's head lowered. Her silken hair trailed over his skin, and she kissed one of his scars.

His hands grabbed her hips. "Cassidy…"

She kissed another scar. Her lips fluttered over him. So careful, as if she feared hurting him. But she couldn't hurt him. He didn't think Cassidy could *ever* hurt him. She was kissing what another woman had hated. Tenderly stroking what others thought made him into a monster. Taking away the rage and hurt and putting something else in its place. Something he couldn't even name.

Down, down she went. Her hands slid toward the snap of his jeans.

His muscles strained with the effort to hold back. He wanted to grab her, roll her beneath him, rip her panties away, and plunge deep into her.

She pulled down his zipper.

No underwear for him. He'd been in a hurry when they changed at the rundown motel. He'd showered away the soot and ash. Cleaned the new scratches on his arms. Yanked on fresh jeans and a shirt and she was...*Fuck me.*

Her fingers closed around his eager dick.

A long, thin line went right over his left hip and dipped toward his cock. The sonofabitch had threatened to cut his dick off at one point during the torture session. He'd thought that threat would make Titan break.

*Instead, I put a damn knife through your throat.*

Because Titan didn't ever show fear. And he got his vengeance.

Cassidy kissed that thin line. She followed it toward his cock and then she was taking the tip of his cock into her mouth. Opening her lips wider. Licking the straining head. Tasting him.

His teeth ground together.

She took more of him into her mouth. Licked. Sucked him. Her head bobbed toward him, and because she'd insisted that the lights stay on, he could watch her.

He was so freaking glad those lights were on. He loved to watch her. The sight of Cassidy taking his dick into her mouth. Past those plump, gorgeous lips...

Her hair fell over his thigh. His hips arched toward her.

She took more of him. Her mouth slid along his length.

*Cassidy!*

He couldn't hold on. Too much. Too good.

He caught her shoulders and gently pushed her back.

"Was that...did I do it wrong?"

Wrong? Not in a million years had that been wrong, but no way could Titan manage speech. He rolled her beneath him.

*Panties and bra have to go.*

He yanked down the bra straps. Her tight nipples thrust toward him. Titan took one into his mouth even as his other hand yanked her panties out of the way. The sound of cotton tearing seemed extra loud.

"You keep doing that." Her husky, breathy voice. "I'll run out of panties at this rate."

Perfect. She could stop wearing them. Faster access.

Speaking of access...his fingers slid between her legs. Yes, *yes*, she was wet. Wet and hot.

"Tasting you...turned me on," Cassidy admitted, voice soft.

His head lifted.

Her breath caught at whatever she saw on his face. "Titan?"

"Tell me..." He forced those words out. "If I hurt you." He still wore his jeans. Mostly, anyway. Titan left her long enough to kick out of them, then he remembered the condoms in his bag. He spun away from her and marched for the bag. In seconds, he had a foil packet in his hand.

"It's good that you're prepared." She ditched her bra and levered up onto her elbows. "Back in the day, you were a Boy Scout, weren't you?"

He tore open the condom. Rolled it on as she watched.

"This is gonna be a tight fit," she whispered.

What he was fucking counting on. But there was a difference between tight and pain for her. Titan wanted no pain. So, he'd better make sure she was extra ready.

He caught her legs.

"Titan?

He pulled her to the edge of the bed. Then he spread her legs wide and put his mouth on her.

*"Titan!"*

He stopped her when she nearly flew off the mattress. His tongue swiped over. Licked her clit. Again and again.

"OhmyGod."

Then he drove into her with his tongue. Her taste made him wild.

"You. In me," Cassidy gasped. "Now. Now, now, now, now..."

He licked her again. Then once more.

"*Titan*!"

She started to tremble and quake, and he knew her orgasm was coming. Perfect. No pain. Only pleasure. He lifted his head. Put his dick at the entrance to her body, and he thrust deep.

Just as she started coming.

Her sex squeezed him in quick ripples of contractions. Her eyes snapped shut as she arched up against him.

He withdrew, only to sink into her again.

"Yes! Yes! Keep doing that!"

Oh, he intended to. His thrusts were drawing out her orgasm, and the feel of her core squeezing around him had Titan going out of his mind. Over and over, he slammed into her. Her hands grabbed for his arms even as her legs wrapped around his hips once more.

He put a hand on the mattress to brace himself, but his other hand slid under her hips so that he could lift her up. Ah, yes. That angle let him go in even deeper.

She screamed his name. Then bit him on the shoulder.

Titan pounded into her, and his release poured from him. The pleasure churned through every cell in his body. It consumed him. Raged from the inside, out, and when it was over...fuck, when it was over...

His head lifted. He stared down at her.

The gold burned in her stare.

When it was over, he just wanted her again.

Titan slowly withdrew from her.

She winced. "Titan?"

He stalked to the bathroom. Ditched the condom. Went back to her because he needed more. Deliberately, he went to his bag and took out another foil packet. That was the whole supply. He would need more, STAT.

"Titan?" Cassidy called his name again.

Her legs still sprawled over the edge of the bed. She was completely open to him. The sexiest thing he'd seen in his life.

She blushed and hurriedly snapped her legs closed. "You, ah...you have another condom?"

In his hand, yes. “Did I hurt you?”

Her head moved in a slow, negative shake.

“Can you take me again?”

A nod. A teasing smile. “Can you take me?”

Abso-fucking-lutely, he could.

He rolled on the condom. Pulled her hips to the edge of the mattress. Her legs wrapped around him. Her heels pushed into his ass even as her upper body remained on the bed.

He sank into her. If possible, she was even tighter, even wetter now. *Slick and swollen from her orgasm.* This time, Titan went slowly. Inch by inch. Her head tipped back. Her breath shuddered out.

“Titan...*all* of you.”

Oh, she’d get everything he had to give.

But he kept going slowly. He was savoring this. When you’d been in hell as long as he had, you knew the value of heaven. You wanted to stay in paradise for as long as you could.

His gaze didn’t leave her face as he filled her completely. She was so gorgeous to him.

Absolute perfection.

And the way she felt around his dick...

He sank fully in her. Didn’t move. Just lodged inside.

“You’re driving me crazy!” Cassidy’s cry as she tightened her inner muscles around him.

*Fucking perfect.* His hands slammed down on the bed. He knotted the sheets in his fists.

She kept squeezing him with her inner muscles. So incredibly good. Nothing in his life had ever felt like she did.

“Titan! Stop playing with me!”

He wasn't, but that sounded like a fabulous idea to him. His left hand flew away from the sheets and pushed between their bodies. He went straight to her clit, and, oh, yes, he started to play.

Her mouth dropped open in a startled *O*. Her eyes widened. And then she was shoving her hips up against his hand feverishly. She kept squeezing him with her inner muscles. So wet and hot and *tight*. And he knew he was going to have to thrust. Withdraw and thrust. Because he could not hold on, but he sure wanted her to come for him once more before he—

She broke. He saw the pleasure crash over her face as she ground her sex against him. She trembled and moaned and he was done. Titan heaved out of her, then plunged back. Out. Back. Hard enough to have the bed shuddering. Hard enough to lift her hips from the bed.

Her head thrashed on the mattress. "Too good, too—"

No such thing.

He rammed into her. Again and again. The ripples from her climax spurred him on. She was still coming. And he was close. So close. But he hated for it to end and—

*It won't end. I won't let her go.*

He erupted into her.

***

"Told you the bed was big enough for two." A yawn punctuated Cassidy's sleepy words. "Do not even think about bunking on the floor again."

He wouldn't dream of it. Not when he was *holding* a dream. Cassidy had snuggled against him. Her body was soft and warm, and she had one arm casually draped over his stomach like being cuddled with him in bed was the most natural thing in the world for her.

He hadn't shared a bed with a woman in...shit, too long. He'd fucked, yes. Not like he'd been a saint. But he hadn't stayed with anyone. Not like he'd wanted anyone to wake in the light of dawn and get a good look at him.

Yet with Cassidy, he didn't care. They'd only just turned out the light.

One of his arms was around her. She felt right. Natural. She felt like someone he could get addicted to wanting. He knew that was a mistake. Major red flag.

In that moment, Titan just didn't give a fuck.

"Thank you," Cassidy whispered. But her words were slurred.

His head turned on the pillow.

"For moving the rose petals. Sweet..."

He smiled at her. Not like moving the rose petals had been any kind of major deal.

"If I...wake up screaming...sorry..."

"Don't worry about it," he murmured back. "I can handle it."

Her breathing evened out. She fell asleep in his arms.

His lips brushed over her forehead. He didn't think she'd have bad dreams. Not that night. And if she did...

*I'll be right here.*

***

"No! No! *Titan, stop!"* Her terror-filled scream woke Titan right before Cassidy's fist came flying toward his jaw.

He managed to catch her hand, to hold her gently, even as his heart raced. *So much for no bad dreams.* And what was happening? Was he scaring Cassidy in her sleep? Had he become a nightmare? "Baby..." The endearment kept slipping out with her. He cleared his throat. "Cassidy. Wake up."

Her eyes flew open. Her breath rushed out with a whoosh. She blinked quickly, and he knew that she was trying to adjust to the darkness. Her body stiffened, and she tried to yank her hand away from his.

*Christ. She may not even realize it's me.* "Titan," he said quickly. "You're with me. And you're safe. You know I'll keep you safe."

Her breath came harder. Choppier.

He wasn't calming her down. He'd never particularly been the calming type. "I...think I gave you a nightmare." He let her hand go.

But that hand of hers flew back. This time, it went to his chest. Pressed over his heart.

"You're alive," Cassidy rasped.

Well, yes, he was.

"You'd better stay that way," she ordered him.

"I have zero plans to die."

"Good. That's good." She pressed her body close beside him. "I'm sorry." Softer. "Did I scream?"

"Only a little." *You were dreaming about me being hurt?*

"Did I...do anything else?"

"Just tried to nail me with a punch to the jaw. No worries. You missed."

"Sorry." Her body had gone stiff. "I can sleep on the couch. Or I can be the one on the floor. Or I can—"

"Stay right where you are? Yeah, excellent idea." He faked a yawn. "Night, Cassidy."

She remained tense. "Did I say anything?"

Now he hesitated. "You want to tell me about the dream?"

"No. I want to forget."

Fair enough.

He tried to transition his breathing into an easy, deep rhythm so she'd think that he'd gone to sleep. Titan didn't want Cassidy worrying that he might grill her. He had put his arm back around her, and she was curled against his side. He liked her pressed against him that way.

The tension slowly faded from her body as she softened against him. He thought she might be asleep, so he started to relax, too, and—

"Please don't die." A soft whisper from her, barely more than a breath. "I just don't want you to die."

# CHAPTER FIFTEEN

"Something is different." Oliver peered at Cassidy, then sent his frown to Titan. "What the hell is different? I only left you two for about seven hours."

What was different? Only that they'd had sex. And Cassidy was feeling super awkward because she wasn't exactly sure how to handle Titan in the bright light of day. Especially after he'd given her three—maybe four orgasms? The pleasure had all blended together and she couldn't even be sure how many times she'd come during the hours of darkness.

And the fact that the sex had been far and away the best of her life? That Titan had just set all of her future sexual expectations way, way too high? Another problem.

"Nothing is different." Titan's rumble. "You're just being your usual weird-ass self."

Boom. That was the other thing. Titan almost seemed extra grumpy. Sure, Titan on a good day was solemn and a little grim, but something else was going on. Cassidy was terribly, terribly afraid that he regretted what had happened between them.

Meanwhile, it had been the best night of her life. Well, not the part where she'd had to put her soul bare for Oliver as she answered question after question for him. The part after, with Titan. *That* had been the best ever.

Oliver was still studying her far too intently. So Cassidy flashed her widest smile at him. "What could possibly be wrong? You brought bagels. The day is a win." She'd even managed to choke down the whole bagel. That was a definite win. "I'm assuming you have a game plan for us?" Because the sooner they got down to business, maybe the weight in her stomach would ease.

"A win, huh? Right. Well, I do have a game plan. Though I suspect Titan already knows what it is." Oliver rubbed his jaw. "Don't worry, though. You'll have plenty of backup. Called Memphis last night after I left you—"

"You called Memphis?" Cassidy cut in because she was lost. "As in, Tennessee?"

"No, as in Memphis Camden. A person, not a place." It was Titan who explained, "He's a lead Ice Breaker."

She waited for more. There, of course, wasn't. Sighing, she waved her hand toward Titan. *More, please.*

A furrow appeared between his brows, but he added, "Former bounty hunter. Really good tracker."

"*Almost* as good as Titan," Oliver chimed in to say.

"In his dreams," Titan returned.

She pinched the bridge of her nose. "You called in this former bounty hunter to help us?"

"Him and Smith Sanders," Oliver said.

"Hell." Titan shook his head.

"What?" Oliver frowned. "Your old friend is good, and you know it. You guys and your special ops routine always get shit done."

So...Smith Sanders was special ops. Just like Titan? She wanted to ask so many more questions.

But Oliver announced, "And I've got two FBI agents who will be helping us, too. Special Agent Jon Kimura will be running point with me. He's already down in the lobby, trying to blend, and we'll have Special Agent Mae Silva joining us soon. Most of the team will remain on the periphery. Not like we want to scare off our target." His gaze seemed to become extra intense as he told Cassidy, "We want Blake Normandy to believe that the only person between him and you is—"

"Me," Titan cut in.

"Exactly." Oliver nodded. "So we're set."

"Uh, no," she disagreed. "We aren't. You just rattled off names that mean nothing to me. I'm sure those people are great FBI agents, but I know zero about them. And I know next to nothing about this Smith person or Memphis—"

Oliver's brow furrowed. "Told you, he's a former bounty hunter—"

"I trust Titan." Trust him so much that she'd had sex with him. Twice. She felt heat rise in her cheeks. "And, Oliver, I trust you because Titan does. But as for these others..."

"You can count on Memphis," Titan assured her. "And Smith. Smith covered my back more times than I can count."

Okay, now *that* was the kind of reassurance she needed.

"I worked with Jon before. Good man. But I don't know a damn thing about Mae Silva." Titan shrugged.

"Thanks for that, buddy." A grumble from Oliver. "Way to reassure the witness. Couldn't you have just said Mae was good to go, too?"

Titan simply gave another shrug. "I won't lie to Cassidy. Don't expect me to."

That was why she trusted him. "What's the plan? You're getting this mini-army into position, but what's the agenda? We don't know that Blake followed me to Vegas. Titan switched cars, he made sure there was no tracker on the new vehicle, and after I shot at Blake in Utah, he might have decided to just get far away from me." Did she sound too hopeful? Maybe.

Oliver shook his head.

Her heart seemed to wither as hope fell. "He's...not getting far away from me?"

"Maverick is awake," Oliver said. "Your deputy friend from Nowhere? He's gonna be okay."

The news startled her. It was great to know. Wonderful, in fact, but kind of left field to just announce when they'd been talking about—

"I spoke with his sheriff before I came to see you and Titan this morning," Oliver added by way of explanation. "Maverick is conscious and talking, and he remembers what happened before the tornado came barreling at him." The faint lines near his mouth deepened. "See, the tornado wasn't what hurt him. It saved him. According to Maverick, he spotted what he thought was a disabled vehicle on the side of the road. A truck. He stopped to help and met a man wearing glasses and a ball cap."

Glasses and a ball cap? *Disguise.*

"Maverick tried to help him, and in return for that act of kindness, the man stabbed him."

She took a half step back.

"The guy wanted to know where you were, and it seems he did not like hearing you were safe with your boyfriend."

Helplessly, her gaze slid to Titan.

She found him watching her. For a moment, his stare blazed with emotion and—

Shut down. Whatever that blazing emotion had been, it was gone in a flash. She forced her focus back to Oliver.

"I traced the rental truck that was left in Nowhere. Of course, it was rented under a bogus ID, with a stolen credit card. And the man who rented it avoided all security cameras. But I think we can confidently assume it was your ex." Oliver's gaze flickered to Titan. "Also talked to the family you saved in Utah. Neither the mom nor the dad saw who set the fire or nailed the window shut."

"It was Blake," Cassidy said, voice shaking. *It's always him.*

Oliver nodded. "I agree. Blake Normandy has been tracking you for a very long time." Oliver's voice was certain. "He's not going to walk away.

He will keep hunting. We're just going to make the hunt a little easier for him."

"I'm sorry." Her wide smile came again, but it felt shaky because she felt shaky. "Did you say you were going to make it *easier* for him?"

Oliver nodded once more. "Exactly."

He seemed to like that word.

"He knows you're traveling with Titan." He pointed to a silent Titan. "What Blake probably didn't realize—until you rushed back toward a fire and then shot at your ex instead of eagerly taking his hand—well, what he didn't realize is that you've fallen in love with your marshal."

This time, she took two full steps back. "I—"

"You haven't," Titan said flatly. "That's just what we want Blake to believe."

*You haven't.* She pulled in a breath and hoped that she had schooled her features. Unlike Titan, she wasn't so good at controlling her emotions.

Oliver gave Titan a long look, then slowly glanced over at Cassidy. "What we want him to believe." A shrug. "Whatever. The point is that Blake will assume you are still with Titan. Titan will be the one he tracks. He doesn't need a GPS on the car to figure out that Titan is in Vegas. He can track Titan's credit card usage or his phone."

"But that's illegal!"

Oliver's brows climbed. "So is being a serial killer."

Seriously? Her eyes narrowed on him. Was he mocking her?

A sigh escaped Oliver. "Come on. You must have thought Blake could track your credit cards. You didn't use them any when you were on the run." Oliver shoved his hands into the pockets of his suit coat. A dark blue suit today. "I suspect that he had access to your credit cards long before he even met you. You can learn a whole lot about a person when you check their purchases. You can learn when they buy flowers. Their favorite restaurants. Favorite bands...You can learn so much that you don't seem like a stranger the first time you meet someone. You seem perfect."

Titan rolled back his broad shoulders. "The guy is tech savvy. That's what Oliver is saying. Another piece of his profile."

*He's saying that Blake had already ripped into my life long before we first met.* She sucked in a breath as she absorbed that info and tried to follow along. Licking her lips, she asked Oliver, "And you're thinking he will hack Titan's accounts now?"

"Yes, and that's why the hotel suite might be under a fake name, but the account will tie back to Titan's credit card statement. I took care of that issue for us last night before I went to bed."

Hold up. Her heart lurched. "You've already started setting the trap? You could have warned me first!"

"I'm warning you now."

She glared. "You don't warn someone after the fact. You do it before. That's how this works. It's *polite.*"

He waved that away. "You and Titan will go out and about today. I want you to do everything that you would normally do, you know, if you were in Vegas for fun and not because you are fleeing a psychotic ex."

Her temples throbbed. Unable to stop herself, Cassidy walked toward Titan. His head turned as he looked down at her. The force of his electric blue eyes seemed to steal her breath. "Is he...is he serious?" she asked Titan.

"As a heart attack," Oliver cheerfully assured her, answering before Titan could.

She didn't look at him. Her focus remained on Titan. There were lots of problems with this plan. "Blake isn't going to buy that I'm just *tra-la-la-ing* my way around town. I've been hiding for months. He'll suspect something if I suddenly do a one-eighty on him." Oliver's plan was crap. She'd expected more from the Fed.

"You didn't have Titan before," Oliver reminded her. "You do now. You're a woman in love."

She could feel the blush rising in her cheeks. "Stop saying that."

Titan's eyes narrowed on her.

"A woman in love doesn't hide," Oliver said. "She lives her life."

*Not if she's trying to keep her lover from dying*. Because the memory of her last brutal nightmare? Too bold and in horrible living color as it spun through Cassidy's mind.

"I'm not asking you to wave a big, red flag." Oliver gave what sounded like a forced chuckle. "That would be too obvious. Go out to eat. Play some slots. Maybe put in a booking at a wedding chapel."

Her head whipped toward him. Like that *wasn't* waving a big, red flag? She was pretty sure the wedding chapel was the definition of big, red flag.

"What?" Oliver blinked. Twice. "That was your genius idea last night. When I went down to fix the credit card info, I ran into Kurt. Remember him? Friendly, concierge guy. Kurt said he was gonna send some pamphlets on chapels to you this morning."

That bit to Kurt about getting chapel info had just been a quick cover, not real at all—

"If you pick a chapel and you make a booking with Titan's credit card info, then that's another breadcrumb that will get our killer coming in. He'll want to stop your wedding, I am absolutely certain of that fact."

Great. So now she had a fake wedding where she *might* get killed on her agenda?

"It's more than you bargained for." Titan's words had her attention flying back to him—only to find his intent gaze on her. "When you agreed to help me, you never counted on all of this."

No, he had it wrong. "You never counted on it. I hardly doubt a marriage to me is high on your to-do list."

His jaw tightened.

"Might be surprised by that," Oliver muttered.

Titan sent him a glare that should have left scorch marks.

"Even *if,*" Cassidy clarified, "it is a fake marriage, you can't be excited about this plan." *Who is?* But when it came to Titan... "You strike me as pretty-low key. I doubt you want to be wandering Sin City, gambling, and strolling into wedding chapels." Cassidy paused a moment. "But you're not complaining." She was the one fighting the agenda. "And, honestly, you're the one helping *me*. So I don't see where I can really say anything negative about the plan at all." Did she love it? Hell, no. Was she going to do it? Hell, yes. "You're helping me," Cassidy told Titan again as she reached out and curled her fingers around his. "You're taking a whole lot of risks. You could have walked away. Left me with him." Her stare drifted to Oliver.

"What's wrong with me?" Oliver wanted to know.

*You aren't Titan.* She squeezed Titan's fingers and looked into his eyes once more. Would she ever get used to that powerful blue? Probably not. "I'm just a job. One that, apparently, you did freelance." The words she spoke felt hollow. "You've already gone above and beyond the call of duty. And..." *Say it.* "I shouldn't have made you promise that you wouldn't just drop me off with the Feds and leave. I pushed for that promise because I was scared, but it wasn't fair to you." She let him go. Stepped back.

Titan just watched her.

*Finish this.* "You can leave. You don't have to do more for me. Oliver and I can find some other flag to wave. Sooner or later, Blake will find me. At least now, thanks to you getting me to the Feds, I won't be on my own." And... "Someone finally believes me."

"Lots of someones," Oliver assured her.

Titan's brows pulled down low as he studied her.

She waited for him to say something. Or to walk away. She figured he'd have to do one of those options.

He didn't. The blue of his stare seemed to heat more.

Her arms wrapped around her stomach.

"You...want me to leave?" The halting question from Titan almost had her jumping.

"No," Cassidy responded immediately. Why couldn't he try that? Instead of leaving a person in suspense, why not just say things in a fast and straightforward way? "No, but I don't want you staying because I made you give a promise that you don't want to keep."

"Oh, that's cute." A laugh broke from Oliver. This laugh sounded way more real than his previous chuckle. "You think Titan does things that he doesn't want to do? Have you met him? Seriously?"

"Oliver talks a lot," Titan told her.

She leaned toward him. "So do I."

"Yeah, but I like it when you talk."

Oh, that was sweet. Her lips started to curl.

"I always intended to stay with you until we had Blake Normandy in custody. I'm not going to let you be hunted any longer."

So he wasn't leaving her. He wanted to stay. He wanted to help. He wanted—

"The job isn't over."

Her chest felt like a balloon was deflating inside of it. Titan wanted to finish the job he'd started. Because that was who he was. Not like he was personally involved or emotionally invested in her—uh, in the case. The man had endured torture to protect another witness. Staying with her now—this was who he was. He stuck his neck out for other people. Went the extra mile. Did the hero bit.

Just because he'd given her the most amazing orgasms of her life, it didn't mean anything was personal between them. "No, not over." Why did those words come out sounding sad?

"Excellent." Oliver clapped his hands together. "Enough chatting. Time to get down to business. Let's go draw out a serial killer. Favorite part of my job."

***

The bedroom door shut quietly behind Cassidy, and Oliver instantly lost his bright and positive expression. He stormed toward Titan. "What. The. Hell?"

Titan frowned at him. "Where's the problem? I'm going along with your dumbass idea." Gambling? Booking a wedding chapel? *Hello, bullshit plan.*

"Uh, first, not my dumbass idea." He jerked his thumb over his shoulder. "Your girlfriend was the one to tell the concierge that you needed a wedding chapel."

She had. But... "Because you booked us as man and wife. And using the name of Robert Price, really? You still locked onto your horror movie addiction?"

"First, Robert England was terrifying in his role as Freddy Kreuger. He scared the shit out of me back in the day. And Vincent Price? The man was a genius. And, second, it's not some addiction. You know I like horror movies because I need to see monsters that are even worse than the bastards I hunt every single day. I *need* something else." His cheeks puffed out as he exhaled. Oliver seemed to settle down a bit before he muttered, "You didn't correct me."

Titan's gaze had strayed to the closed door. Cassidy had just asked for a moment to freshen up. She'd looked plenty fresh to him, so he didn't know what was up with her sudden rush from the room.

"Uh, Titan? Big T? You didn't correct me when I called her your girlfriend."

"She's...not."

"Uh, huh. Why don't you try saying it like you mean it?"

Why would he do that? His stare cut to Oliver. "I thought the plan was for us to pretend to be getting married."

Oliver looked toward the ceiling as his eyes rolled. "You like jerking me around. I know you do. Stop it." His stare snapped to Titan. "You're sleeping with her."

"Don't see where that is your business."

"Shit. Sonofabitch. *Shit.*" Low. "You didn't deny it. You were supposed to deny it. Why, why are you sleeping with our witness?"

A simple reason. "Because I want her."

Oliver's mouth dropped open. And then hung open.

Titan waited for the other man to collect himself.

"You...she...I mean, I get it. I do. She's attractive."

Gorgeous.

"And she's been through hell, but she's still going strong. She evaded a killer for thirteen months. I could see where the fighter aspect of her character would appeal to you."

"She pulled a gun on me when we first met." Titan smiled at the memory. "Then she ran from me. And kicked me in the dick."

Oliver choked. "Yeah, total love at first sight. I get that now."

"I had to cuff her. I—" He stopped. "You keep mentioning love. Stop. It's not. It's just..." His words trailed away.

"Just what? Sex? Sex with a witness? Just you crossing lines and not caring and not learning from my epically bad mistakes?"

It wasn't just sex. Sex didn't leave you feeling hollowed out and completely lost in someone. Or at least, sex in the past hadn't been that way for him. And just saying...sex, just calling it *sex*—that made it seem like he didn't care. He did. He would walk through fire to protect Cassidy.

*I did that for strangers at the motel. Hell, yes, I'd do it for her. In an instant.*

But...no, the reason he wanted Oliver to stop talking about love... "Cassidy doesn't love me."

"No, she doesn't. She's just got one major case of hero worship. Her feelings are all over the place, and you need to watch it."

Titan stiffened. "She doesn't have hero worship."

Oliver's mouth dropped. After a moment, he sputtered, "Yes, yes, she does. I have eyes! I can see how she watches you. The woman looks at you like you're hanging the stars or some shit. She is getting emotionally involved. You're not. When the case is over, and you leave her, what then? You think that just because she's safe, it will be okay if her heart is broken? Screw that shit. I'm telling you, I have been where you are going...*you will regret this.*"

He hadn't been anywhere near where Titan had been or where he would go. "You lied to Lark."

"Oh, dammit! There you go, saying her name. Don't do that. You say her name, and you summon her. Don't you know how this works?"

Titan could only shake his head. "For a man of science, you can say the craziest shit."

Oliver straightened his shoulders. "I didn't lie to Lark. It wasn't my fault the way things ended."

Bullshit. "You misled her." A big difference between him and Oliver. "I've been honest with Cassidy from the beginning."

Oliver surged closer to him. "You think I don't see how *you* look at her? Man, be careful." Pain roughened his voice. "You don't want this to blow up on you. Listen to me, I am trying to help you."

The bedroom door opened. Cassidy had pulled back her hair. Twisted it in some loose knot that made her neck look enticing and extra feminine, and faint tendrils of hair had already escaped to tease the edges of her face.

She was beautiful, and he just wanted to rush to her and pull her into his arms.

Instead, his hands clenched into fists.

“That way.” A disgruntled whisper from Oliver. “That’s the look I’m talking about. The way you are staring at her right now. It’s the look that says...*I’m fucked.*”

# CHAPTER SIXTEEN

"Seven, seven, seven," Cassidy chanted as she held tightly to the handle of the slot machine. The machine kept spinning, over and over, and then she saw...

Seven.

Seven...

She bounced. Waited...

*Seven.*

"Ohmygosh!" The lights started flashing and a lovely dinging filled the air. Cassidy finally let go of the handle and grabbed for Titan. She hugged him as fiercely as she could. "We won! We *won!*" She might have been bouncing up and down. After a crazy, too-tense and stressful start of her day, this turn of luck was exactly what she'd needed.

"Uh, Cassidy." Titan's hands settled around her waist. "You're playing nickel slots. You didn't exactly strike it rich."

She whirled back to her machine and did some quick calculations. "Forty dollars. To me, that's a big win." Cassidy hummed with excitement. "While working in Biloxi, I saw plenty of people lose, so getting a win...let's just say I'll take it and be happy."

He trailed her as she cashed out her prize, and then they were strolling toward the front of the casino, passing the blackjack and poker tables.

He slowed. "Want to play?"

"Oh, no, I'm terrible."

"You were a dealer."

"Yes, but I'm a terrible bluffer." She looped her arm with his. "That's why I'm so scared that I am going to screw up this whole thing." Were Feds watching them? Cassidy was sure they were, only she hadn't spotted their tails yet. Maybe Titan had.

"You think you're gonna screw up." A hesitation. "Because you don't think you can fake being involved with me?"

"I don't have to fake it. We are involved." But she bit her lip. Because they had very much not talked about what had happened last night. "Unless, I mean...was it just a one-night thing?" She turned toward him. Keeping her voice low, Cassidy said, "If it was, just say so. I'd really like some clarification on what we are."

Yep, she'd just spit that out. Maybe it was the high of winning forty dollars. Who knew? But she just—

"I don't know what we are."

Right. Sure. *Put on a brave face. Smile.* "Then that makes two of us." She threaded her fingers with his. They'd been putting on the show for most of the day. Or trying to. They'd gone out for breakfast. Correction, a decadent brunch. He'd paid with his card. The brunch had included a big, unlimited mimosas extravaganza on the restaurant roof of a nearby hotel.

She'd barely touched her one drink. Cassidy had been far too nervous.

Now they'd just been big—fine, *semi*-big—winners, and she knew the next step was...

*The chapel.*

They were supposed to start scoping out chapels. Maybe she should have enjoyed a little more of her mimosa. Might have made this next step easier.

Titan led the way outside. The streets were already packed. So many people filled the city. It was pretty overwhelming. Titan pulled on a pair of sunglasses and slapped a ball cap over his head.

She figured she should pull out some sunglasses, too. He'd bought her a pair in the hotel lobby. She plopped them on, then just glanced at him from the corner of her eye. Titan walked with total confidence, as if he knew exactly where he was heading. Probably did. Everyone tended to get out of his way, fast, and she wondered if it was because of his size or the whole I-don't-take-shit vibe that drifted so effortlessly from him.

He wouldn't know that she'd completely eavesdropped on his conversation with Oliver back at the hotel. He wouldn't know that her chest had ached when he told Oliver that whatever they had going on...it wasn't love.

But it also wasn't freaking hero worship, either. The Fed was so wrong on that score.

They stopped at the corner. She glanced toward the crosswalk sign. A crowd gathered behind them, and someone bumped into her. Cassidy staggered a little under that bump.

Immediately, Titan yanked her closer against him even while he turned on the person who had—

A woman exclaimed, "Sorry! Lost my footing."

Cassidy glanced back at her.

The woman sent her a sunny smile. Her dark hair was pulled back into a ponytail, and, like Cassidy, she wore sunglasses. "Oh, look," the woman added, voice brightening, "the light's changed. Let's go."

Cassidy peered toward the light. Sure enough. The sign had changed and was now counting down, showing there were fifteen seconds for everyone to get across the road.

Titan and Cassidy started walking together. He kept his arm around her shoulder.

Two teen boys zipped past them.

A guy on a skateboard slid in and out of the pedestrian group, before rushing across the road.

Down to ten seconds.

Why was she so nervous? Why were Cassidy's feet suddenly rushing as if she expected an attack? The cars were all waiting. She'd looked at the drivers. There had been no sign of Blake.

This was silly.

She stepped onto the curb. Titan was right beside her. The woman who'd bumped her rushed away. Cassidy stared after her, aware that something just felt off.

"Cassidy?"

The crowd swallowed the other woman.

She turned back to Titan.

"What's wrong?" Titan wanted to know.

It was silly, really, but... "Did you think she kinda looked like me?" *Stop thinking that every woman with brown hair looks like you or is a potential target. Stop it.* Goosebumps rose onto her arms. Before Titan could reply, she hurriedly told him, "Let's get to the first chapel."

***

Trinity Rae lifted the wallet. "Don't know why you wanted me to target her specifically." She sent a smile to the man who'd been waiting for her. "But that was crazy easy." She and the hot guy had met last night when the strip had been bursting at the seams. At first, she'd thought he was a cop. He'd caught her right after she'd lifted some drunk asshole's wallet.

Trinity had been sure she'd be spending the rest of the night in a jail cell.

That hadn't been the case. Instead, she'd made a new friend. One who had sprung for them to get a super nice hotel room. They'd waltzed inside the fancy lobby and acted like a couple as he ordered the room. He'd even gotten her an amazing breakfast. She would have gladly fucked him the night before because the guy was truly extra hot, but her "gentleman" friend hadn't touched her.

But he had asked her to lift a wallet for him.

He took the wallet and flipped it open. She thought for sure he'd go for the credit cards, but...

He took out a room key. "Perfect."

She was so lost. "You know her or something?" He must because she'd been a very specific target.

"I don't know her at all. Sometimes you think you do...but it's just a mistake." What could have been sadness came and went in his voice. "She has to learn. I warned her what would happen."

Trinity was completely confused. Did he know the woman or not?

He tucked the hotel keycard into his pocket. Tossed the wallet.

"No!" She grabbed for it. "There is cash in here!" Cash but...as she flipped through the wallet, Trinity realized there were no credit cards. Just an ID. "*Cassidy Jacobs.*" She laughed. "Kinda looks like me." She'd had the thought when the woman turned toward her after the little *bump* Trinity had given her. She always did the bump as a distraction technique.

But that big bruiser next to her mark...

*He sure scared the crap out of me.*

Not like her handsome new friend. Her handsome friend wasn't scary at all. He seemed more like a dream. *A guy like this can take me places.*

"You keep the cash," he told her.

She'd planned to.

After tucking the cash into her back pocket, she looked up and found him smiling at her. "Want to have some fun?" he asked.

"Always." That was what she lived for. The nine-to-five-job routine wasn't for her. She loved to party, loved to spend other people's money, and her motto was that each day was an adventure waiting to happen.

"Then come with me."

She laughed. "We're breaking into her hotel room, aren't we? That's why you wanted the key. Are we gonna trash the place?"

"We're going to leave my friend a surprise that she will never forget."

Trinity had a quick worry. "The room number isn't on her card." The name of the hotel, yeah, one she definitely recognized, but no numbers. Numbers were never on the cards. "How are you gonna find—"

"I know what room she's in."

"How do you know that?"

"I have my ways."

That was all mysterious. A little scary. But a little scary could be hot.

"But we have to be careful," he said. "I don't want to be seen slipping inside."

"Oh, I can handle this." He'd come to the right woman. "Sneaking into a hotel is one of my specialties."

He smiled at her. "I knew you were just the woman I needed from the instant I saw you."

She preened beneath his smile.

"You are perfect," he told her. "Definitely my lucky night when I found you."

No one had ever called her perfect before. Her mother had called her a fucking waste of time. Her father had never even been in her life. Her shoulders straightened. "I think my luck has changed, too."

He offered his hand to her.

She was going to get him in and out of any hotel in the city. She'd show him just how valuable she was.

***

"This is one of our most popular venues." The man in the white suit lifted his hands and did a slow turn. "All the beauty of an outdoor wedding, but—"

"But it's inside," Titan finished gruffly.

The man's slow-turn stilled. "Yes, but it *looks* as if it is outside. We have trees..." He gestured to the left. To the right. The twisting trees stretched toward the glass ceiling. "And at night, all you will see are the projection of stars above you. So picturesque. So perfect. Exactly the setting you need..." Now he dropped his hands and crossed to stand right in front of Cassidy and Titan. "For your happily ever after."

Cassidy had to admit, the chapel was quite stunning. And if she was truly getting married, she might go for it.

"What else do you have?" Titan asked.

Their host blinked. "You...you don't like our little slice of heaven?"

Titan shrugged. "Can we see something else?"

This was their fourth stop.

"Of course, of course. Ah...we have a chapel in the Victorian style just down the hallway. Beautiful, elegant, lots of white curtains for purity and promise and—"

Cassidy winced. "I'm not feeling Victorian fun right now." She turned to Titan. "But I do like this chapel." They were supposed to book something, weren't they? Set their trap? And not just spin their wheels all day? "Let's get this."

A muscle flexed along Titan's jaw.

"Come on, honey." She squeezed his hand. "It's why we're in Vegas." *To catch a killer.*

He nodded. His head turned back toward their host. "Do you have anything available for booking in two days' time? Say around nine p.m.?"

"Oh, well, we do tend to book in advance since we are such a popular venue, but...let me see what we might have available. I can make no promises." He bustled away.

Cassidy's head cocked as she watched him retreat into a small office. "I thought people came to Vegas for spur-of-the-moment weddings."

"Not at my venue!" The man had obviously overheard her. "I can book up to six months in advance."

Great.

"But you're in luck! We had a cancellation." He hurried back toward them, beaming. "That poor couple's misfortune can be your gain. Two days from now, at *ten p.m.,* you can be a blushing bride!"

Two days. She knew Titan had wanted that date because he needed time for Blake to track them down. Not like they were actually going to get married. *Just springing a trap.*

"Two days." Titan took out his wallet and handed over his credit card. "Book it, will you?"

***

"Ohmygod! The honeymoon suite!" Trinity danced inside. "This is insane!" She ran straight to the bar and helped herself to one of those tiny bottles of champagne that was always stocked inside fancy places like this. Two guzzles, and it was gone. She dropped the bottle and rushed toward the bedroom. Delighted laughter spilled from her. "The bed is heart-shaped. How amazing is that? Oh, I have got to try it." She ran forward, hopped on the bed, and bounced.

"That bitch."

Her bouncing paused. Her new friend—he'd told her to call him Blake—stood in the doorway of the bedroom. His handsome face had tightened.

And she knew why. Sympathy flashed through her. "It all makes sense now." Everything fell into place in Trinity's mind. "I'm sorry." This was her chance. She just had to seem sympathetic enough. Like she could be his shoulder to cry on. She slid off the bed and sidled toward him. "She was your ex, wasn't she?" They'd crept in through the staff entrance of this hotel. She'd been here before, but never up to this particular level. "You followed her to Vegas."

"I followed her. Tried to ditch me, but she underestimated me."

Trinity's hand flattened on his chest. Oh, the muscles. She bet he'd look killer beneath those clothes. "You don't need her."

"She shouldn't be in the honeymoon suite with him. She shouldn't have chosen him. I warned her what would happen."

She stroked carefully with her hand. "Some people just don't listen." Her tongue slid over her lower lip. "I'm a really good listener. The best. I can be the best you've ever had."

His gaze had been on the bed. At those words, though, his stare jumped to her face.

She smiled at him.

"I saw you on the street," he told her. "I watched you before I approached you. I knew you were looking to either steal from someone or fuck someone."

Now she stiffened. She'd never had sex for money in her life. As for the stealing... "A woman has to make a living—"

"You kinda look like her. But the eyes are off. Not just the color, but the expression in them. You just don't fucking *care* about anything, do you?"

Some days, she didn't.

Some days, she did.

"I'm that way, too," he revealed with a cold smile. "Don't care at all, and that makes things easier."

Unease flickered through her. "What exactly are you planning to do to your ex?" Because they were inside the honeymoon suite, and suddenly, it felt like they were lying in wait. There was a difference between making a quick score and actually doing physical damage to someone else. "I'm not into hurting people." She'd been kicked around enough as a kid.

Maybe he wasn't such a good new friend to have. Attractive or not, it might be time for her to leave. She tried to step around him and get out of that bedroom.

But his hand flew out and caught her wrist. “Too bad,” he told her. “Because I am.”

It took a minute for her to understand his words…

She’d just said…*I’m not into hurting people.* And he—he—

Her eyes widened in horror. She opened her mouth to scream. But she didn’t get the chance. He grabbed her and rammed her back into the doorframe. Her head hit the wood. Once. Twice. By the third time, she could feel the blood sliding down her neck and her whole body was getting heavy.

“I like hurting people…one hell of a lot.”

# CHAPTER SEVENTEEN

"It's not hero worship."

Titan turned his head at Cassidy's low words. They'd stopped for ice cream. Freaking ice cream. Like a normal couple on a date. Not like, oh, we're-trying-to-lure-a-serial-killer-to-us. It *felt* like a date which should have been weird as hell to Titan. Only, it didn't. The sun shone down on them. His chocolate ice cream was melting already, and Cassidy held her cone and casually licked her cookies and cream treat.

*Note to self. Stop watching her lick.*

Swallowing, he jerked his gaze away from her mouth. And tried to ignore the ache in his dick. What had she said? He'd gotten distracted and sort of been wishing he was an ice cream cone.

"I don't care what your buddy Oliver believes. It's not hero worship. I admire you. I like you. And I enjoy having sex with you." She licked the ice cream again. "Wanted to get that out there. I don't expect you to fall in love with me, so you can relax on that score."

Part of his ice cream plopped onto the pavement. Wonderful. She looked sensual, and he probably looked like an idiot. Titan grabbed for the napkins and cleaned up his mess before dumping his cone. "You don't want me to..." He stopped. Shook his head. He just couldn't say the words.

"I don't expect you to love me. I heard what Oliver had to say. It's easy to overhear things when you are deliberately eavesdropping."

Titan blinked.

Another lick of her ice cream, and then, "You don't need to worry that I'm building unrealistic expectations or something in my head. I get that when we catch Blake, you'll go back to your life. I'll go back to mine." A quick lick of her tongue on the ice cream.

*Sonofabitch.* The things he wanted to do with her tongue. The things he wanted *her* doing.

"I'll go back to—to whatever my life may be." Her voice turned musing. His reflection stared back at him from her sunglasses as Cassidy continued, "To be honest, I'm not real sure who I am anymore. Teacher, bartender, blackjack dealer. Maybe I'll become someone else completely new when I start over. Just don't know yet. What I *do* know is that it will be nice not to look over my shoulder for an attacker anymore."

His gaze slid over her shoulder...just because he'd caught sight of a figure moving in swiftly. Titan's eyes narrowed even as he tensed. Someone was running full out behind Cassidy. Titan's hand extended, he grabbed her and immediately shoved her behind him even as he reached for his—

*Oliver?*

Oliver was the one running full speed toward him. Oliver in his expensive blue suit, with the damn thing flapping around him and revealing both his holster and the badge he'd clipped to his hip. *Way to keep a low profile.* The agent was going to blow this whole mission right then and there.

*Unless there's already danger. There has to be, or he wouldn't be coming—*

"Problem," Oliver gasped as he reached them. "Big fucking problem." He strained to see around Titan. "She's good? You're good?"

So far, yeah. "What the hell is happening? Did you see our target?"

"He's killed again. We believe he took out Dwight Asa."

The name rang a faint bell. Titan needed that bell to ring louder—

"Dwight worked at the car rental agency you used in Utah after the fire."

Dwight's image flashed in Titan's head. *Yes, yes, sonofabitch. I remember him. Forties, thinning hair, small moustache, dark eyes that had lit up when he pointed to the picture of his family on the counter.*

"He didn't show up to work today. Boss got worried because he never misses a day. Uniforms went to his house." Oliver peered at the street. Nodded quickly and moved toward the curb. "He was dead inside."

A black SUV pulled to a stop near them.

A black SUV? *Why not just run a siren with all kinds of flashing lights?* The stereotypical ride screamed Feds. Sure, Titan had used an SUV when he was hunting for Cassidy in Nowhere, but at least the damn thing hadn't been government-issue black.

"Dwight had been stabbed. Twice in the chest, then his throat had been cut. Funny fucking thing..." Only Oliver wasn't laughing. He was yanking open the back door to the SUV. "Another guy you both know—Deputy Maverick Thomas—he had wounds similar to those, too."

Titan turned toward Cassidy. "Get in."

She tossed her ice cream in the nearby can and practically flew in the vehicle. He jumped in behind her and slammed the door.

Oliver took the front passenger seat. "This is Special Agent Jon Kimura. Think I mentioned he'd be joining our party."

He'd mentioned that Jon would be staying on the periphery. This wasn't periphery.

Jon turned to glance back at them. His dark eyes raked first Cassidy, then Titan. "Did you see any sign of Blake Normandy today?"

"We need to get moving," Oliver urged him, impatience and what could have been worry biting through his words "Let's drive and talk at the same time. The sooner they are secure, the better."

Cassidy's hands clenched in her lap even as the vehicle lunged forward. "You think Blake killed that nice Dwight guy? I-I remember him from the rental place. He's got those cute twin boys. I saw their picture."

The vehicle zipped through traffic.

"I think Blake realized you got a new ride," Oliver said. "I think there were two rental companies close by for you to use in Utah, and I think he figured out he could make Dwight talk." A ragged exhale. "We have to assume Dwight revealed plenty to him before the poor bastard died."

Cassidy shook her head. "I don't understand. It's not like we told Dwight where we were headed!"

"Rental car companies have to protect their assets," Jon said as he navigated them through the swarm of cars. "Most rental vehicles have trackers on them."

"Dwight was the assistant manager," Oliver added. "He would have been able to access the tracker, probably from his home computer. It would have been easy enough for Blake to get the info...hell, he could have even swiped a laptop from Dwight's place. No way the cops know what—if anything—has been taken from the guy's home yet. They're still too busy processing the body and scene."

Titan heard the click of Cassidy's swallow. "So...Blake already knows we are in Vegas."

"More than that, he would already know which hotel you're staying at. The rental was in the valet lot all night. Dammit, I thought he'd track down credit card info. That was why I wanted a trail left for him." Oliver turned toward them, and his eyes were darkened by shadows. "But he's already here."

Cassidy grabbed the edge of the seat in front of her. Leaning forward, she said, "Jon, I believe it was?"

"That's me," the agent replied.

"Can you drive faster?"

He did.

***

"I like things that are broken."

He tapped Trinity lightly on the face. When her eyes didn't flutter open, he tapped her harder. *Harder.*

Gasping, her eyes flew open.

Not gold. Just muddy brown.

No dimples, either.

And the hair was too thin. He'd yanked her hair from the ponytail. Run his fingers through the rough strands. *Not the same.*

But it was more than the surface that was wrong. "Broken things, broken people." He smiled at her. "Usually, it takes me much longer to find someone who clicks for me. But I've always been lucky. And you just walked straight into my path when I reached Vegas."

She started to jerk up.

Only to stop when she felt the tip of the knife slice into her throat.

Her lips began to tremble.

Begging would come next. It always did. He liked that part.

"I know when people are broken," he murmured. "When they do bad things..."

"I-I'm not bad." A whisper. "*Please...*"

"You steal from people. You take their money. Take their identities—their lives. And you don't care."

"Y-you w-wanted me to t-take—*no!*" A desperate cry when the knife cut deeper.

"I give people a chance to show me who they are. You didn't have to take her wallet. You could have told me no. But that's what you do. You take and take and take..." He leaned over the bed.

*Was Cassidy on this same bed? With that sonofabitch?*

The knife sliced deeper.

Trinity whimpered. "*Please. Please, let me go.* I will do anything you want!"

The only thing he wanted was for her to die. No, not just to die. "You'll send a message for me."

Her eyes flared wide. "Yes!" An eager hiss. "Any message you want! Any—"

He sliced the knife across her throat, going deep. "This message will work."

The blood poured from her. Her eyes widened in horror.

"I like broken things. I like broken people. I see them put together, all jagged and twisted, and I like to cut them apart."

She tried to shake her head.

But couldn't.

***

"He knows you're in Vegas. We have to assume he's already here." Oliver had turned to face the front of the vehicle once more. "First Deputy Maverick Thomas, now Dwight Asa. Attacks on two men? Doesn't fit his MO at all. Not the profile I made." Frustration boiled in his voice. "He should have stuck with victims who looked just like her."

Titan stiffened as he caught the end of Oliver's snarled words. He cut a glance toward Cassidy, just in time to see her pale.

Dammit. Titan reached out his hand, caught her jaw, and turned her head to face him. "Baby?"

The car seemed to go dead silent.

Screw the agents up front. He didn't care what they thought. She mattered.

"Baby, you're safe."

Her lower lip trembled. "Dwight had a family. I saw the picture of his two sons. Twins. Were they...God, were they—"

"They weren't at home," Oliver rushed to tell her. "They'd gone on a trip with their mother. The boys are safe."

She kept looking at Titan. "But they don't have a dad anymore. Because Blake wanted to find me." Another tremble of her lower lip. "I should have stayed with him in Florida."

"No." Titan was adamant.

"He might not have hurt anyone else. I should have stayed—"

"He would have killed you," Titan told her even as he hated the brutal words that came from him. "You'd be the one in pieces. Another woman he left in the woods. You'd be the one who was missing and that no one could find." And that image made him sick. The idea of Blake hurting Cassidy. Killing her.

*No. I will see him in the ground first. I will destroy him. He will not have the chance to ever hurt her.*

His thumb brushed along her cheek. "You aren't committing the crimes. He is. The only person to blame? It's *him*. Don't ever forget that."

"We need a new profile," Jon fired from the front. "The stuff you told us before, Oliver—it's not matching up. You said the target he'd want was a dark-haired woman in her mid-twenties, slender build, no more than five feet five. You said he preferred prey that were weaker in build compared to him. Well, he's taking out men. First the deputy's attack and now the poor rental assistant manager. He's not matching your victim profile at all. Makes me wonder—"

"He's adapting," Oliver gritted out. "His primary choice of prey remains the same. He's not enjoying the attacks with the men. The rush wouldn't be the same. He's attacking to get information. His attacks all go back..." He looked over his shoulder.

*Do not say it. Don't you dare say it—*

"To Cassidy," Oliver finished.

The man had no tact.

"He's like a wounded animal," Oliver continued. "He's taking out whatever is in his way because he has to reach his ultimate goal."

"I'm the ultimate goal." Cassidy's voice held pain.

Titan's thumb brushed over her cheek again. He'd felt a tear on that silken skin. Dammit. He hated her pain. If he could, he would take every single bit of it away for her.

"Yes." Oliver was clearly not in the mood to pull punches.

"Then why the hell," Cassidy's words came out low and angry, "am I in this vehicle? Shouldn't I still be parading around town with a big neon sign on my body? Screaming for him to come and get me?"

Silence.

Titan saw Jon's stare flicker to the rearview mirror.

"The public street wasn't contained enough." Oliver faced the front. "We needed an environment with more control. We didn't expect an attack so soon, and the news we received at the Bureau today indicated we had to change our plans."

*You thought he would come at her in public. That he would get past me. That he would kill her on the street before any Feds could reach her.* "Not happening," Titan swore.

He felt Cassidy jerk beneath his touch. "What isn't happening?" she whispered.

His hand fell away from her. "You're not getting out of my sight, you understand that?" If he had to pull out fresh cuffs, he would. No way was the woman getting away from him.

From the front, Oliver cleared his throat. "I just said plans had changed, marshal."

Oh, hold up. Had Oliver just gotten all official with the "marshal" BS? Never a good sign.

"You're not leading the case," Oliver told him gruffly. "While the FBI certainly appreciates your cooperation, your involvement is purely temporary. If necessary, Cassidy will be moved to a location that is deemed safe by the FBI."

In other words, Oliver had just said he might take Cassidy away. Stash her in a safe house and kick Titan to the curb. He couldn't help it. Laughter rumbled from Titan. "I'd really like to see you try."

"So would I," Jon added softly. "Because I don't think that shit will fly."

Titan grunted. He'd actually run some cases with Jon before. The agent was calm under fire, feared very little, and didn't stand for BS. Traits that Titan always admired. Back in the day, Jon's father had met a female soldier who'd been stationed in Japan. They'd fallen in love, moved to the US, and Jon had been born a few years later. Unfortunately, Jon's mom had been killed on a mission when he was just five years old.

How did Titan know that? Because he'd met Riku Kimura, and the man had proudly shown him all of Helen's medals. He'd also embarrassed the hell out of Jon by pulling out every photo he'd ever taken of his son.

"Titan stays with me," Cassidy suddenly declared, voice tight. "That was the deal. And we're not changing the deal."

Titan glanced her way. He nodded. "We're not changing the deal."

*No fucking way.*

***

The SUV braked in front of the hotel. Titan climbed out first, but Oliver joined him almost instantly. Before Titan could walk around to

Cassidy's side of the vehicle, Oliver was in his path.

"I don't think you get what's happening here," Oliver said softly.

"I get plenty."

Oliver stood toe-to-toe with him. "I'm worried that *you're* the next target. He will mow down anyone who is in his way in order to get her."

"I'm hard to mow down." He stepped around Oliver.

"Dammit!" Oliver grabbed his arm. "This is bigger than you."

"Few things are." He shrugged free of the agent's hold.

"Oh, great," Oliver muttered behind him. "Now you get a sense of humor, and it's a real shitty one. We're talking about danger—" But he shut up because the valet was rushing forward. "Nope. We do not need your services. My friend will park our ride. Thanks."

Titan opened Cassidy's door. He took her hand. "You good?"

"No." She hopped out. "But as long as you're not ditching me, I'll make it."

No way was ditching her in the cards. He whisked her past the valet staff, aware of Oliver on their tail. They hurried straight for the elevator, and Titan hauled out his keycard.

As they slipped into the elevator, he noticed Oliver nodding toward a woman who sat perched on the end of an elegant couch. One of her high heels swung lazily, and she barely seemed to even see Oliver.

But Titan suspected he'd just seen the second agent, the female one Oliver had referenced the night before. Mae Silva. So she was keeping her eyes open in the lobby. Good.

The elevator doors slid closed. Oliver exhaled. "I hate fucking casualties. Jon was right. The profile has to change." He ran a hand over his face. "I think Blake is going off the rails."

"That doesn't exactly sound like a clinical term," Titan said. He used the keycard to gain access to their floor. The elevator started to rise.

Oliver's hand fell. He zeroed in on Cassidy. "Why are you different?"

"I'm not."

"He is obsessed. Can't cut his losses. Will take out anyone in his way. He's going up against prey that isn't as physically weak as his normal choice. He's not taking the kills that bring him pleasure."

Cassidy swallowed. Disgust slid over her face. "Maybe every kill brings him pleasure."

Oliver shook his head. "Figured a woman like you played prominently in his past. A mother, an older sister, the girl he crushed on who wouldn't give him the time of day when he was a kid. Someone who looked like you—usually the predator attacks that same individual over and over again. But something threw off the pattern with you." His features twisted. "Why? *Why?*"

The elevator dinged. The doors opened. Titan stepped out first and swept the hallway. All clear. His head dipped so the others would move forward. Titan led the way, with Cassidy in the middle, and Oliver pulling up the rear.

Titan's steps didn't slow, not until he was right in front of their door. He pulled out his keycard—

"My wallet is missing." Cassidy's startled voice had him looking back at her.

Her hand had shoved into her purse. Her head tilted down as she raked through the bag. "It's not here. I put it in this morning—when you bought me the bag in that little lobby shop—I put the new wallet inside. It had my room key and my cash and—"

"It's okay," Oliver soothed her. "Maybe it fell out. Let's just get the hell inside."

But unease settled heavily around Titan's shoulders. Before he opened the door, he pulled out his gun. "Do not let her in until I say it's clear."

"What?" Cassidy grabbed his arm. "What's happening?"

"I'm going in. You're staying here with Oliver." He pressed his keycard to the little pad above the door handle. The light flashed green.

"We have no cover in the hall," Oliver grumbled. "You need to—"

"Stay," he ordered, then stepped inside. All of the lights were out. He knew they'd turned off the lights when they left, but...

Titan turned on a lamp.

Why was there a small bottle of champagne on the counter? The top had been twisted off, and it looked as if the bottle had been emptied.

*Fuck.* There was no sound in that suite. Not even the rustle of air from the central cooling system. Keeping his weapon up and at the ready, he swept the den and the kitchenette.

Not a lot of places for someone to hide.

Except…

The bedroom door was slightly ajar.

He took a step toward the bedroom.

***

"I don't like this," Cassidy whispered.

Oliver glanced back down the hallway, then toward the suite's door. The door was open just an inch, maybe two, but only because Oliver's foot was pressed against the bottom. Titan had disappeared inside, and the twisting in her gut grew worse with every single moment that passed.

"Titan has this," Oliver assured her.

"He needs back up." The exact same thought she'd had at the motel in Utah.

She took a step forward.

"Nope." Oliver snagged her around the shoulders and pushed her behind him. "That's cute, but it's not happening. Keep your ass out here, sunshine. I say again…Titan has this."

***

Titan pushed open the bedroom door. Darkness waited inside. The curtains had been pulled, completely blocking the sunlight.

His shoulder brushed against the door as he opened it wider. "US marshal," he snarled. His grip on the gun never wavered. "I'm armed. *Show yourself.*" He lunged to the right even as his hand swept out and hit the light switch. He crouched down, angling so that he would be in a new position when the illumination flooded the room and he could see the target—

Blood. On the bed.

In her hair. Her dark hair that slid over her face.

He rose to his full height. Took a staggering step toward the bed.

So much blood. It soaked her. Soaked the white, silk sheets beneath her. Turned their color a dark red. His hand reached for her neck—

*Cut open. You're not finding a pulse here. She's…*

He grabbed her wrist, looking for a pulse. She was still warm. Sonofabitch. All that blood. And the wound in her neck was so deep. Thick, like—

Something fell from her hand. She'd been holding it, but when he searched for her pulse, her fingers had slid open a bit. The plastic card fell onto the bloodstained sheets.

A plastic keycard.

A hotel room key.

Cassidy's missing hotel room key?

"Titan?" Oliver yelled. "What the hell is happening in there?"

His fingers pressed harder and he found—

She gurgled.

*Fuck.* "I need an ambulance!" he roared. "Now! Now, *now!*" Titan grabbed for the sheets near the bottom of the bed. He shoved them against her wound.

Footsteps pounded.

"Nine-one-one!" Titan blasted. "We need an ambulance right now!"

A shocked gasp came from the doorway.

Titan's head whipped toward the sound. Oliver rushed closer to him, but Cassidy had frozen in the doorway. She stared at the woman in the bed, and Cassidy's eyes seemed to swallow her face.

Oliver hurried to help Titan.

"*Ambulance!*" Titan snapped. "Cassidy, call them—"

She raced to the side of the bed, and she picked up the phone. He heard her shaking voice asking for help, saying that a woman was injured.

*Her throat is cut from ear to ear. It's a miracle she's alive. If we had gotten here just a few minutes later...*

The thought froze him. "He's here," Titan snarled. "The sonofabitch...he must have seen us arrive." The suite and its damn view of the fountains. If the killer had been watching outside, he would have seen them pull into the valet area.

"Honeymoon suite," Cassidy said. "Hurry, there's so much blood. Please, *hurry!*" She dropped the phone.

"Don't you dare leave this room, Cassidy!" Titan didn't take his eyes off the victim. "Don't you *dare!*" Because the killer had to be close.

And maybe he was just waiting. Hoping to grab Cassidy. Hoping to take her. To kill her.

Titan's gaze remained on the woman on the bed. The woman covered in blood. The woman who hadn't opened her eyes. Who'd only made that one sound.

*The woman who could have been Cassidy...*

# CHAPTER EIGHTEEN

Chaos.

That was the way to describe the hotel's lobby. The first time she'd entered the place, it had been beautiful and serene. Her gaze had been caught by the beauty of the flower sculpture above her. It had been like stepping into a dream.

But, as was so typical for her, the dream had turned into a nightmare.

The woman who'd been in the bed—she'd been rushed away moments before. Cops had swarmed. The hotel staff members buzzed madly. And guests were whispering and staring and holding up phones to take pictures of the chaos.

Cassidy stood there, feeling numb. There had been so much blood in that bed. Her bed. The bed she'd shared with Titan the night before.

*He put that woman in the bed deliberately.* Cassidy knew Blake had sent her a message. She knew exactly what the twisted freak wanted to tell her.

*Her death is on you.*

Fuck him. Fuck him to hell where she hoped he burned forever.

"Hey, you okay?"

The soft, feminine voice had Cassidy turning her head toward Mae. Special Agent Mae Silva. Small, petite, with light brown skin, carefully styled hair, and worried brown eyes. Mae was on Cassidy's right, while Special Agent Jon Kimura hovered on her left. Her guards.

Titan and Oliver had rushed out with the ambulance. They'd been barking orders at the EMTs.

"Cassidy?" Mae prompted.

Right. She should speak. But lying and saying she was okay or fine—not really what she wanted. "She's not going to make it."

Mae and Jon shared a look.

Cassidy knew what the look meant. *No, she's not.* Had the woman even been alive when she'd been rushed out? How could you live with that much blood loss? But Titan hadn't given up on her. He'd been frantically working on her every moment. Telling her to stay. To fight.

The dead couldn't fight. That was the job of the living.

*Come for me, you sonofabitch.* Her gaze scanned the lobby. He had to be close by. This was just like the motel fire. He'd created chaos at the motel in Utah in order to draw her out. To distract. He'd left the woman upstairs in the honeymoon suite, knowing chaos would follow. Titan had been separated from her, and now...

Now it was just a matter of time until Blake closed in. "I need a gun," Cassidy said. She'd had one at the fire. This time, she could be a better shot. She'd wait until Blake got closer. She'd shoot the bastard right between the eyes so that there could be no mistake—he'd be the dead one.

Jon cleared his throat. "What do you want to do with a gun?"

She rolled her eyes and turned her head his way. "Kill someone, of course."

He blinked. "Of course."

He didn't give her a gun, even though there was one right there in his holster. She could see the bulk beneath his suit coat.

Mae also made no move to give Cassidy a weapon. Annoying. A disgusted sigh slid from her. "Do you both want me to just be a sitting duck? At least give me a fighting chance."

"You're not a sitting duck," Mae replied quickly. "We're here with you—"

"You've got me smack in the middle of the lobby where everyone is filming with their phones and posting on social media. You want Blake to see me." Cassidy wasn't an idiot. "Trust me, he does see me. And he's coming. I can't run from him. Tried that. Failed. People are just going to keep dying. It has to end." So, back to her request. "Give me a gun."

They didn't.

Screw that. This was Vegas. She'd find a weapon on her own if they weren't going to give her one. "You both probably have backup weapons on you. Don't you want me to at least have a fighting chance?" She returned to that point.

Mae flinched. "No one is sending you out unprotected. Titan and Oliver want you to wait here. We are with you. We're protecting you."

How fantastic. Time for her to come up with her own plan. Her gaze raked the massive lobby. She tried to peek at every single face. But there were so many faces. Too many.

"If you see him," Jon said, his voice barely a breath, "tell us immediately."

Of course. Why else would they be hanging out there? Everyone thought Blake was coming in for the kill. *My kill.*

But first, he'd killed the woman upstairs. *Or come very, very close.* That was all he could do. Kill. Over and over again.

Her gaze drifted from person to person. But the lobby was truly too packed. Men and women in uniform rushed left and right. Families poured from elevators and paused just long enough to gape. High rollers were whisked away by security.

Cassidy backed up a step.

*I'm just prey.*

She had to get out of there. Finding a weapon was job one. Job two—staying alive. Having the weapon would make that job so much easier—

Titan marched through the crowd. People parted for him, instantly moving to the side. Oliver trailed behind him, but then Oliver paused briefly at the concierge desk. Both Titan and Oliver wore grim expressions...and blood. Both men wore blood.

Cassidy swallowed. Blood was on Titan's shirt. On Oliver's shirt.

For the first time, Cassidy looked down at herself.

*OhmyGod.* No wonder so many of those phones had been sent her way for filming. She was bloody, too, because she'd tried to help the woman upstairs. Cassidy's body started to shake. "I-I have to change." She stumbled back.

But Titan surged forward. His hand closed around her wrist.

*No blood on his fingers.* There had been earlier, though. She remembered seeing it—

*Blood had been everywhere.*

"Do you see him?" Titan growled.

She shook her head. *I just see blood.*

"We've got officers searching the hotel and all nearby buildings. They are canvassing the streets. They're going door to door in the hotel." A muscle flexed along his jaw. "We're pulling security footage. There is no way he should have been able to get in our suite."

"She was...the woman who bumped me." A chill raked over Cassidy's body. "When we were at the crosswalk, she was the one to bump me. Do you think she got my wallet then?" She must have.

Titan looked back at Oliver. The Fed had hurriedly left the concierge area and joined them.

"No ID on her," Oliver returned. "We'll run her prints. Get info soon enough. She is—"

"Is she dead?" Cassidy asked.

"She was still alive in the hotel room," Titan replied.

*But was she alive when she got loaded into the ambulance?* She bit back the question. "I'm tired of being on display. Can we please get out of here? Or do I need to be bait longer?"

The muscle jerked again along Titan's jaw.

"I think the red flag has been waved. He knows I'm in this hotel." Not just in the hotel.

Blake knew which suite she'd used. *He's so far ahead of us.* "We've got the blood-soaked sheets to prove he knows." And she had the blood on her clothes. "I want to change. I want to shower. I want—" *To kill Blake.* She'd crossed over. Gone so far there was no way she could come back. She wanted him dead. If he was dead, then he would never be able to hurt anyone else.

Not in jail. Not getting some *therapy* someplace. She wanted him dead.

"There's another suite she can use," Oliver spoke quickly. "Just confirmed it with the concierge. It's two floors above our previous room. Already have the key. I can get fresh clothes brought up, and while you're guarding her, I'll start reviewing the security footage."

Titan nodded. "We're changing, Cassidy. Then getting the hell out of here. The security at this place is compromised to hell and back." Titan tugged her forward. "Come on, baby."

She kept her spine straight and her chin up as they made their way to the elevator. Titan on one side, Oliver on the other. Mae and Jon followed behind them. It was like she was walking with her own wall of security.

The elevator doors opened.

A woman stepped out. A woman with long, almost perfectly black hair that skimmed beyond her shoulders. A stylish, red dress snugly fit her body.

*Blood red. I see blood everywhere.*

The woman froze. Her eyes widened in surprise as she took in their group.

*Right. Now she's seeing blood.*

But the woman shook her head and sent her sleek hair flying. "You sonofabitch," she snarled. Then she slapped Oliver right across the face.

The slap was sudden and brutal and Cassidy had no idea what was happening. Why was this woman attacking Oliver?

Titan swore beneath his breath.

Mae and Jon surged forward to grab the woman.

"No!" Oliver's low voice. "Don't touch her."

The woman's hand dropped. Fisted. The elevator had closed behind her.

"Uh, that's assaulting a federal officer," Mae pointed out.

"No, it's personal." Oliver's voice remained low. His gaze also remained on the mystery woman.

"All right." Mae didn't miss a beat. "Then it's domestic violence. You don't just *slap* someone who—"

"He's innocent," the woman said flatly. Her bright green gaze burned as she glared at Oliver. "You used me. You locked him away. Now he's with murderers and drug dealers and he's in hell when he never did anything wrong. My brother isn't a killer. You think you know criminals so well?" She stepped closer to Oliver. "You don't. You were wrong about him, and I will prove it." Her head turned toward Mae. "You want to arrest me? Do it."

Oliver shook his head. "Mae, no."

"Then get the hell out of my way," the woman demanded.

Oliver stepped to the side.

"Blood on you," the woman drawled as her stare raked him. "How not surprising." She stormed away.

Oliver watched her go. And his expression…

*Torment. Need.*

Cassidy shook her head. "Yeah, look, I'm kinda in the middle of my own nightmare. Chase after her if you want, but I am getting out of this damn lobby." She jabbed the elevator button again. The doors swung open.

Oliver shook his head, as if waking up from a dream. He hurried into the elevator. So did Titan and Cassidy. But Oliver pointed to the other two Feds. "Stay down here and check with the local cops. See if they turn up anything. Have a uniform sent up to Titan and Cassidy's new suite. I want him standing guard in front of their room." He rattled off the room number. "They are the only suite on the floor. I'll be right back down because I want to view the security footage."

Moments later, the doors slid closed.

"What the fuck was Lark doing here?" Oliver shoved a hand through his hair. Cassidy noted the faint tremble in his fingers. "That's the last thing I need now. Dammit, I warned you. Say her name, and you summon her."

Summon her? Cassidy let that bit go and focused on what worried her. "What were you wrong about?" Cassidy asked him. *If he's been wrong about one killer…*

"The elevator won't move unless you use the keycard," Titan growled.

Swearing, Oliver swiped the keycard, pressed the button for their floor, and they started to rise.

Titan's arm brushed against Cassidy. She realized that he was practically on top of her. When her head turned, she caught—

*Torment. Need.*

There one moment, gone in the next blink. Titan had been looking at her the same way Oliver stared after the woman he'd called Lark.

"She shouldn't be here. *Why* is she here?" Oliver muttered.

"Fucking *focus,*" Titan snapped back at him.

Oliver jerked to attention. "Once you're in the new suite, clean up as fast as you can. I'll have fresh clothes sent up. Told you that shit already, didn't I?" His hand swiped over his face. Like Titan, he'd already washed the blood off his fingers. "There will be a cop at your door. And you were right, we can't keep staying here. Not secure enough. We'll find a safe house to use for the time being. First, though, I want to go look at the footage and get eyes on the honeymoon suite once again and...*shit*. I underestimated him. I don't like to be wrong."

The doors opened. Oliver led them out. As they all approached the door to their suite, Titan drew his gun.

"I want one of those," Cassidy told him. "Immediately."

He nodded. "You can have mine."

Kind of him to offer, but... "No, I want you to have one, too. I want my own." It would be way better if they were both armed.

Oliver unlocked the door. She noticed that he went in with his gun up, too.

"Not taking any chances," Titan said.

But it wasn't like Blake was psychic. They'd just gotten this suite. Hardly possible for him to be lying in wait. Right? But the men still searched thoroughly, and it was only after they gave the all clear that Cassidy was able to rush for the shower.

"I'll be right here," Titan promised.

She shut the bathroom door. Finally got a look at herself in the mirror.

*Blood on my clothes. Horror in my eyes.*

Her hands gripped the edge of the sink. Even though she feared the worst, Cassidy still sent up a desperate prayer. *Please, God, let that woman live.*

***

"There is no way she's going to live, you know that, right?" Oliver asked. Then... "Fuck me!" He whirled and drove his fist into the wall. "He shouldn't have gotten inside. He shouldn't have *killed under our noses*. He should be in a cell. And Lark should fucking not be here!" He drove his fist into the wall again.

Titan's brows raised. He'd already reholstered his weapon. "Anyone ever say you have anger issues?"

Oliver's shoulders stiffened. "I loved her and lost her. When you lose Cassidy, come back and tell me how that shit feels."

*I won't lose her*. "Never said I loved her."

Oliver whirled around. "You don't have to say it. It's on your face. In your eyes." He strode toward Titan. "You want to kill him right now, don't you?"

*The world won't be safe for Cassidy as long as he's living in it.* Titan shrugged.

"Let me rephrase. You're *planning* to kill him, aren't you? Because when you walked into that bedroom and you saw the woman on the bed, you knew Blake had left a message. One for Cassidy and one for you. Fuck, one for me, too. He wants Cassidy to think every death will be on her. He wants you to see what it will be like when he kills Cassidy. And he wants me to know that I can't stop him. That we're all screwed."

"He will not kill Cassidy." But, hell, yes, Oliver was right. When Titan had gone in that bedroom, when he'd seen the blood and the body, he'd lost his sanity for a time.

"You get you were working to save a dead woman, right?" Low, just for Titan.

"No, she was alive."

Oliver's expression darkened. "You lost it because you imagined Cassidy. All that blood being hers. *Her,* being slashed in that bed. He killed her where you fucked Cassidy."

Titan's fists were clenched so tightly they ached. "He will not get her."

"I don't want to be wrong. But I have been. I thought we had more time before he arrived in Vegas. I didn't anticipate that he'd go after the rental assistant manager in Utah. Shit. *Shit.* Cassidy thinks the deaths are on her. She's wrong. I should have stopped him. I should stop them all. They keep hunting and killing, and I feel like I am drowning because I'm trying to take them out and there are so many of them...*but what if I'm wrong?"*

Titan couldn't afford to have Oliver doubting himself. "Tell me his profile. Every bit of info you've got." Though he'd read the profile before. As he'd hunted for Cassidy, Titan had tried to learn as much about Blake Normandy as possible.

"He stalks his victims. I believe he discovers as much about them as he can before the initial meeting. The way he already knew Cassidy's favorite band and her favorite food—that confirmed my suspicions. But the woman in the honeymoon suite—there couldn't have been time for him to stalk her. Something else made her click for him. It must have."

"Sure. She had the right hair. The right build." Cassidy had even said, *"Did you think she kinda looked like me?"*

Oliver adamantly shook his head. "No, no, it's more than that. It has to be—my gut is *screaming* that I just need to look deeper and see—"

"Then if you want more on the woman in the honeymoon suite, start looking through police records. She lifted Cassidy's wallet, and she was holding the keycard in her hand when I found her in bed. The bastard left it in her hand because he wanted us to know he'd used her to get access. She lifted the card that took her to her death."

Oliver staggered back a step. "Police records. That's it. Sonofabitch. I was too narrow."

Titan frowned at him. "What are you talking about?"

"Cassidy was never charged. Just suspected. Because she's not fucking guilty. Maybe he doesn't think he's guilty of doing anything wrong, either. Maybe he's taking out the women who are guilty." He shook his head. Grabbed Titan by the shoulders. "I could kiss you right now."

"Don't."

"I have to check—I need the security footage. Got to make some calls. *Do not leave this room until I get back.* Guard her with your life—hell, what am I saying? You already look at her like she is your life." He spun for the door. Yanked it open and almost slammed into the uniformed cop already out there.

"Excellent!" Oliver exclaimed.

Titan had a quick flash of the cop's surprised face. Young, a little soft around the jaw. Red hair.

Oliver grabbed the cop's shoulders and pushed him to the side. "If anyone without a badge tries to get in this room, you pull your weapon and—" The door shut, cutting off the end of his order.

For a moment, Titan didn't move. His hand fisted and released. Fisted and released.

His chest still burned. He'd washed the blood off his hands downstairs, but he swore he could still feel it. He'd washed the blood away and ditched the suit coat he'd been wearing. For most of the day, he'd worn the coat to hide the holster under his arm. But there had been no point in hiding it any longer, not after he'd walked into that bedroom and seen the blood-soaked sheets.

*Not Cassidy. Not Cassidy. Not.*

Cassidy was safe. She was showering. She was alive. He was going to protect her.

*Cassidy.*

He stalked to the door. Engaged all the locks. Then he turned and glanced around. Another giant suite. Except this one was twice as big as the one before. Had a freaking piano in it. A pool table. To the right of the pool table, a massive dining room table waited. Champagne was chilling in a silver bucket in the middle of that table. *Does this place always have champagne at the ready?*

Titan ignored the champagne, and he headed for the bedroom. When he crossed the threshold, he realized there was no heart-shaped bed.

*No blood-soaked woman in the bed.*

The woman had not been Cassidy. Not her.

He took off his holster and put his weapon on the nightstand before he approached the closed bathroom door. After a brief moment passed, Titan realized that he didn't hear the flow of water. He didn't hear anything at all, and panic flared. It burst inside of him, and he twisted the knob and threw the door open. *"Cassidy!"*

She spun toward him. She'd just been stepping from the shower. Water clung to her skin, and her eyes flared in alarm.

Hell. "Sorry. I scared you."

Her tongue snaked out to lick her lips. "No, you've never done that." A pause. "Well, maybe the first time we met. Just briefly because I didn't know you were the hero back then."

"I'm not."

"Liar."

He yanked open the buttons on his shirt and shrugged it off. A toss had the shirt sailing toward the corner. The blood on the fabric chilled him. *Could have been Cassidy's.* The shirt was a freaking biohazard. Needed to be collected as part of the investigation. Everything was fucking madness. Doing shit by the book?

There was no book.

*I wanted to save her.* The woman in the honeymoon suite. He'd wanted to help, but feared he hadn't.

*What if I can't save Cassidy?* No, no. Titan shut down the thought. He would save Cassidy. There was no other option. Cassidy had to be protected.

"You need to shower, too," Cassidy told him. She didn't seem to care that she was completely naked, and he was eating her alive with his eyes. She reached back and turned the water on once more. It thundered out in a powerful stream.

Titan finished stripping.

Cassidy's gaze swept over him.

His was still on her. Drinking in every single inch. "Do not leave this room."

Her stare whipped back up to meet his.

"I need to keep my eyes on you." For the few moments he'd been away from her as he talked with Oliver, his mind had kept running right back to her. The truth? He was afraid. Fucking terrified. He hated that fear.

*I can't lose Cassidy.*

"I'd like to keep my eyes on you, too," she whispered.

He stepped into the shower. The door was made of glass so he could see her through it. Cassidy reached for a towel and wrapped it around herself.

Unnecessary. He'd wanted to keep looking at all of her.

He bathed quickly. Thoroughly. He wanted to be perfectly clean when he reached for her again. He could not touch Cassidy with blood on his hands, not ever.

Titan had thought the water might cool him down. Might settle the rage and the fear that kept twisting so hard within him. It didn't. When he yanked the water off, and the *drip, drip* filled the air, he sucked in a deep breath. He pushed open the door.

Cassidy had hopped up onto the granite counter. She sat there with the towel around her and with her eyes on him.

Water slowly dripped down his body. Cassidy could see every inch of him. *Was* seeing every inch, and he didn't care at all about the scars. She looked at him, and there was need in her eyes. The same dark and almost desperate need that he felt.

"I know this is wrong," she said.

With quick strokes of a nearby towel, he dried off. Mostly. Then he ditched the towel and stalked toward her. His hands lifted and flattened on the countertop. One hand on either side of Cassidy. The position caged her.

"I shouldn't want you right now, but I do." Her husky voice flowed over him like a touch. "I'm scared he's closing in."

*Because he is.*

"I'm scared something will happen and I'll get pulled away from you, and being with you? It's sort of been the best thing that has happened to me in ages."

He'd been hanging onto his control with every bit of strength he possessed. Her words broke him. *You are my best thing.* "Spread your legs."

Her eyes widened. Her legs spread. His right hand moved to shove her towel out of his way so that he could see her. *Sweet. Beautiful. Mine.*

That was how he'd come to think of Cassidy. Not as his witness. His charge. Just...*mine.* "You're my best thing." Ever. Did she get that? Probably not. Too soon. Too fast. Nothing about their partnership had been normal. There was no normal for them. There was just need. A longing that cut past everything else.

"Sometimes, Titan, you can say the sweetest things." Her hands rose to curl under his jaw. "Tell me I won't lose you."

"You're not losing me." *And I won't lose you.* He should step away. He absolutely was not going to do so. Not unless Cassidy told him to back the hell off. "It can't be you."

Her dark lashes fluttered.

"It won't be," he swore, and Titan kissed her. Not with finesse or gentleness, but with a savage demand because he felt savage. Emotions battered at his core. Needs and dark desires spiraled through him.

Primal. Possessive. Protective. He wanted to fight for her. To kill. To do whatever it took to keep her safe.

And he would.

Cassidy kissed him back with frantic passion. No restraint. Just the same consuming need that he felt. Her hunger fed his own. Drove up the wild lust.

*She's safe. She's alive. She's in my arms.* But it wasn't enough. He needed *in* her. "Cassidy," he rasped against her mouth. "No...no condom, dammit." He should let her go. *Now.*

"You...you don't have to worry. I *always* used condoms before and...Titan, I want you."

He wanted her. More than breath. More than life. More than anything else at all.

His hands locked around her waist. He pulled her even closer to the edge of the counter. She was spread wide for him. His dick shoved at the entrance to her body. And he *pushed...*

Cassidy gave a quick gasp, and he stopped instantly.

*Tight. Too tight. She's not ready.*

His teeth clenched as he lifted his head so he could stare down at her. "Baby..."

"I want you. Don't stop. Please, don't."

She wasn't ready. He would not hurt her. Not fucking ever. Every muscle in his body seemed to strain as he held back. His cock stayed lodged inside her, but only just the head. His left hand snaked between them. Went to her clit. He rubbed. Stroked. Squeezed with his thumb and forefinger. He was not moving another inch, not until she was ready.

His mouth pressed to her throat. Licked. Kissed. Sucked lightly.

*Blood. A throat cut open*—no!

He banished the image. Kissed her softly. Cassidy was alive. Cassidy was safe. Cassidy was *his.*

His fingers kept stroking her. She began to soften around him. To get wet. Slick. Hot. He pushed his cock in a little more.

She trembled. The good kind of tremble because she moaned at the same time.

And she took him. He slid home and was lost.

No more holding back. Not for either of them. Cassidy's nails dug into his shoulders and her hips shoved up against him. In and out, he drove into her, and he kept working her clit every moment with his fingers. Her breath came faster. The towel she'd worn fell between them. He couldn't get in her deep enough. Not at this angle. So with one hand still curled around her waist, he lifted her up. Took two steps and pinned her against the wall.

She cried out as she came. The contractions of her release were a sensual stroke over his cock that sent him careening into oblivion. He held her against the wall and lost everything—his mind, his last thread of control, his soul—as he poured into her. He kept thrusting because he didn't want to stop, and as he thrust, she moaned and opened her mouth for him in a passionate, crazed kiss.

Pleasure destroyed everything else. Everything, but one thought.

*I won't lose her.*

# CHAPTER NINETEEN

"When Tracy Eldridge was sixteen years old, she was involved in a hit and run. She was drinking, and the elderly woman she hit died at the scene." Oliver glanced around the busy lobby, then focused his attention back on Jon and Mae. "The records were sealed because she was a juvenile, but I got the info from a relative when I was interviewing the family." *Tracy Eldridge.* The victim Cassidy had found in Blake's kitchen. The woman who had later been discovered by Dr. Antonia Rossi. Oliver exhaled slowly, then revealed, "The victim today—she stole Cassidy's wallet. A pickpocket. And Cassidy—she was suspected of killing her parents." The pattern was right there. And it was so much more than hair color and a similar build.

Jon frowned at him. "I don't get—"

"The vic who was found in South Carolina—Judith Trace—I need to know if she had run-ins with the law. If she was ever suspected of committing any crimes." Her record had come up clean, he knew that already. But he also knew that they needed to dig deeper. Especially if she'd only been *suspected* of a crime. "Jon, get on this. Leave no stone unturned, got me?"

"Where are you going with this?" Mae asked. "What does it matter if these women—"

"It matters to him. To Blake Normandy. I looked at the crimes wrong. Dammit, the whole thing is *wrong.*" That one word from Lark had sent his brain spinning. "What if he killed the other women because they were guilty?"

Mae gaped. "Guilty of what?"

"Small crimes. Big crimes. Whatever sins he felt they'd committed." Like being a pickpocket. Or committing a hit and run. "He studied his victims, got to know them, maybe even got them to confess...they were guilty."

Mae and Jon looked at each other, then back at him.

"They died." *No, they were brutally murdered by their judge, jury, and executioner.* "Cassidy wasn't killed. She was different because maybe she was the only one not guilty in his mind. Maybe the only one worthy of him. She got to live. He wanted someone to be *good." And you found that someone, didn't you, bastard? Only she left you when she realized what a monster you were.* "He couldn't handle that," Oliver muttered. "So he had to hunt her. He will never stop hunting her."

"Special Agent Foxx!" The chief of security ran toward him. "We think we caught something on a surveillance video. A man and woman snuck in through the staff entrance earlier—"

"Show me." But first...He pointed at Mae. "We need to make sure the local cops are doing a thorough floor-by-floor search. And by thorough,

I mean I want them in every single room in this place. Hell, I want them to check twice."

Her jaw dropped. "You don't actually think he's still here?" She waved her hand toward the chaotic lobby. "With this much of a police presence? He'd have to be crazy."

*Uh, Mae, he cuts up bodies for fun.* Not like their perp was the picture of perfect mental health. "He'd have to be obsessed," Oliver corrected. "And that's exactly what he is. The object of his obsession is here, so he *has* to be close." That made him worry even more. "One cop isn't enough." He'd left the uniformed cop with strict instructions to guard the door to Titan and Cassidy's new suite. "I want two. No, make it three. Get one guarding the elevator on Titan's new floor and one on the stairwell. Get me constant radio contact."

Mae nodded and backed away. She already knew which floor Titan was using.

Oliver pointed to the chief of security. "Show me. Now."

From the corner of his eye, he saw a familiar figure in a red dress heading for the exit. Cops were near the doors. Oliver hesitated. "Detain her," he ordered Jon.

"Excuse me?"

"The woman in red. Don't let her leave. Make sure she has a guard at all times."

"Uh, she doesn't look like his type..."

*I will take no chances.* "Detain her." And just like that, he'd be giving Lark another reason to hate him. Oh, well, at least she'd be safe.

*Alive and hating me is one hell of a lot better than dead.*

***

The thunder of his heartbeat echoed in Titan's ears. He still had her pinned against the wall and was still buried balls deep in her.

Sonofabitch. Wrong time. Wrong place. What in the hell had he been thinking?

"Thank you," Cassidy murmured. Her lips pressed to his throat. "I needed that."

To be taken hard against a wall? No, she needed care and a gentleman and not some jerk who jumped on her after a freaking murder scene. "Baby, you need more than I am." He slowly withdrew from her and gently lowered her until her feet touched the bathroom tile.

He kept his hands on her to make sure she was steady, and his gaze swept over her to make sure—

"Fuck. No protection." He was a bastard. Through and through. He grabbed a cloth from the sink and put it under hot water. Tenderly, he tried to clean her thighs and moved up toward her sex.

Her fingers curled around his wrist. "I'm healthy. I told you, ah, before, you don't need to worry about that."

"So the hell am I." She'd been the first he'd ever fucked without using a rubber. "But what about pregnancy?" The image of Cassidy pregnant, smiling, happy, those dimples flashing...*I have never wanted anything more.*

"I'm protected, Titan. My birth control will last another year. You don't have anything to worry about on that end."

His chest ached. "Of course." He tossed the cloth aside. "You might want to shower off again. I'm sorry if I was too rough."

Her hand rose to press against his chest. "You aren't too rough for me. You aren't too demanding. You are exactly what I need."

He'd just gotten caught in her gorgeous eyes. "This wasn't the right time."

"You made love to me like it was."

And his eager dick jerked when she said the magic words of "made love to me" in that breathy voice of hers. He cleared his throat and tried to function like a rational person, and not a crazed lover who was desperate for his woman. "Cassidy..."

"Titan."

She just stared at him with those dark, golden eyes.

"I was scared," he heard himself say.

What the hell?

Her head dipped in the faintest of nods. "So was I."

The ache in his chest got worse.

"When I'm making love with you, though, all the fear goes away." The darkness of her eyes lightened a bit. "I can't think of anything else for a little while. Nothing but you."

"Baby, I just fucked you up against a wall."

Her golden stare hardened. "Baby," Cassidy tossed right back, "you call it what you want, but to me, we just made love against the wall."

"You...you don't love me."

"How do you know how I feel?"

Titan shook his head.

"Most days, I don't even know how I feel," she said.

He should back away. They were both naked. He was still practically trapping her against the wall, and making love wasn't some primitive mating where he plunged desperately into her and took her against the wall. Making love was something tender and slow and not born of desperation because he'd been frantic to prove that she was still alive. Still safe.

"I know this, though." Cassidy's tone turned certain. "When I'm with you, everything seems better. Even in the middle of my worst fears, I'm better. Because I'm safe with you." Then her dimples flashed. "Relax, Titan. It's not like I'm asking you to love me back."

*Why not?*

***

The elevator doors opened.

Officer Liam Kelly automatically tensed. The special agent had given him strict orders not to let anyone near the governor's suite—only people with badges—and he was damn well not going to be slacking. His eyes narrowed even as his fingers automatically went to his weapon.

But a figure in a uniform just like Liam's stepped out of the elevator. The cop gave him a friendly wave as he headed down the hallway. The man wore a badge. *He's safe.*

Liam exhaled. "Did the Fed decide he wanted two of us on duty up here?"

"Three, actually," the cop replied as he closed in on him. He pointed toward the stairwell. "One of us is to take the stairs, one the door to the suite, and the other should be stationed near the elevator. The Fed is really freaking out."

A nod from Liam. "Tell me about it. But, it's a serial killer. Like...a real one." And it made him nervous as hell, not that he'd show that nervousness to anyone. "Heard the room downstairs was a real bloodbath."

"Yep." The cop's head lowered as he fiddled with the taser on his belt. "That's what happens when you cut the carotid and the jugular. Didn't get them both at the same time. Had to work a little at it. Things got a bit...sloppy."

Liam's eyes flew wide. "What—" He didn't recognize this guy. He didn't—

The cop's hand lifted, and he drove the taser right at Liam. Liam's body jolted and rammed into the door of the governor's suite.

***

Titan tensed. "Did you hear that?"

Cassidy shook her head. "Hear what?"

A thump. Or maybe...maybe a knock at the door? Definitely had been from the front of the suite, and the sound had been very faint. "Stay here."

"You're often telling me that, you know."

"And you're often *not* staying." He whirled. "You're naked. You should put on a robe."

Fuck. He grabbed the robe and yanked it on. And he tossed one to her.

Her nose scrunched. “I might shower first.”

“*Stay here.*” He scooped his gun off the nightstand.

“I want my own gun immediately,” she called after him.

Right. Yes. On it. But first...He rushed toward the front of the suite. Titan put his eye to the peephole. He could just see the profile and half the body of the uniformed cop. Still in position. Still keeping guard. Good. But what the fuck had that thump been? On high alert, Titan yanked open the door. “What happened out here?”

“Some bastard tried to get inside. I stopped him.”

*What?*

But the cop pointed toward the elevator, and Titan’s gaze automatically whipped to follow that signal.

And...

A figure was slumped just a few feet away. Just beyond the doorway of the suite. Only it was a figure wearing a cop’s uniform and—

Electricity jolted through him. It started at Titan’s neck and streaked through his whole body, making him shudder and shake.

“Drop the gun, bastard. Drop it now!”

Titan managed to turn his head, but he already knew who he’d be seeing.

Different haircut. Different color. Same sonofabitch face.

Blake Normandy.

And the fucker was *tasing him.*

Full freaking force. Titan could feel the charge even in the fillings of his teeth and it took every bit of control he had—

"*Drop it!*"

Titan staggered back a step, sliding into the hotel room. The electricity had him shaking, but he lifted his weapon with a trembling hand and fired.

# CHAPTER TWENTY

Cassidy froze. The sound of the gun blast echoed in her ears. A sound that had been far, far too close.

She hauled on the robe and ran through the bedroom. Her feet flew over the carpeted bedroom floor. Her heart slammed frantically in her chest. "*Titan!*" She burst out of the bedroom.

Titan filled the doorway to the suite. He'd opened the main door, and he stood there, body jerking and twitching and then he fell back. He crashed onto the floor. Cassidy screamed.

She ran toward him and—

A police officer. He kicked Titan's legs out of the way and hauled the front door shut. *Trying to get Titan away from the threat.* He flipped the locks even as she fell to her knees on the floor beside Titan. Her hands flew toward his chest.

"What happened?" Cassidy demanded as her gaze swept Titan. "Who hurt him? Who fired the shot?"

"I did."

Ice poured through her veins. She froze with her hands on top of Titan's partially open robe.

"Tased the bastard, and can you believe he still thought he would be able to shoot *me?* Even the big boys fall hard. I twisted his hand back. The bullet hit him, not me."

She could see that. Because the white robe was soaked red on the left side.

"He's not dead, but I am sure ready to finish the job—"

"No!" Cassidy plastered her body over Titan's. "No, dammit! Blake, *no!*" Because she knew that voice. It was the voice that haunted her nightmares. The one that haunted *her*. Her ex was right there. In the room. And Titan was bleeding out.

One of Blake's hands clamped over her shoulder with bruising force. "Get the fuck off him."

She was covering Titan's heart. She needed to cover his head, too. Because Blake could fire at any moment and—

A knife. At her throat.

"I don't like guns. So freaking loud. And not nearly as intimate as a knife."

"Th-that shot will have cops running up here. Other people will have heard it. You need to get the hell out—"

"I have an exit strategy, don't worry. And no one beyond this floor heard a thing. This is the VIP level, sweetheart. The place for rock stars to party their fool heads off all night long." The blade bit into her neck. "You think the owners of this building didn't invest in some soundproofing so the people on the level beneath this one could sleep? Think again. Now, *get the fuck up*. Or I will slash your throat right here, and you can bleed all over your new boyfriend."

She couldn't help Titan if she was dead.

And Blake was holding the knife on her with his left hand. He was left-handed. If he had the knife in his left hand and his right gripped her shoulder, no way could he fire a shot at Titan. *He can't be holding a gun.* She could get up and attack him. This was her chance.

"I-I'm getting up. *Please,*" she injected as much fear into the plea as she could. Luckily, Cassidy had plenty of fear. "Don't cut me." *Move the knife away so I can fight you.* She needed a weapon, STAT. *Where* was a weapon?

She rose. Slowly. He kept the blade at her throat, but it wasn't biting into her skin any longer. He'd eased his hold. She needed him to ease it more so that she could attack him.

She'd just made it to her feet when Titan's eyes flew open. His bright blue stare immediately locked on her. And then fell to the knife at her throat.

Titan started to lunge—

"Hero, you come at me, and I will cut her from ear to ear," Blake snarled. "You know I will do it. Saw my handiwork in the honeymoon suite, didn't you? I wanted you to know what I can do. What I will do."

And the blade made a small slice across her skin.

Titan froze.

The red on his robe spread. How bad was the gunshot wound?

Blake's hand lifted from her shoulder. "Put these on," he thundered to Titan and tossed a set of handcuffs at him.

Handcuffs?

Titan grabbed the cuffs. Glared at Blake.

"What can I say?" Blake laughed. "They came with the uniform. Just like the taser and even a gun. Damn convenient. I mean, there I was, sitting in my newly acquired room, minding my business, and this helpful young cop just knocked on my door. Seriously, if you're going door-to-door looking for a killer, don't be surprised when someone comes out with a knife and drives it into your gut."

Cassidy flinched.

"*Put on the cuffs!*" Blake yelled.

The knife sliced a little more.

Staring—glaring at Blake—Titan put on the cuffs. They snapped into place on his wrists.

Wait, had that just been *one* snap? She thought maybe it had. It looked as if Titan had both cuffs snugly in place, but she wasn't so sure...*I think he only snapped one.*

"Now stand up. Nice and slow. And take four steps back. No, five. I don't want you too close to us."

Titan stood up. Nice and slow. And he took five very slow steps back even as blood dripped on the floor. His robe was quickly getting soaked.

*Distract Blake.* "Y-you have a room here?" Cassidy asked, and she didn't have to fake the quiver in her words.

"Had to hide after the cops rushed the place. Barely had time to get in there after I left my little present in your honeymoon suite."

*That wasn't a present. She was a person.*

"Wasn't going to leave, not until I had you back. The GPS on that dick's ride led me to the hotel. Heard the concierge talking about the couple in the honeymoon suite who wanted to get married—the woman with the pretty smile and the scarred boyfriend. Fucking *pissed* me off, Cassidy." Rage burned in his voice.

She felt blood slide down her throat.

"But then I thought...has to be fake. He's the marshal. It's just a cover. *Has to be fake.*"

She clamped her lips together. *You keep telling yourself that it was fake, asshole.*

"What were you doing in here, Cass?" Blake asked silkily. "Why are you in a robe? Why the hell is the marshal in the robe? *Were you in here fucking him? Because this shit doesn't seem fake!*"

Her breath shuddered. "There was blood on our—our clothes. We tried to help the woman in the honeymoon suite. W-we had to change. Clean up."

Laughter spilled from him. "Should have saved yourself the effort. There is no helping Trinity. She wasn't worth your time." He spun Cassidy in his arms. A fast move and she was suddenly in front of him, staring up at him even as the blade pressed to her throat. "Damaged goods. They all were. Twisted and broken on the inside. I see the broken pieces when I meet them.

And when I'm done with them, I *put* them in broken pieces so that everyone else will see, too."

*OhGod. OhGod.*

"Thought you were like them at first. But you weren't, were you? You didn't hurt your parents."

Cassidy shook her head. Once more, the blade slid over her skin. She barely felt the slice.

"And you kept fucking wanting to *help* everyone when we were together. You remember when you found out one of the kids in your class didn't have money for new shoes? You left shoes on his doorstep. Like you were some freaking guardian angel. Shoes. A backpack. And I know you brought in extra lunch every day because there were kids you worried were hungry." He smiled at her. "You were soft when the others had been hard and brittle. All those broken pieces, so jagged and twisted. You didn't have those pieces."

What was Titan doing? She didn't dare look away from Blake. Different hair. Same handsome face. But his eyes were so terrifying to her now.

"She left me hungry," Blake told her. "Left me locked away some days. Never cared if I had good shoes or a backpack for school. Too busy with whatever guy was in her life. They thought she was charming. Perfect. Didn't see that she was broken and twisted. I showed them in the end. I make it so no one could ever doubt how broken they all were."

She fought the nausea rising in her throat. "You cut them up."

"Because they're already in broken pieces."

*OhmyGod.* She almost vomited on him. Maybe she should have. Maybe she should let that be the distraction they needed—

"I was mad at you for shooting at me when I found you at the motel."

*When you set the motel on fire?*

"But then I realized, you couldn't do anything else, could you? Because...because I went after the kids. You and kids—that soft spot you have."

"You could have killed them!" Titan hadn't made a sound behind her. *What is he doing?*

"I could have killed them." Blake shrugged. "I didn't. They got out."

"Blake—"

"It's time for us to leave. More cops will be coming up here. I heard the guy downstairs give the order for more protection. You and I will be gone before they arrive."

"The hell she will," Titan snarled, breaking his silence.

Blake's head whipped toward him. His eyes narrowed. "I don't need to cut you into pieces. I can see you're broken from here. Scars all over you. Broken and stitched together, but you'll never be whole."

Really? Blake was going to talk to someone else about being whole? "You have no clue," Cassidy spat.

His stare flew back to her.

"You're the one who isn't whole," Cassidy snapped at him.

The blade bit deeper. She didn't care. And she knew how to break him apart. Into a million pieces. "I was fucking him."

Blake blinked. The knife pressed harder.

"*Cassidy...*" Titan growled.

She lifted her chin, giving Blake better access to her throat. Staring him straight in the eye, she told Blake, "We were fucking in this suite. That's why we're in robes. Sure, we had blood on our clothes. So we ditched the clothes. We showered and we fucked—no, we made love. Because I wanted to be with someone who was whole. Someone who made me feel safe and valued. Someone who pushed all the dark parts and fears aside. Someone I could love—"

At that last word, Blake's eyes went wild with rage. She knew she was dead. Or, she would have been, but Cassidy had waited for this moment—

She kicked him in the dick as hard as she could. And she threw herself to the side. The knife sliced over her. There was more blood and pain that she refused to acknowledge. Cassidy didn't know how deep the wound was. She couldn't care about that now. She crashed into the floor even as Blake roared his fury and pain.

She looked up and saw that he'd drawn back the knife. He gripped it tightly in his hand and, face twisted with hate, he brought that knife down toward her.

Her hands flew up to block him.

But the knife didn't hit her. Because Titan hit *him*. Titan drove his body into Blake's, and they thudded back against the closed suite door. Only one cuff was around Titan's wrist, and he grabbed both of Blake's shoulders.

Blake drove the knife into Titan's chest.

*"No!"* Cassidy screamed as she lurched to her feet.

"I will carve you up. Every fucking inch." Blake yanked out the knife. Drove it into him again. "You'll be in pieces—"

Using his hold, Titan jerked Blake forward, only to ram him back into the door. Over and over again. With pounding, brutal force. Blake's head hit the door. Slammed into it again and again.

But he was still slicing with his knife.

*No, no, no.*

There was blood everywhere.

She grabbed a champagne bottle. There'd been one chilling in another silver bucket on the dining table. It was the only weapon she could find. Cassidy rushed toward the fighting men and lifted that bottle because she was going to slam it into Blake's head.

But...Titan was between her and her target. She twisted to try and get closer.

"Won't touch her," Titan spat. "Won't hurt her...ever...*ever...*"

Blake brought the knife down again—

But this time, when it sank into him, Titan's right hand flew out and he locked it around Blake's wrist. Using his hold on Blake's wrist, Titan yanked the knife out of him. And then he—

He twisted Blake's wrist, and, in a flash, he drove that knife into the soft skin beneath Blake's chin. Drove it into that skin and straight up.

Brutal.

Savage.

Terrifying.

Blake's eyes went wide. He gasped. Clawed at the knife.

But Titan was already stepping back.

And all Blake could do was fall.

He fell, and the champagne bottle Cassidy had gripped slipped from her fingers. It hit the floor with a crash, and glass and champagne exploded everywhere.

But she didn't care about the broken pieces of glass. Titan—Titan was falling, too. Titan shouldn't fall, but he was. His knees gave away, and he hit the floor.

*So much blood.*

"Get...out," Titan told her. "*Find...Oliver...*"

She was going to call for help, that's what she was going to do. She wasn't leaving Titan.

"Not...*dead.*"

He'd damn well better not be. Cassidy grabbed Titan's hand as she dropped to her knees beside him. She put his arm around her shoulders as she tried to support him.

*"Not...dead...Get out!"* Each word seemed dragged from him, and she realized—

Cassidy's head snapped back toward Blake.

He'd sagged near the door, but his hand was still clawing at the knife Titan had driven into the underside of his jaw. And he was...

*Pulling the knife out.*

Holy Mother of... "He's blocking the door." There wasn't another way out. Was there?

"B-bedroom. L-lock door...c-call...*h-help...*" His words were slurring. But Titan had stiffened. He pushed at her. She knew he was going to try and fight Blake.

Titan had fought before, had nearly died protecting one witness.

*He is not dying for me.*

Blake had the knife out. Blood covered his neck and soaked his cop uniform. A uniform that she now realized was a little too tight.

Blake's breath shuddered in and out. He locked his gaze on her.

And smiled.

Titan staggered upright. Cassidy rose on shaking legs with him. He weaved even as he shoved her behind him.

Blake came at him with the knife.

*Hell, no. No!* She'd told Titan over and over that he was not to do anything stupid like die for her.

She grabbed the champagne bottle from the floor. A scream of rage and fury erupted from her. She tried to rush around Titan, but he caught her shoulders. He pushed back again—

But it was too late.

Blake had surged forward, moving a few steps away from the door. He hadn't been going after Titan with his knife.

*He was coming for me.*

Fair enough, she'd been going for him, too.

His blade sliced across her arm.

The broken champagne bottle pierced his chest. Because when she'd picked it up, she'd only picked up half the bottle. *Broken edges. So sharp.*

The broken bottle didn't sink deeply enough, though. She could tell that immediately. It barely pierced him and it had to go—

*Deeper.*

Titan caught the top of that bottle and drove it in deep. Deep and he twisted it.

Blood spilled from Blake's lips.

And that was when the door crashed in behind Blake.

"*FBI! Freeze!*" Oliver yelled as he drew his gun.

A team of uniformed cops crowded in behind him.

Blake didn't freeze. He still had the knife in his hand. Had a champagne bottle shoved into his chest. He staggered to face Oliver with the knife extended—

Titan tackled Cassidy. They hit the floor, and he covered her.

A gunshot rang out.

***

"Cassidy..."

"She's going to be fine." Oliver's fierce voice. "You both are, hear me?"

His eyes blinked open. He was lying down, but...moving. And Oliver was seemingly racing along beside him. "Are you...holding my hand?"

Oliver squeezed his hand. "He's dead. You don't have to worry about Blake Normandy ever again."

Titan became aware of the pain pulsing through his body. Not just one spot. Everywhere. "Cassidy..." Where was she?

"Lift him up." A different voice. One he didn't know. "Need more hands here! This guy is big!"

He was lifted up and shoved—wait, he'd been on a gurney? Because now he was in an ambulance, and he was strapped down and... *"Cassidy!"*

Oliver had climbed into the ambulance with him. "So, you keep coming in and out of consciousness. I've told you this already. She's hurt—"

"*Cassidy!*" Titan roared. He heaved against the restraints. Felt one snap.

Someone swore.

Oliver pushed him back down. "Same reaction every time. That's why you're strapped so tightly. Though the straps clearly aren't working and—hey, where are the pain meds? My friend is freaking cut open!" Impatience and worry bit in his words.

Cut open? Didn't matter. He'd been cut open before. What mattered was... "Cassidy."

"Yeah, I get she's the only thing you can say. And understand me—she is going to be all right. They are taking her in a separate ambulance. She's not as bad off as you, but she needs attention, okay? When you wake up at the hospital, she'll be there."

Cassidy needed attention? "Cassidy!" But her name was weak because his eyes were sagging closed.

"I have to go secure the crime scene. They are going to take care of you. You got the bad guy. He won't hurt anyone else again. Hell, before the uniform with me got trigger happy, the dude was already falling. Pretty sure you shoved that bottle into his heart. And you did all that shit in a robe.

Though your dick might have been hanging out a bit at the end, just so you know."

He couldn't understand all of Oliver's words. Darkness was growing. Pain spreading and he just wanted—

*Cassidy.*

A siren wailed.

# CHAPTER TWENTY-ONE

He was in a hospital. Titan knew it before he even opened his eyes. The smell was always the same in a hospital. Antiseptic. Sterile. A machine beeped from somewhere nearby, and the slow, steady sound was what had drawn him back to consciousness.

For a moment, he just wanted to keep his eyes closed. Because when he opened them...

*Cassidy.*

What if she wasn't there?

His head turned to the side. Toward the beeping machine. His eyes slowly opened. Titan had to blink against the bright light that spilled through the blinds over the window. The light fell onto the chair right beside the bed. An empty chair.

The machines beeped a little faster as his breath sawed out.

"Hey, handsome, want to look over here?"

His head immediately whipped to the left.

Cassidy stood beside the bed. She wore a hospital gown, and she'd pulled a big, metal stand—and an attached IV bag—with her. The bag fed into a little tube that had been taped to her hand.

"Hi." She smiled at him. Shadows lined her eyes, but her dimples flashed.

He drank her in. He could see the bandages on her neck. Bandages on her arm. She was pale, but so beautiful. So perfect. Her dark eyes were full of worry, but she was standing there. Alive. Safe.

"They didn't want to let me in, but seeing as how I'm your fiancée, they didn't really have a choice." She lifted one hand toward him—the hand not attached to the IV line—and carefully ran her fingers over his arm. Over his arm, then down to rest over the back of his much larger hand.

Her touch sent pleasure pouring through him. *Cassidy is safe.*

"We *do* still have that reservation at the chapel. Though I doubt we'll be able to make it. You know, what with you being stuck in a hospital bed and all." Her smile slipped for a moment as the worry deepened in her eyes. But she quickly rallied. Her shoulders squared, and her dimples peeked again. "But I'll just take a raincheck on that chapel date, shall I?"

She was smiling for him. Trying to be brave and act like things were fine...for him.

All he wanted to do was pull her close. His hand turned so that he could hold her fingers with his. "You're...okay?" His voice came out even worse than normal. Wonderful. Probably meant a tube had been shoved down his throat at some point.

But Cassidy's smile deepened, as if his voice *was* wonderful to hear. "I'm better than okay. He's dead, Titan. Blake won't hurt anyone else again."

*Good.* Should he feel bad for killing a man? He didn't. Maybe it was the drugs still in his system or...

*Maybe it's the fact he was a murdering psycho who chopped up women.*

"And Trinity is going to pull through."

Who the hell was Trinity?

"The woman you saved in the honeymoon suite? Her name is Trinity, and she made it through surgery. The docs are saying it's a miracle that she didn't die." Cassidy licked her lips and hauled her IV stand closer as she inched nearer the bed. "The cop who was stationed outside our last suite is okay, too. He was tased and stabbed, but he got help in time." Sadness swept over her face. "Officer Clint Patrick didn't survive. Blake attacked him when Clint was searching rooms at the hotel. He killed him and took Clint's uniform and then he came up to kill us..." She leaned over the bed. "But you stopped him."

No. It had been a team effort. "You...shoved the bottle at him."

"Don't think I pushed it in far enough. Thanks for helping out with that."

If he'd had his way, he would have cut out the man's heart and dropped it at her feet. Too savage? Probably. Maybe it was good he'd passed out before Titan had decided to do that bit of madness. But at the time...

*I wanted to destroy him.*

"Oliver found Clint's body. That's what sent him and the others rushing to the rescue, though, apparently, more cops were supposed to be coming to stand guard and they just all sort of arrived at the same time. They kicked in the door and...Blake was raising the knife at them. A uniform fired but—"

But Titan could remember Oliver telling him that Blake had basically already been dead.

*I did that*. And he'd do it again, no hesitation.

"Did you hear me, Titan?"

Fuck, he'd zoned out. Stupid medicine. He squeezed her fingers.

"There are a lot of people outside who want to see you. A guy named Smith Sanders said he's known you for years. And a kinda intense man named Memphis is here, too. Told me he was an Ice Breaker. I think you told me before that he was the bounty hunter? Oliver is out there, as well. Everyone wants to make sure you are back with us." She bit her lower lip. "But I wanted to see you first. I needed to be here when your eyes opened."

His eyes were open. They were on her. "How...bad am I?" He hadn't looked down at the damage. Mostly because he didn't want to look anywhere but at her.

"Not bad at all." She lifted their joined hands and pressed a kiss to his knuckles. "In fact, I think you're pretty amazing."

He had new stitches. He could feel them. New scars. The knife had pierced his chest again and again.

Cassidy kissed his knuckles once more. "It will take you a few days to feel well enough to do anything like...go dancing."

He'd never been much for dancing. He tended to just lurch about.

"Bet you'll be amazing on a dance floor," Cassidy told him.

He shook his head.

"Oh? Don't think so? I'll just take that as a challenge. As soon as you're out of here, we'll go dancing to find out. It's a date."

A date.

Titan knew what she was doing. With her overly bright voice and the deliberately flashing dimples, Cassidy was trying to reassure him. But he could see the fear and worry in her eyes. Not fear *because* of him. Fear for him.

There was no revulsion or horror. Just his beautiful Cassidy as she tried to reassure him.

He could not fucking love her more if he tried. "A date," Titan agreed.

Her breath eased out. "Good."

This time, he pulled their hands toward his mouth. He kissed her knuckles. "I won't forget about the raincheck...either."

Her head tilted. A little furrow appeared between her brows.

"One day, when you're ready..." His voice was still rough as hell, but talking was getting much, much easier. "We'll make that appointment at the chapel."

Tears filled her eyes, but she blinked them away. "Don't you dare make a promise you can't keep."

"I never do." He was staring at his world. "I love you."

A sob burst from her lips. And she leaned over the bed and pressed her mouth frantically to his. "You scared me so much." Another kiss. Even more desperate. "They took you away from me." Another kiss. "I had to sneak out of my room with this stupid IV. It's still hooked up to me." Another kiss. "I love you so much, and I know it was fast, but *I love you.* I was terrified. I felt like I couldn't breathe until I saw you again." One more kiss. "Do not *ever* do this crap to me again. My heart can't handle it."

She'd handled a psychotic ex. He was pretty sure Cassidy could handle anything that came her way.

But her head lifted. She stared into his eyes. No sign of her dimples. "I don't want to handle life without you. Be safe. Be with me."

With her? That was the only place he wanted to be. "Always."

"I love you." And her mouth crushed to his.

God, he loved this woman. She was his soul.

He heard a door creak open behind her, but he didn't stop kissing Cassidy. If it was a nurse, she could see that he was fine.

"Oh, yeah." Oliver's too loud voice. "We can stop the prayer vigils, guys. The man is gonna be just fine." A laugh. "Just fine, indeed."

The door creaked again as it closed.

And Titan kept kissing Cassidy.

***

"You're a bastard, you know."

Oliver tugged at his collar. He'd already released the top two buttons, but the damn thing still felt entirely too tight. "Look, I explained about the other day—"

Lark snapped, "When you had me arrested—"

"When I had you detained—"

"Because I slapped—"

Oliver paused. "You *did* assault a federal agent."

Her emerald eyes narrowed. "Sorry," she bit out.

"Yeah, you don't sound like you mean that apology."

She shoved back the chair and leapt to her feet. They were in a small interrogation room at the local Bureau office, and he'd gone to meet her after finally being assured that Titan was going to fully recover.

*He was kissing Cassidy as if he'd never stop. The man will be fine.*

Now Oliver had to put out a fire of his own. A fire otherwise known as Lark Lawson.

"Sorry I slapped you," she gritted. "I lost control. I know I shouldn't have. But when a man lies to you, fucks you, then arrests your brother and tells the world that he is a *serial killer*, well, things can get a little out of hand."

He tugged on his collar again. "I detained you at the hotel for your own protection."

"Right. Like you care about protecting me." She snorted, and, dammit, the sound was oddly sexy. His problem? He'd always found everything about Lark to be sexy.

Always had. Always would.

And she hated his guts.

Fabulous. “There was a killer on the loose at that facility. I wanted you safe.”

She shook her head and her dark hair slid over her shoulder. “There were hundreds of people in that hotel. Why did I get special treatment?”

*Because you are special.* Even though she hated him, she was special. “I just wanted to—to explain what happened.” Did that sound desperate? Probably.

“What happened? At the hotel?” She took a step toward him and brought her tempting jasmine scent with her. “Or when you made my whole world implode?”

His lips pressed together.

“I meant what I said,” Lark told him. “My brother is innocent. I’m going to prove it. And I’ve got help. You ever hear of the Ice Breakers?”

Oh, wait. *Fuck.*

“I’m going to get them to help me prove my brother’s innocence. He’s not a killer. The real murderer is out there, and I am not going to rest until Lane is free. Now, get the hell out of my way, *Special Agent* Foxx.” Her tone had gone glacial.

For a moment, he hesitated. He didn’t want out of her way.

*I want her.*

But you didn’t always get what you wanted in this world.

He stepped aside.

And Lark walked away.

# EPILOGUE

*Six months later...*

"We could have gone anywhere," Titan told her.

Cassidy sent him a sunny smile. "But we'd already made the appointment here."

He was helpless against those dimples. "That appointment was for six months ago."

She simply shrugged. "Better late than never."

*Hell, yes.* She was right on that score. Better late than never. Because what was he about to do?

*Marry the woman of my dreams.*

The man waiting for them cleared his throat.

Titan turned toward the minister who patiently stood in the little Vegas chapel. A small ceremony. Just close friends. Some Ice Breakers.

Titan pulled the ring from his pocket. "Mind if we go ahead and get to this part?" He really wanted his ring on her finger. He wanted to be married to Cassidy.

A delighted laugh came from her as he slid the ring into place.

The minister stammered a little. Maybe people didn't usually change the order of things on him, but Titan just hadn't been able to wait. After a few more stammers, the guy launched into the ceremony. The words rolled over Titan, and he heard himself saying, "I do forever," at one point.

And Cassidy said something like, "I happily do."

Everything else was a blur.

The last six months had been a blur. A happy blur of loving Cassidy. Of realizing that, no, Oliver had been wrong. What he and Cassidy felt—it wasn't some adrenaline fluke because of the case. Not some hero worship. Not something weak that would fizzle away after the case ended.

He loved her more every single damn day.

And he knew that his love for her would just keep growing.

"Uh, don't you want to kiss her?" The minister appeared confused.

Titan blinked.

"We're married," Cassidy told him. "You get to kiss me now."

Hell, yes. He leaned in and pressed his lips to hers. He swore he could taste joy and love on her lips. Joy and love.

*My Cassidy.*

***

The after party had ended. Titan thought that probably wasn't the right description of the event, but he didn't really care. After the ceremony, Cassidy had changed out of her white gown. She'd kept on the string of pearls that she'd told him had belonged to her mother, but she'd dressed in a body-hugging black dress. He'd kept his tux on, and they'd gone dancing at a bar his buddy Smith Sanders had rented out for them.

The entire bar.

He'd held Cassidy close. Danced in front of their friends and hadn't cared about how many eyes were on him.

There was no honeymoon suite waiting. No heart-shaped bed. That was a nightmare he didn't want brought back to Cassidy. Instead, he'd gotten them a cabin just outside of the city. Cabin, mini-mansion. Same thing. Smith had handled the booking for him.

She stood on the deck and watched the stars.

He slid up behind her and put his hands on her waist. Immediately, her body softened as she pressed back against him. His head bent and his mouth feathered over her neck. Her hands rose, curled over his. "I really like our friends," Cassidy told him. "But I'm also really, really glad they're gone." She turned in his arms. "I love you."

*I love you.* Sometimes, he didn't think love was even the right word. It seemed too tame. Too weak. Cassidy consumed him. She was his whole fucking world. Everything good? That was his Cassidy.

Blake Normandy's real name had been Blake Haskel. The Feds and the Ice Breakers had found an old house that belonged to him in Georgia. Inside that house? Twisted souvenirs. Mementos of madness. Even a sick journal of his crimes.

Thanks to that journal, the remains of his other victims had been found.

The nightmare was over.

And, with their marriage today, the future waited. To Titan, that future seemed incredibly beautiful.

"I love you," Cassidy breathed, "and I have been wanting to get you naked all night long."

He smiled at her. "There's a hot tub about four feet away from you."

"I did notice that."

"You have on too many clothes."

"I noticed that, too. Unzip me?"

Gladly.

"And let's get you naked, too," Cassidy said. "Because I really, really want to make love to my husband."

*Make love.*

His fingers trembled as he unzipped her. The dress fell at her feet, and she daintily stepped out of it. Then she caught his hand and led him toward the hot tub. He stripped off his clothes and didn't give a thought to any of his scars. How could he? He was too busy looking at his beautiful wife. Too busy being grateful for the life they had.

*And I would kill in an instant to protect her.*

Nothing mattered more to him than Cassidy.

*His* good dream. His life.

His wife.

**THE END**

# A NOTE FROM THE AUTHOR

Thank you so much for reading FORGED FROM ICE! I hope you enjoyed the latest cold case romance. I've always been a cold case addict, and I've loved having the chance to explore these mysteries. Titan was such a fun character for me—I always fall for the tall, dark, and dangerous heroes! From the minute that Titan appeared in TRAPPED IN ICE, I knew he had to get a book of his own.

If you'd like to stay updated on my releases and sales, please join my newsletter list.

*https://cynthiaeden.com/newsletter/*

Again, thank you for reading FORGED FROM ICE.

Best,
Cynthia Eden
*cynthiaeden.com*

# ABOUT THE AUTHOR

Cynthia Eden is a *New York Times*, *USA Today*, *Digital Book World*, and *IndieReader* best-seller.

Cynthia writes sexy tales of contemporary romance, romantic suspense, and paranormal romance. Since she began writing full-time in 2005, Cynthia has written over one hundred novels and novellas.

Cynthia lives along the Alabama Gulf Coast. She loves romance novels, horror movies, and chocolate.

**For More Information**

- *cynthiaeden.com*
- *facebook.com/cynthiaedenfanpage*

# HER OTHER WORKS

**Ice Breaker Cold Case Romance**

- Frozen In Ice (Book 1)
- Falling For The Ice Queen (Book 2)
- Ice Cold Saint (Book 3)
- Touched By Ice (Book 4)
- Trapped In Ice (Book 5)
- Forged From Ice (Book 6)
- Buried Under Ice (Book 7)

**Wilde Ways**

- Protecting Piper (Book 1)
- Guarding Gwen (Book 2)
- Before Ben (Book 3)
- The Heart You Break (Book 4)
- Fighting For Her (Book 5)
- Ghost Of A Chance (Book 6)
- Crossing The Line (Book 7)
- Counting On Cole (Book 8)
- Chase After Me (Book 9)
- Say I Do (Book 10)
- Roman Will Fall (Book 11)
- The One Who Got Away (Book 12)
- Pretend You Want Me (Book 13)
- Cross My Heart (Book 14)
- The Bodyguard Next Door (Book 15)

- Ex Marks The Perfect Spot (Book 16)
- The Thief Who Loved Me (Book 17)

**Wilde Ways: Gone Rogue**

- How To Protect A Princess (Book 1)
- How To Heal A Heartbreak (Book 2)
- How To Con A Crime Boss (Book 3)

**Trouble For Hire**

- No Escape From War (Book 1)
- Don't Play With Odin (Book 2)
- Jinx, You're It (Book 3)
- Remember Ramsey (Book 4)

**Death and Moonlight Mystery**

- Step Into My Web (Book 1)
- Save Me From The Dark (Book 2)

**Phoenix Fury**

- Hot Enough To Burn (Book 1)
- Slow Burn (Book 2)
- Burn It Down (Book 3)

**Dark Sins**

- Don't Trust A Killer (Book 1)
- Don't Love A Liar (Book 2)

**Lazarus Rising**

- Never Let Go (Book One)
- Keep Me Close (Book Two)
- Stay With Me (Book Three)
- Run To Me (Book Four)
- Lie Close To Me (Book Five)
- Hold On Tight (Book Six)

**Bad Things**

- The Devil In Disguise (Book 1)
- On The Prowl (Book 2)
- Undead Or Alive (Book 3)
- Broken Angel (Book 4)
- Heart Of Stone (Book 5)
- Tempted By Fate (Book 6)
- Wicked And Wild (Book 7)
- Saint Or Sinner (Book 8)

**Bite Series**

- Forbidden Bite (Bite Book 1)
- Mating Bite (Bite Book 2)

**Blood and Moonlight Series**

- Bite The Dust (Book 1)
- Better Off Undead (Book 2)
- Bitter Blood (Book 3)

**Mine Series**

- Mine To Take (Book 1)
- Mine To Keep (Book 2)
- Mine To Hold (Book 3)
- Mine To Crave (Book 4)
- Mine To Have (Book 5)
- Mine To Protect (Book 6)

**Dark Obsession Series**

- Watch Me (Book 1)
- Want Me (Book 2)
- Need Me (Book 3)
- Beware Of Me (Book 4)

## Purgatory Series

- The Wolf Within (Book 1)
- Marked By The Vampire (Book 2)
- Charming The Beast (Book 3)
- Deal with the Devil (Book 4)

## Bound Series

- Bound By Blood (Book 1)
- Bound In Darkness (Book 2)
- Bound In Sin (Book 3)
- Bound By The Night (Book 4)
- Bound in Death (Book 5)

## Stand-Alone Romantic Suspense

- Monster Without Mercy
- Kiss Me This Christmas
- It's A Wonderful Werewolf
- Never Cry Werewolf
- Immortal Danger
- Deck The Halls
- Come Back To Me
- Put A Spell On Me
- Never Gonna Happen
- One Hot Holiday
- Slay All Day
- Midnight Bite
- Secret Admirer
- Christmas With A Spy
- Femme Fatale
- Until Death
- Sinful Secrets
- First Taste of Darkness
- A Vampire's Christmas Carol

Made in the USA
Las Vegas, NV
19 September 2023

77814272R00184